Dear Reader:

If you want to know something about an author, look at who's holding her book.

Don't ask the people who, after buying it, prop it on shelf with their other polite purchases. Instead, go find the people who crease the binding and perhaps leave crumbs in the cracks.

Don't ask the people who buy a book "just to be nice" or the people who like the *idea* of reading more than the experience of reading.

Don't research polite comments left on digital billboards or seek out marketing magicians whose sleight-of-hand can make an author appear more (or less) than she is.

Never ask the author directly, for she will likely blush and look away and doubt herself for having the audacity to write a story in the first place.

Avoid reading the first and last pages by themselves or hunting for bad words, hoping it will deliver the writer's world view in a neat envelope.

I especially ask you not to ask the people who only buy a book for extra credit, since any insight purchased at the price of ten points is not likely to be worth much.

If you really want to know something about an author, fall into her story and stay there for a while. Meet her characters, listen to the rhythm of her sentences, and discern the truth of her narrative.

Then you are a bit closer to knowing who wrote this book.

Karsen Kipp

(2019, SOMEWHERE IN CALIFORNIA)

This is a work of fiction. The characters, places and incidents portrayed, and the names used herein are fictitious or used in a fictitious manner. Any resemblance to the name, character, or history of any person, living or dead, is coincidental and unintentional. Product names used herein are not an endorsement of this work by the product name owners.

Copyright © 2019 by Karsen Kipp. All rights reserved.

No part of this book may be used or reproduced, stored in a retrieval system, or transmitted in any form or by any means, electronic, mechanical, photocopying, recording, scanning, or otherwise, without written permission from the publisher except in the case of brief quotations embodied in critical articles and reviews. Permission for wider usage of this material can be obtained through Quoir by emailing permission@quoir.com.

1st Edition

Cover design and layout by Rafael Polendo (polendo.net)
Cover image by storyblocks.com

ISBN 978-1-938480-40-9

This volume is printed on acid free paper and meets ANSI Z39.48 standards.

Printed in the United States of America

Published by Quoir
Orange, California

www.quoir.com

The Multiplication of Elmer Whit

for Alexandra...
"Love always multiplies!

(aka FERD)

KARSEN KIPP

Just a Note

Writers sit in empty rooms a lot.

Me? Not so much. The rooms I sit in are often full of people, and I am grateful for them. Rafael Polendo sat at my table this year, bringing the kind of collaborative, professional genius that every writer hopes for. On the walls hang portraits of imaginative people: mentors, parents, ancestors, writers. My sons and daughters pulled up their chairs, showing me how to love, think, and feel nearly every day. My husband, positioned at the head of the table, gives me the fancy chair whenever I want. Did you know he even does the dishes?

But the room of this project is mostly crowded with teenagers. Lots of them.

They are the Elmers and Elenas, the crowd-sourcing masses, my subconscious descriptions, and the insecurity in my characters' voices. God brought me the dreamers and the idealists, the jaded ones, the addicts, and the adolescents sitting on the fringe. They are the collective energy of this story, and I can't separate them from this book.

Nope. I'm never alone. Thank you, Jesus. My table, like my classroom, always needs more chairs.

I am grateful.

Table of Contents

"God does not care about our mathematical difficulties;
He integrates empirically."

ALBERT EINSTEIN

$$[1,2,4,2] \quad 1+2+4+2 = (9)$$
$$\Sigma$$

CHAPTER ONE
The Sum of One's Parts

When Elmer Whit's mother first discovered there was a baby growing inside of her, she did what most fifteen years-olds would do. She fell into a dark hole and stopped breathing. While turning blue in that hole, she remembered what started the whole thing—a trashy man-boy named Carl who said her panties were pretty. She waited underground until she could no longer hold her breath, and when she finally emerged after three long days she decided she would tell no one, not even Carl.

In other words, Elmer was a zero.

Her soft stomach grew firmer each month, swelling imperceptibly as though God attached an air nozzle to an under-inflated tire at the Exxon station. She wore her clothes loose at school and when she could no longer fasten her jeans, she took rubber bands and looped them around the metal button and through the slot on the other side. In the month of October, the weather changed just in time for Talia's coats and sweatshirts to camouflage her truth. No one asked why she ate more and cried more—don't most teenage girls do both when they're depressed? —and when her mother noticed her daughter's widening hips, she chalked it up to the family's hefty DNA and the arrival of womanhood.

In the eighth month, Talia felt the child begging for air himself, moving around so violently inside of her that she wondered if he would kick his way out. She spent her days hiding her belly under the school desks and her nights rolled on her side on top of her twin bed, dreaming about the day she would give birth to Carl's son. He would be pink and round and perfect and twice the man his father was. She would surprise the world by dressing him in a cream-colored, rich-boy romper and presenting him in front of the student body during an assembly where she would announce how he would be the next Nobel Peace Prize winner. Then everyone would chuck their fingers under his chin and wiggle his toes and tell Talia how lucky she was to have given birth to such a fine son.

When the time came sooner than it should, that teenage mother felt her body crack open like a hen's egg. She crawled down to the basement when no one was home and laid beside the telephone, spreading out beach towels side by side. The boy slid out while Talia screamed. He was slippery and chalky white, and the side of his face was splattered with purple paint in the shape of a continent. She looked at the tiny boy-on-a-leash and called the emergency operator who told her to "stay right there," an instruction that seemed rather unnecessary.

Her mother arrived at the same time as the paramedics. Elmer's new grandmother flung herself on the sofa and wailed louder than her daughter had. The EMT snipped the leash and brushed off the blood, but the purple shape on the baby's face did not go away. Talia cried and said that her baby boy was supposed to be perfect. It's just a birthmark, said the man with rubber gloves. He is beautiful anyway.

It was the second time that a man had lied to her in just eight months.

Elmer Whit entered the world curled in the shape of a zero. Like his mother, he lived underground in a hole where it was dark and moist with very little beauty in it. Elm had the terrible misfortune of being born into a labyrinth of tunnels, a place of horrible darkness.

When Elmer was three, his biological mother and father decided to join forces yet again, this time in unholy matrimony. They had everything in common, like brown hair, a fondness for mac-and-cheese, and two bastard sons between them. Apparently, teenage girls were Carl's specialty. Five-year-old Ed was Carl's first son, but Talia was so desperate to play house that she took them both. They pretended to be parents for six months before the lack of sunlight wilted their hopes. Daddy Carl eventually split for higher ground, and the two boys stumbled along in their underground life, two little nothings

Elmer was no different from other boys except for one small item: a tiny little variation that showed up during the mysteries of cell division in his mother's womb. With God looking on, and even with his approval, Elmer's DNA experienced a tiny blip. It was the reason that the peculiar birthmark on Elmer's lower jaw was the color of new bruises. It was the reason that he loved repeating simple math problems but couldn't read big words. It was the reason that he was secretly brilliant and beautiful and so freaking nice. It was the reason that he was slow and strange and wonderful. Even when the dark soil of his family altered his brain chemistry even more, he was still a work of art. True, Elmer's DNA was different from most other kids' but then again, whose genes are perfectly aligned anyway?

When Elmer started pre-school, he escaped the basement but continued to stumble through the darkness. He later trudged through middle school and finally staggered along with the nameless, teenage mass moving every 55 minutes through the hallways of Sun City High School. When he turned seventeen, the hallways of Sun City High School still felt a lot like the tunnels of Elm's life. Dark. Random. Dangerous. He moved from 7:30 to 3:00 like a worm in the soil, with the distinct feeling that at any moment a classmate's spade or a noisy lawn mower might cut him in half. To be stalked or ridiculed is to be valued in a way, but to be ignored is an even harder fate. Usually the teenage mass ignored him. Like scientific organisms that follow natural patterns, most of Elm's peers shut their eyes to the brown-haired boy with the backpack-on-wheels and eventually forgot about him. By tenth grade, the laughter died down. Not many asked questions about his face or his brain. Few bothered anymore.

He finally had a dream that one day he might push through the clay and find the sun—a mythological orb that coaxed flowers to grow and handed out suntans to pale boys and assisted vitamin D to do what it was made to do. In other words, Elmer knew that his time was coming.

In high school, Elmer learned to navigate his struggles with a certain measure of finesse. He picked a random happy song every morning and sent it rattling around in his head. He packed his own lunch—even if that lunch was day-old bread, cucumber slices and a slap of cheap, bright-yellow margarine. All the while, he ignored the eternal droning of his mother's grief. He was born with a fierce optimism, not to be subdued by bullies and con artists or the occasional jackass, thanks be to God.

Oh, and maybe thanks be to Gloria Christenson.

Miss Chris, as everyone called her, was a teacher made of uncommon goodness. She was neither attractive nor homely—just a moderate shade of pleasant, the perfect neutral against which to frame her vibrant inner character. No one knew how old she was: was that a streak of silver in her hair—or just an illusion of precious metal? Were those wrinkles, or merely the places where her smile embraced her cheeks? She could be thirty; she could be fifty. Her chronological age was so entirely irrelevant that no one ever asked about it or even speculated. Few women can ever simply *be*. And Miss Chris simply was.

She had been born to a Scandinavian family long ago whose parents' strong backs and hardy resolve had rowed a boat across the sea to find a new life for themselves. With five brothers, she had learned that boys need to fight epic battles and women need to leave them alone while they do it. Her mother had taught her about compassion and her father about justice, a combination that can change the world.

No one knew why she never married. No one asked. Perhaps they knew what the answer would be, that Miss Chris might not be a real person at all but simply one who had been cast out of heaven, not as a punishment for pride or self-glorification like Lucifer's fate, but because God needed someone who could help him scoop up the dirt, shake it through his fingers, and unearth the creatures living there.

To do such a preposterous thing, every morning between 6:45 and 7:30, Miss Chris followed a very strict routine:

6:45 – Take her keys off the hook by the back door (a lucky horseshoe nail forged into a J)

6:46 – Start the car and drive to school

6:55 – Arrive at the door of Room A-8

6:56 – Place her purse in the cabinet, her grade book on the podium, and her lessons on the whiteboard

7:00 – Pray for miracles

7:20 – Spray for germs

7:25 – Awkwardly fist-bump all the humans as they walked through her door

And it just so happened that Miss Chris and Elmer were destined to collide.

———————

Elmer woke each school day with the single-minded focus of an athlete. He wasn't fussed over like other kids whose moms hid sweet notes in backpacks. Instead, he had learned to live in a rather solitary world. He had conversations with himself—sometimes monologues, too—and he didn't mind the company. When he walked outside in the morning, the air felt better than his suffocating bedroom.

His thoughts were usually packaged in straight lines like rows of cookies. *The breeze is good today. My hair is doing something stupid. Don't make noises when you eat lunch. Will I find a place to eat? Why is the string on my sleeve a different color than my shirt? I hope Charley is there. My left ear hurts.*

On the first day of school in August, he unrolled the paper scroll he had fashioned out of his school schedule to see where he should go. He saw the name *Christenson* and her classroom number: *Seven.*

When he finally walked into Room Seven at 7:42 am, he felt the air change. Elm loved it, breathed it, drank it like water. Miss

Chris had artfully posed a shrine of portraits from Einstein to Curie, cell models, a standing rack of lab coats, a row of microscopes like a military line-up, mobiles swinging with cheap Styrofoam planets, and glass cases holding secret experiments. The entire place celebrated the patterns of God, the predictability of the world, and the anticipation that there was more to learn. The smell in her classroom was not the deathly fog of formaldehyde, but the quieter scent of life.

She also taught math, having not been able to decide which of the glorious disciplines—math or science—she would rather tinker with each day, so she was certified in both. Alongside the gorgeous collection of science doodads were math posters of various kinds. It was a classroom of impeccably straight lines dancing with the curves of art. Her classroom was beautifully appointed with the things she loved, and in this house of formulas and discovery was something even more astonishing: hope.

He slipped into his desk. It vibrated with good things, but he didn't know why. Miss Chris, of course, had spent her time hovering over it that morning with whispered prayers, electrifying it with a divine voltage. He did not know this. He just knew that during the first week, he walked from death to life as he crossed the threshold of her door, feeling the sun on his face. Their first conversation was a beautiful thing.

"And you are Elmer?"

"Yes, ma'am."

"I can't wait to hear more about that name. Can you stay a moment after class?"

"You want me to stay?"

"If that's okay with you."

"I'll stay."

"Do you have your textbook yet?"

"Um…I don't have my ID card. I don't like pictures, really."

"Oh, I think you'd take a great picture, Elmer. In fact, let's go over there together at lunch, and I'll show you where they take ID photos."

"Really? Do I really need one?"

"Yes. If you check out a book from me, you have to show your ID."

"All right."

She and Elmer walked over to the library at lunch just as she promised, and he smiled into a camera. The laminated card popped out of the machine, and Miss Chris took one look and said to Elm, "Why I think I might see you on my wall someday as a famous mathematician."

"Yes, I think you just might," he said.

———————————

Elmer never understood why high school was named such.

It certainly wasn't the highest school you could attend; there were plenty of others that ranked much higher, such as Wonder Valley Community College or maybe a place named Yale. It wasn't really high in the narcotics sense either, since actually getting high inside the high school was really difficult to pull off (unless you were Dylan Arbuckle who artfully wrote "Get Wasted in Civics" in the *Yearly Goal* box of his free school planner).

High school didn't have high morals, it rarely demanded high standards, no one ever used high diction, and the morale among the teachers was painfully low. So after Elmer's first three months of ninth grade, he was sorely disappointed that a place such as this had so woefully misrepresented itself. Yes, three months into high school and Elm had discovered that one can never assume too much about a name.

Unless your name is Elmer, in which case everyone assumes plenty. *Fudd* was the obvious weapon of choice, the blunt, punishing association used by the least clever peers in school. Fudd was easy. It was a given. It was the nickname that the simple-minded bullies used, a leftover relic of 1950s hand-drawn animation when Porky Pig and Elmer Fudd roamed Saturday mornings.[1]

On one fall day, all of Elmer's irregularities were on full display. He was moving his rolling backpack along the corridor at school, humming some song to himself. He felt the *swish swish* of his shorts as he moved, keeping his eyes down and watching the concrete change from gray to black to brown.

Wearing jeans shorts to campus (not the socially acceptable ones, but the ones that grandmothers snip out of your used denim) was the high school equivalent of a beef cow being tagged for the slaughterhouse. Elm's brain didn't make the connection between his clothes and his social punishment, but every time he pulled those shorts over his thighs, he felt a vague uneasiness. His mother, believing somehow that she was redeeming him from a cruel father who could not buy his son new clothes, made it worse by hemming those unholy denim cut-offs with sturdy white thread.

Matched with a T-shirt emblazoned with the fading words *Fashion Fiesta Mall Albuquerque*, Elm's clothing ("psychopath couture" as one girl labeled it) invited all manner of oppression.

---

1. A long, long time ago, cartoons were vicious and disturbing portraits of human nature made of anthropomorphic creatures who preyed on weaker victims. These cartoons were much closer to reality than the modern creations of politically correct optimists.

His mother didn't realize it. His sympathetic aunts continued to send odd little items, like parachute pants with zippered compartments, 1980's faded striped shirts, and freebies like T-shirts from the American Cancer Society. For adults, the purpose of clothing was strictly utilitarian; for the rest of Sun City High School, clothing was essential to one's survival.

Elmer saw the crowd ahead of him. He was used to the nausea, used to moving in slow motion toward the nameless, faceless oppressors who subtracted his value. Crowds of teenagers meant diarrhea. *Do they know that my brain is different? Do they even know my name?*

Suddenly a kid named Kelton, Sun City High School's Chief of Pricks, answered his question. "Hey! Hey, you there…Fudd!"

Elm knew better than to turn around.

"I said *Fudd!* Are you listenin' to me, Fuddrucker?"

Elm said nothing. He kept humming to himself.

"Oh, geez, you're making me look like an idiot now. Is this how you treat all your friends?"

A small cluster of onlookers began to feel the buzz and crackle of conflict. In a high school, it's irresistible. So the people gathered, and the King Prick kept it up.

"We saved a seat for you at lunch, E-Dog. How come you didn't show up?" Kelton, annoyed by the slight and empowered by the crowd, gathered momentum. There was no turning back on this growing provocation. "You gotta be kidding me, fag-boy. Are you deaf AND stupid?"

One girl's voice from the middle of the crowd squeaked out a weak little counter-weapon: "C'mon, Kelton, you're being a jerk now. Quit it."

Elm had not turned around the entire time. He was floating above the action, as he had learned long ago. But this time the intensity and perseverance of his enemy just might pull him down to sea level.

"That's right, slow down and listen to your buddy. Are you gonna turn around and talk to me or what?"

Boys like Kelton aren't powerful; they simply terrorize small habitats like tiny, ugly reptiles in the desert who feed on rubbish dumps or scrawny rodents. A perverse idea slithered into Kelton's head and worked its way to his hand. He drew a pencil out of his backpack, not unlike a video game avatar drawing a sword. He swept into position behind Elm and grunted against him with the point of the pencil pressing into the back of his jeans. "I'll bet you like that, Fuddrucker. Now I gave you something to dream about tonight."

The crowd squirmed. The air was thick with brutality.

Inhale exhale inhale exhale. I am zero, he thought. *I must keep walking I must not look I must keep my face to the sun.* His stomach leaped up to strangle his throat, and Elmer struggled to breathe. *Get to the corner get to the door get to the exit get to the fresh air.*

Kelton and all the reptiles watched as Elmer, back straight and face set to the sun, left the building.

———————

In the quiet safety of Miss Chris's room, his mind fiddled with a Rubik's cube made of only three colors: Kelton-the-prick, his warped mother, and a man whose sperm was his only qualification for fatherhood. He could not think of Study Skills or World History. Only these three.

Elmer dreamed every day of his new name, the name that God would someday give him in heaven. The scene would look something like this:

God: How are you, Elmer? You're looking rather dead today. How about a resurrection?

Elmer: Boy, that'd be cool.

God: As a bonus, I'll give you a new name. Would you like that, too?

Elmer: I'll say.

God: All right, Andrew Weldon Carmichael. C'mon inside and join the party.

As for Elmer's mother, she had snapped long ago. More than a few men had dumped their own shovels of black dirt over her air supply as well. With two sons and an addiction to her own unhappiness, she knew nothing except for hollering and sleeping. When she was asleep, she was no mother at all, and when she was awake she was a persistent nag.

Elm, get yourself out of bed, child.
(silence)
Elm, get yourself going—it's time for school.
All right.
You got those clothes I washed for you? The jeans shorts?
Yes, mother.
You'd better thank Aunt Kitty for those the next time you see her. She bailed us out with those clothes since your father left us with nothin'. ELM! GET OUT OF THAT BED! That dumbshit don't know if he's asleep or awake.

While sitting in Miss Chris's classroom, he added to his thoughts the arrival of his father two weeks ago, an unexpected visit that further smothered him.

Geez, E, can you put away your crap here? It's all over the living room.

It's not mine—it's Ed's.

Tell Ed that the two of you pigs aren't welcome in this house.

I'll tell him.

You steal my Crown Royal? That stuff ain't cheap, y'know.

No, Dad, I don't drink.

That's what they all say. Hey, E?

What.

You're a good son, you know that?

Sure.

When you're not screwing things up, you're not too bad. You might be messed up in the

head, but I say he's a good tax credit, that Elmer.

Silence.

I said you were a good son. You hear me?

Yeah.

We should do something sometime. Go somewhere when your mom doesn't know.

Silence. Are you going to live here now?

Are you crazy, boy?

I was just wondering.

With his dad coming in and out like the tide, Elmer's life was unpredictable and often disrupted. He had never known the steady life, never known the certainty of a daily sunrise. His father was as damaged a man as you will find, with his grandfather equally broken. In this way, Elmer would have to be rescued from the long ancestral record of self-loathing.

Carl Whit was a builder. Not the kind with craftsmanship in his blood, or engineering in his head, or a natural love of cross beams and mahogany, but the kind of oxymoronic builder who lives to tear stuff down. His rage and disappointment with life were relieved, in part, by the daily hammer blows he laid down. He worked to be paid, and with that payment he consumed his whiskey and porn, pissing away any respect that comes from merely being someone's daddy.

Carl was a dirty man. First, he was dirty in the physical sense with grime buried in the half-moons of his fingernails and ball caps etched with the salt of forehead sweat. Showers rarely helped. His jeans—some six or seven pair of Levis with indistinguishable markings—were stiff and polluted, and on the floorboard of his 1992 pick-up truck were scattered months of neglect. Unlike the men who find art and dignity in their physical labor, Mr. Whit found nothing but contempt for himself. His own father was dirty, too, the master having taught a young apprentice.

But such dirt was not merely streaks on the skin and clothing. It had seeped into his heart and changed its color to ash. He had never allowed love to scrub his heart clean, so Elmer's father carried around a dark soul wherever he went. It had stained his wife, ruined his friends, and soiled his sons. They all lived underground in a big pile of dirt with the address 4863 S. Bedford Road.

As a testimony to Elm's deeply tragic beginnings, that little boy had buried in his psyche that afternoon at the age of five when his father took him to buy a milkshake. On the day before kindergarten started, Elm was excited, having remembered few outings that promised a reward. He ordered strawberry—it was just a cup of too-pink frozen chemicals purchased at the cheapest neighborhood joint. But for Elm, it was heaven. His father never bought him anything.

On the way home, the truck hit a speed bump and Elm's dreams fell to the passenger floorboard in a sticky puddle, mixed with the detritus of his father's miserable life. His father said nothing, simply pulling over to the side of the road. His anger was spilling over in strange and silent form. He opened his car door and moved to the passenger door where he instructed his son to step out of the truck.

"Get out," he shouted.

Elmer slid down from the cab, barely tall enough to land without hopping.

"I said drink it," he repeated. "You spilled it, you idiot. Now you get to have your milkshake."

The boy, bewildered by his father's command, looked up at his dad.

"Drink it," he demanded.

The minutes that followed—the vile, outrageous minutes that shrink a boy into a worm, the minutes that make some men into beasts, the minutes that teach a child's spirit how to die— defined Elm's childhood forever. That young boy bent his head into the grainy pink puddle and lapped and lapped and lapped until his father finally let him free.

On the way home, some said they saw a little boy leaning his head out of the passenger window, vomiting up the day's reward in a long pink stream.

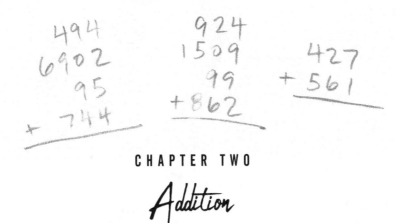

CHAPTER TWO

Addition

It wasn't long before Miss Christensen decided that Elmer needed more than a paid professional to love him. He needed a real friend. She was determined to find him one. This was a mission requiring some creativity—and maybe a flat-out miracle.

Miracles were rare in high school. She had learned that adolescence is about fear and hopelessness and exaggeration. It is childhood purity melting into puddles of wax, set on fire by internet flames and the proximity of so many firm bodies. She discovered that high school is fourteen-year-old girls vomiting up their beauty into secret toilets. It is man-boys like Kelton-the-Prick warping their consciences for the sake of position and power. It is not merely pep rallies and preparation for college, but a four-year experiment to test the limits of the world and find out where they might end. Miss Chris had come to learn all of this about high school, and it reinforced her belief that desperate men need a good God.

Elmer lived and breathed in a different social stratum, one whose selection of friends was limited at best. The geo-dome called *Special Education* was biologically irregular. He had seen enough people curve their two fingers on each hand when they said the word "special" to know that it was hardly so. The breadth of students who warranted special education was vast. They ranged from Elm with his marginally scrambled brain chemistry, to Belinda, a wheelchair- riding, twisted, frail little thing with the mind of a two-year-old who was escorted every day from a technologically tricked-out van over to her day class in the B building.

The two teachers who were in charge of Elm during his "special hour" were reasonably pleasant, although at times it seemed their specialized training was simply bureaucratic. If these two women were ever caught in an Olympic competition involving the educational legal code, they would certainly bring home the gold. But when it came to the kind of love that could change someone's life, well, Mrs. Trotter and Mrs. Alvarez couldn't compete for squat. They shuttled him politely from room to room, enforcing extended test time like the Special Needs Gestapo, and keeping track of folders in mysterious colors.

Belinda and the other eight severely disabled students looked like they could be nineteen or twenty. Two of the young men had visible beards, and the group of them formed a beautiful community of human anomalies. Some hunched over, others vacant-eyed, a few in wheelchairs—they were the fringe of humanity, completely isolated from the rest of the campus.

The Normies (as his brother Ed used to call non-special-ed students) would offer a disturbing inventory of comments as they walked past the wing, often peering into their classroom.

"Aw, crap…they've got a *fridge in* there? And a sofa? I should fake some psychopathic shit just to get admitted."

"Look at that one! He's got freaking sideburns from the 1970's. Dude, I'm gonna wear that at prom this year."

"That's crazy, man. I'd hurt myself if I wound up in a class like that. Just go ahead a shoot me, bro, if I ever start drooling like that."

The insanity that spilled from the lips of the so-called Normies walking past the special education wing was a monstrous study in irony, but few would ever notice. When Elmer had observed the special day class last year as a freshman, he was at first overcome with compassion and sadness for the residents who spend their time there. But now he was almost jealous of their beautiful isolation and the care given them by the faculty. As one of the recipients of the state's special education money, Elmer felt at times even more freakish than Wheelchair Belinda. He had one foot in the mainstream and one foot in the loony bin. Neither group considered him one of its own.

Since Miss Chris was on a mission to find Elmer an authentic friend, she first considered two locations: his physical education class and the cafeteria. She wasn't particularly hopeful. These are the black holes of public education where anything less than normal gets sucked into its frightening anti-matter.

Physical education class was rough. Despite the fact that every student wore the same uniform—a gray shirt with the five pillars of good character on the front, matched with shiny burgundy drawstring shorts—Elm looked different in his. It swallowed him up. He walked differently than the others, adopting no arrogant strides or particularly masculine poses. He slipped into the locker room every day alone, looked down at his skin which was the color and texture of beige socks, and changed his clothes just in time for the others to arrive. There were no clichéd gym teachers with thick socks and whistles who shouted at him to run faster. No teams that picked him dead last or big kids who put his head in the locker room toilet. That's just 80s movie mythology. Instead, it was the small, relentless erosion of Elm's value as a human being that subtracted his value.

As for the cafeteria, there were some opportunities to make alliances, but these weren't typical. On the days when Miss Chris was not in her classroom, Elm would take his place in the cafeteria line for lunch. Evangelina, a cafeteria lady (who believed in a divine calling which happened to be named *Food Service*) loved seeing Elm in line. She was one of the few people who talked freely with him.

"Hey, Elmer," she would say. "So you didn't bring a lunch today, eh?"

"No, ma'am," he said.

"Would you like a little extra cake?" she whispered.

"Sure."

And Evangelina would cut a special slice off the giant sheet cake for him. *Hey, that's not fair!* another kid would say, but Evangelina would have none of it.

"When you start being as nice as Elm, I'll give you a bigger piece, too," she joked.

The cafeteria lady came to learn that Elm's birthday was on the twelfth of November, that he got an 72% on his recent grammar test, and that he liked to look at the pictures in Japanese graphic novels. She noticed when his hair was different and asked how tall he was compared to last year. If he was absent for too long, or brought his lunch five days in a row, she would look for him in the morning among the breakfast crowd.

"Hey, Elmer! Where've you been, my friend?" she would ask when he finally showed up. "I've missed you!"

One time, another cafeteria worker asked Evangelina why she paid so much attention to "that one kid" when there were 2000 kids at the school.

Evangelina simply replied, "because I can't possibly know all the other 1,999."

As the weeks went by, it seemed that Elmer's best chance for finding a real friend lay in the compassion and maturity of old people. But Miss Christensen knew that this was less than ideal.

What 17-year-old can survive without belonging to his own species?

———————

Elmer continued his survival techniques. Living about seven blocks from the Sun City campus, he would roll his backpack over the broken places in the sidewalk, avoiding the insects as he went. This kind of precision required great concentration, head down, eyes focused on the world below.

During the two-mile walk home each day, he was in charge. He was bigger than the insects, able to save or crush them at will. Passing through the microcosm of high school was no different from living in the real world where the hierarchies are almost scientifically fixed. Didn't he read this in his science book? *Human matter starts complex, filled with potential, and then it breaks down systematically into simpler forms when confronted by pressure.*

And every day while Elmer walked home, Miss Christensen was shutting down her classroom for the evening. With the same precision as Elm's, she planned the next day's lesson, re-arranged the chairs sent askew by the final bell, and gathered her belongings. If the morning was for prayer, the late afternoon was reserved for gratitude.

Some had called Miss Chris's mission hopelessly naïve. This quixotic[1] temperament had been one of the reasons she had stayed single for so long. One young man long ago had

———————

1. Don Quixote (pronounced key-HOE-tay) was a swashbuckling character in the 16th century created by Spanish writer Cervantes. His name, transformed into the adjective *quixotic*, is synonymous with romantic idealism and ridiculous optimism in the face of grim reality. In other words, every public school teacher in America is either *quixotic*—or close to retirement.

wondered if he should make Miss Chris—or Gloria, as she was known to suitors—his bride. But they had differed on important matters, such as what color one should paint a kitchen, and oh yes, the source of hope in the world. He believed in the total goodness of man and she believed in the total goodness of God. Some said that they could both be right, but in the end, these were irreconcilable differences.

Alone and powerful, Miss Chris was now allowed to pursue a singular vision, which is why some people should never marry at all. It allowed her to do more for a boy like Elm than others might; her solitary life allowed her to scan the horizon for misfits and rescue them at just the right time. But before God can give you a brilliant idea, sometimes you just have to try conventional wisdom. So rather than asking God for help, Miss Chris first worked very hard to find a friend for Elmer the old-fashioned way.

Bribery.

Her first attempt required the assistance of Sophia and Tessa. They were some of Sun City's finest examples of Whisper-Girls— girls who never spoke out of turn, loved to impress the teacher, and went home every night to update their college resume.[2] She arranged her seating chart so that Elmer was flanked on both sides.

Miss Chris was certain that Sophia and Tessa would show kindness to Elmer, no matter what. They had a long reputation for doing the teacher's undercover psychological work all through elementary school: sitting with the new kid during lunch, bringing the sick kid to the nurse at recess, or standing next to the

---

2. They are also the ticking time bombs just waiting to explode at their first sorority party, but that's another theory entirely.

smartass during choir performance to subdue the beast. Miss Chris falsely reasoned that if she asked them to be kind to Elmer, he would feel loved and valued. It was a rookie mistake.

"Tessa?" Miss Chris called out softly from her desk during seatwork time. "Can you come here for a moment?"

Tessa slid out of her chair and came to stand in front of the teacher's desk. "What is it, Miss Chris?"

"Can you come in the hall with me for a moment?"

The two of them scooted out into the hallway where Miss Chris presented her audacious request. "You might have noticed that Elmer has a little trouble making friends."

Tessa nodded, looking a bit frightened. This might be beyond her entry-level pay grade.

"I was hoping that you and Sophia could go out of your way a little to, you know, show some extra kindness to him. He isn't always treated well at school."

"Umm, okay." She waited, her mind so accustomed to following directions that it struggled to sort this one out on its own.

"I'll mention it to Sophia, too." Miss Chris smiled, but she was already sensing her misstep.

"What exactly do you want me to do again?" Tessa asked.

"Well, nothing specific, really. Just be his friend. Ask him some questions. Help him out if he needs something."

"All right. I can do that."

"Why don't you tell Sophia to come out in the hall also. I'll speak to her about it."

Tessa walked back into the room saddled with another task. *Would she get extra credit?* She whispered to Sophia, who turned and looked back toward the door. Miss Chris gestured for her to come into the hallway where she repeated her admirable but utterly misguided plan.

Sure enough, the Whisper Girls made good on their promise. For two weeks Elm was suspiciously popular as he sat between them. He was offered extra pencils, helpful answers, and free mannequin smiles, but nothing flowered for real. Miss Chris was grateful for their mechanical acts of kindness, but obedience does not fertilize friendship. You can't fault Miss Chris's sincerity, but in the end, while she had hoped to give birth to a meaningful friendship, the artificial insemination had failed miserably.

This friendship mission would have to work another way.

"And so, do you miss your brother, Elmer?" Miss Chris was writing on the whiteboard while she asked.

"Oh yeah. It feels weird without him."

"What does your mom think about him leaving?"

"My mom? My mom cries a lot, but I think it's because of me and not because of my brother."

"How do you know that?" Miss Chris had a way of asking questions without ever sounding accusatory.

"I just know. I've always made her sad." He got up and poked around her bookcase.

"Tell me a little more about your mom. You said your dad isn't home very much. Do you think she's sad about that?"

"Oh, I don't know." He waited a very long time to speak again. "My dad isn't a good person." It was such a simple admission. It was one of the great tragic truths of Elm's entire life, of any boy's life. He repeated it. "My dad isn't a good person."

"I'm sorry, Elm. I believe you when you say that," Miss Chris replied.

"But I still think my mom cries because of me. My mom and I—we don't talk much."

Miss Chris stopped writing on the board and went over to the bookcase to where Elm was standing. Her older eyes stared right into his. "You know what? I've been teaching for a long time, and I don't know too many boys your age who talk a lot to their moms. I think you're completely normal, if you ask me. And as for your mom crying, I can guarantee that she's crying like crazy over missing your brother. It's not you, Elm. Believe me, it's not you." She stared right into his eyes, never once diverting her gaze to his distracting birthmark.

It's not you. It was such a beautiful phrase.

Elm ate his sandwich quietly for a few minutes while Miss Chris fussed and puttered around her desk. It was often like this during lunchtime. A little bit of talking. Some questions perhaps. Elm never worried about being quiet and neither did Miss Chris. At the end of lunch she would often open the bottom drawer of her file cabinet and pull out a silver box. They knew the routine. "Would you like a piece of candy before you go?" she would ask.

"All right. Thank you. Thank you."

In truth, Miss Chris did not know the complexity of Elmer's brother Edward Whit. It might be said that Ed had even less of a chance to survive above ground than his younger sibling. Ed was brighter, more attractive, and a great deal more stubborn than Elm, so this might surprise you. However, the more a young man knows, the more he suffers, and Ed's brain was unfortunately in tip-top shape.

Ed had graduated last year from Sun City. As a child, he had endured some of the same abuse as had his brother, but as the oldest son, he had escaped some of the selfish indifference his father developed toward the second child. Even so, he had also known the front lines of combat. Lost and angry, he had spent two years as most troubled boys do, sneaking out to empty spaces late at night to drink cheap beer and talk a big game.

In a fairytale, one might expect the two brothers to share a bond together, an abiding contract that says *I got your back,* but it never quite worked that way. Ed did from time to time run interference for his little brother by deflecting attention away from Elmer's intellectual shortcomings. Once when Ed was in the sixth grade, he discovered that Elm's fourth grade classmates were plotting a kid-sized conspiracy against the stupid kid. Their half-witted plot, inspired by the highbrow literature of Captain Underpants[3], involved some underwear and magic store doo-doo made of plastic. When Ed figured out they were going to humiliate his brother by luring him into the boy's restroom to make an ABSOLUTELY HILARIOUS discovery, he foiled the scheme through some clever deception of his own.

But elementary pranks are only the easy stuff, as he soon discovered. In junior high school, when the entire world passes through the Valley of the Shadow of Death, Elm's status dropped into the adolescent chasm. Not even Ed could reach down and pull him out. His teachers were sincere, and the other middle school screwballs threw down a couple of rope ladders for him, but he would not climb out of there. His rolling backpack and fashion choices alone would have disqualified him for full rescue.

Out of his own survival instinct, big brother Edward had determined long ago that a marginally retarded brother, a wacko mother, and a counterfeit father weren't enough to glue him to the city of his birth. The day after graduation, he put all his things

---

3. The Captain Underpants series was listed as the 6th most frequently challenged books when it was published. Apparently, its hardcore insensitivity to inferior groups and its tendency to incite rebellion in young readers concerned many parent groups. This wasn't the only big news that year; 2002 also brought Iraqi violence, corporate corruption, bombs, global drought, and the increasing AIDS crisis. Thank God we cleaned up *Captain Underpants.*

in four paper grocery sacks and placed them in the trunk of his 1989 Chrysler Lebaron. On the seat was a map of the United States with a snaking red line written in red magic marker running smack through the middle of it. His first stop: the forgotten town of Handley, where a friend he once knew in eighth grade had escaped with his mother to start a new life.

The night before, he had brought his graduation cap into Elm's room and propped it on one of the knobs on his headboard.

"Brother, I'm leaving. Your time is coming," he said. He was stuffing one last memento into his satchel.

Elmer, strangely proud of his brother's middle-finger-salute to their home city, nodded politely. "When will you come home again?"

"I don't know. I just know that it won't be soon."

"Are you going to find a girlfriend?" Elm asked innocently.

"Aw, shoot. I got no idea. But now I'll have a chance. That's all I can ask for."

Ed sat next to his brother on the twin bed and gave the graduation cap a twirl. It spun for several seconds without stopping. "You know what, E?"

Elmer looked at him as though he had some wisdom.

"Give it two years. Two more years is all you've got to take. Something good is coming for you." Ed, who never touched his brother except maybe to harass and posture, took the burgundy graduation cap and rested it on his brother's head before putting out his hand in an awkward gesture of gentlemanly farewell. The younger boy reached out his hand and clasped his brother's.

As if aware of feeling like a sentimental movie scene, Ed retracted quickly and turned for the door. "Holy crap, Elm. I'm outta here," he said as he left.

The men in a family leave a legacy for the younger ones. Two Whit men had fled; the third was merely waiting for the right time.

$$ax^2 + bx + c = 0 \qquad x = \frac{-b \pm \sqrt{b^2 - 4ac}}{2a}$$

CHAPTER THREE

Quadratic Equation

Halfway through Elm's tenth grade year, Miss Chris stepped up her mission impossible. The passive kindness of one middle-aged teacher would not be enough to find a legitimate friend for Elmer Whit. It would require an army.

The result?

Team Elm.

She assembled a cracker jack team of experienced misfits who had *been there, done that* when it came to high school rejection. They were all old and experienced, the OG's[1] who had survived high school and lived to tell about it.

Her first choice was the lead custodian, the only guy who knew the entire school better than anyone else. Angelo held all the keys. His skills and ambition almost drove him out some years ago until he figured that janitors often did more for kids than district superintendents. So he stayed put. Angelo was a small man with a bit of mischief in his eyes. His love for the underdog had driven him to secret but extraordinary acts of

---

1. White suburban students are particularly fascinated by the idioms of hip-hop. When a Caucasian male who lives in a cul-de-sac says "That motha's an OG," it sounds like when a California tourist visits Tijuana, sees a cactus, and says *Ser un cardo.*

kindness. This year alone he had scrubbed half-a-dozen hate messages on lockers shortly before they broke someone's heart. He and his magic sawdust saved the reputations of at least four kids afflicted with vomiting. Only Angelo could be so shrewd as to throw the wet towels into the industrial clothes dryers during PE, thus destroying the plans of bullying towel-snappers everywhere. When Miss Chris, who knew all things related to love, decided to assemble a team of Elm supporters, Angelo was the best man to for the job.

Miss Chris summoned Angelo to her classroom during her prep period, and she shut the door like a secret agent thwarting spies before pulling up two chairs to face each other. "We've got to do something extraordinary to find a real friend for Elm."

"I'm in."

"You might think I'm crazy," she answered.

"Too late."

"You've met Elmer, right? Do you know who I'm talking about?" She was testing him, making sure he understood the high stakes.

"Sure. The kid with the purple birthmark on his face. He's a prince. You gotta love that kid." Angelo, with all his 48 years, was getting excited.

"That's Elm. The kids don't know him at all. They just see what's different about him; they don't really *see* him. I want to change all that."

"All right. I like what I'm hearing. How you gonna change anything?"

"This is big, Angelo. Are you ready to hear my plan?"

"C'mon, now, baby. Give it to me straight." Angelo grabbed the back of a chair and spun it around like a dancer. He straddled it and listened.

"You ready?" she asked. "SUN CITY MATCHMAKER!" Miss Chris waited for the reaction.

He squinted his eyes at her. "What the hell is *that*?"

"Sun City Matchmaker! It's brilliant. It works like this. See, I'm gonna interview a bunch of kids to be Elmer's friend. We will pick the sincere ones and then arrange for them to meet. We will have a committee to choose the best one." Her conviction was palpable.

Angelo stared at her for ten seconds. Then he stood up, walked around the chair, and sat down again. "Miss Christensen, you are the damn craziest woman I've ever met, you know that?"

"Uh huh."

Angelo looped his fingers through the enormous key ring on his belt, jangling the metal while he spoke. "Friendship doesn't work like this." He shook his head. "You can't force friends, you know. Elmer will know we're bribing kids to be nice to him. Kids are like chemistry, right? They only bond when it's natural. It's weird when adults get involved."

"Well, when you put it that way, you make it sound like a flop already. But you've got it wrong. I'm saying that kids don't know what's good for them until you show it to them. You gotta trick 'em a little, get them to see the beauty of things by accident. I just know that if the kids really knew who Elmer was, they would love him."

Angelo looked at her. "I'm not buying it. Let's just say that we somehow get enough kids to consider signing up for this little matchmaker scheme. It doesn't even make sense. How do you even advertise something like this?"

Miss Chris got up from her seat and wandered over to the fourth desk from the back on the left side of the room. She said nothing but sat down in that desk and stared straight ahead for at least a minute. A dream-like haze swirled around her head as she began to speak.

"I always wanted to be a research scientist. Did you know that?"

Angelo said nothing.

"I wanted to discover the cure for something big when I was a kid. I thought that I could experiment and find out what caused big, ugly things like cancer or leprosy or malaria. That was my dream." She turned to look at Angelo. "Do you understand me?"

He nodded faithfully but said not a word.

"And so I went to school and figured I would learn all about cell division and mutations and disease. I was going to cure something, let me tell you. It was all I thought of. I was sure that God had called me to rid the world of something ugly, some cancerous, wicked mutation that stole the life out of people." She gazed through the empty air and back into the past. "Are you still listening?"

Angelo could not speak, but he raised his thumb to the ceiling slowly. At that moment, the air compressor in the building whirred and hummed to life, and the mobile of planets flickered in the gentle current of air. Nothing else moved, not even Angelo.

"But you know what, Angelo? I had it right all along. I don't work in a lab. I didn't get hired by a research hospital, but I'm trying to cure something ugly every day, my friend."

Angelo looked up at Miss Chris and tilted his head slightly as if to ask *What? What is it?*

"You don't know?" She looked at him with surprise. "When you've had time to think about it, you can tell me."

———

"How will we decide potential matches?"

It was a good question. When Miss Chris had asked Evangelina from the Food Services Department to join their mission, she had a suspicion that her planning instinct would serve the group well. Now she was part of Team Elm. Evangelina was already a grandmother at age 40, and she had a maternal instinct that matched her sweetie-pie accent and her matriarchal bosom.

"We haven't figured that out yet."

Evangelina was confused. "You gotta give them some incentive. I'm still not sure that being Elmer's friend is all that exciting. Don't get me wrong—I'm not trying to be mean here—but we love Elm because, well, we love kids. All of them. But most kids think Elm is kinda creepy. We're taking a big gamble."

Evangelina did have a point. The idea that human beings are scientific preservationists, that they create alliances with other human beings because they need to survive and because they need to enhance their position in the universe, didn't allow for the spiritual mysteries of love. Yet it was this very mystery that Miss Chris believed in. She would not budge.

The three of them sat awkwardly in the desks designed for smaller people. Evangelina's belly pressed against her chair-desk combo while Angelo's man-legs sprawled out from under his. They readjusted.

"I know what you mean, sister. But let's give it a shot. Stay with me. It just might work. Elm is worth it," Miss Chris said. "Elm is worth it, I tell you."

He heard.

The trio looked up and saw Elmer himself standing in the doorway of the classroom, his rolling backpack leaning against his leg, sandwich bread poised for a bite. *Elm is worth it.* It sounded so beautiful.

The group looked at Elm and he looked at them.

"Hey," he said. He stood awkwardly in the doorway.

"Hello, Elmer," said Miss Chris, clearing her throat. "We were just talking about an idea." She got up and walked over to him. "We want to teach Sun City High School what friendship is. Kind of like an experiment." She glanced at Angelo and Evangelina while poking Elm on the shoulder with an emphatic index finger. "And *this* is the kid to do it."

Elm looked at the trio, all misfits like him.

"Hey, Elm, come on over here and sit with us." Evangelina offered the desk beside her. "We thought it would be good to find some kids who might want to hang out with you at lunch. What would you want to know about a kid who's trying to be your friend?"

He walked to the fourth seat and lowered himself into it. He rattled off a string of requirements as though he had been rehearsing this list for a long time. "I think they need to write an essay first. Then they need to have an interview. And finally, they need to spend an afternoon with me."

"My heavens, he's a genius!" Miss Chris was delighted. "It's perfect. An essay, an interview, and an afternoon with Elm."

"I think Elm's exactly right. The essay will show some effort. It'll tell us if a kid is serious or just trying to be stupid," Angelo offered.

"And the interview…what do you think? Shouldn't we conduct the interview—the three of us?"

"I want to be there," Elmer announced. "I should be there."

"And what kinds of things would you want to do—if you and a friend hung out?" Evangelina asked. "What would you want to do, Elm?"

"I'd want to see something new."

"Something new?"

"Yes. I want to see what other kids do." It was painful to hear this deep alienation from what was normal and ordinary.

"Yup. That's just perfect," answered Miss Chris.

As the four of them sat beneath the classroom poster bearing Einstein's iconic mustache, it was quite possible that a new theory was emerging. Not relativity or gravity, but the Quantum Theory of Friendship in which the universe is made of a myriad of tiny particles called human beings.

"All right, here's another question," added Angelo. "What about the essay? Kids don't usually like to write essays."

"And *that's* why we invented something called EXTRA CREDIT."

The classroom went quiet for a moment. Elmer finally spoke. "I—I want to know if…" he started. "I want to know if the person is good."

Miss Chris looked at him, curiosity rising. "Good?"

"Yeah. I want to know if someone is good. You know what I mean?"

"Do you mean good at being a friend, Elm?" Evangelina asked.

"No, I mean just *good.* I want to know if their heart is good. If they will be nice to me. Being a friend means they shouldn't hurt me. That's what makes someone good."

The four of them went silent, letting the word wash over them. *Good…good…good.* It was so simple, really. Elm was right. The winner needed to be good. He didn't have to be attractive, or brilliant, or popular. A friend of Elm would have an intact soul, with an undamaged heart and virtue in his pocket. Goodness was terribly simply, but awfully rare.

Miss Chris's heart rose up within her. "I've got it. Elm is right. We don't need to know what their accomplishments are or even their motives—"

"They'll just lie anyway," Angelo whispered.

"—or their goals. Instead, we should tell them to write an essay about the most important thing in the world," she said. "Surely this will tell us about their core, right? If you tell us the most important thing in the world, then you've gotten to the center of a person. Everything else won't matter."

The group seemed content with this requirement.

"All right, so we're working out the essay details, and Elm gave us his thoughts on spending the day with him. Now, what about the interview?"

"We will have to come up with a list of questions for them. Really good questions that will weed out someone who's in it for the wrong reasons."

Miss Chris waited while they considered the idea. No one was ready to offer a suggestion. Finally, she spoke. "How about we go home and come back tomorrow, each of us with a list of interview questions. How does that sound?"

Everyone agreed.

"You, too, Elmer?"

He nodded.

That night, when Elmer climbed under the sheets that had been washed only twice that year, he thought about the friend on the horizon. He twitched his foot under the covers and dreamed about sitting comfortably beside someone at lunch, laughing about nothing important, unscrewing the top of an Oreo and handing it to someone else. This would be fantastic. This would be normal. This would be something.

He pictured his friend from fifth grade, remembering the underrated joy of walking to a familiar lunchtime spot only to find that same guy waiting for you every day. He and Devin sat together in peace under the oak tree at lunch for sixty-seven consecutive days. They played thumb wars and threw crumpled leftover tin foil balls into the branches to see if they would stay in the trees. They poked each other with sticks that became light sabers and made up a new language using only animal names. It was the best two months he had ever known.

That night, for the first time, his dreams were actually scattered with hope rather than nightmares.

———————

Team Elm reassembled the next afternoon, Evangelina had brought cinnamon bread[2] from the cafeteria and Angelo set out a six-pack of Coke from the custodial office stash. Miss Chris had written SUN CITY MATCHMAKER on the whiteboard.

"Okay, folks. How are we going to get a list of friend candidates for Elm without sounding desperate or weird?"

"You guys do these crazy conferences all the time," said Angelo. "You can use one of them as a front."

"What do you mean?" asked Miss Chris.

"I mean you guys do these conferences where you use statistics and crap to get people to do what you really want. You know, pretend it's research."

"We don't need a *conference*. We just need teachers to submit names of kids that we can interview."

"Isn't it better if the kids sign up on their own?" Evangelina asked.

"Yeah, but what kid wants to be Elm's friend? I mean, for real."

---

2. Huge flats of industrial cinnamon bread are the cost-effective catering choice of public school gatherings from Alaska to Maine. In meetings where the superintendent is present, the cinnamon is sometimes replaced with bright orange cheese.

They sat in silence and Angelo popped a Coke can.

Miss Chris started tapping the desk. "Maybe we can trick them into thinking they might get some sort of reward."

"Reward? What kind of prize do kids want these days? Being Elmer's friend won't be a reward. They might think it's a punishment."

"Wait a sec—" said Evangelina. "We're overlooking our secret weapon." Her brain was fiddling with the answer. "What's the number one way that kids generate interest in something?"

"You mean…"

"Yeah, I mean the magic of the digital age, the electronic highway, the promise of exposure and attention—"

"You mean social media?"

"Of course! You can't just hang a sign any more and hope that kids show up. This attention-seeking stuff's like nicotine, heroin, and cocaine all wrapped up in a hand-held device."

"She's got a point, Gloria," admitted Angelo. "I think we gotta leave the old-fashioned methods behind."

By the time Team Elm had finished its planning session, they had masterminded the entire scheme. Sun City Matchmaker needed to be a thing. They would hire a consultant who knew all the stealth techniques. If kids could be tricked into what to wear, buy, and think, then it wouldn't be long before being a Friend of Elm would be Sun City's biggest trophy.

$$12 \times 1 = 12$$
$$x \times 1 = x \qquad 6x \times 1 = 6x$$

CHAPTER FOUR

Multiplicative Identity

Team Elm hoped that finding a social media consultant could turn their awkward mission into an irresistible teen magnet. They admitted their limitations and ironically found a company named *Torch Marketing Consultants* in the Yellow Pages. Their owner Bryson "The Spark" Copeland showed up to the high school on a Thursday afternoon, bringing his millennial magic with him.

Bryson's tattoos entered the room 1.2 seconds before he did. He wore his skinny jeans with confidence, and his earlobes were set at a modest 16-gauge. Mrs. Madeline in the front office was reluctant to give him a visitor's badge at first, but Miss Chris assured her on the classroom telephone that he was part of her curriculum-building team.

Hopped up on cold brew, Bryson walked through the door. He grinned behind his carefully groomed beard. "Are you the creative force behind *Sun City Matchmaker*?"

"That would be us," Miss Chris said, extending her hand.

"This is Evangelina, our head of food services here at Sun City—" Evangelina acknowledged the introduction "—and *this* is Angelo, our lead custodian." Both men shook hands.

"And you are Gloria Christensen?"

"Yes, Sir."

They all walked to the circle of chairs and Bryson laid out his pitch. "Well, let's get right to the point, shall we? I've read your proposal, and even though it was—" He paused to glance around the room. "—oddly written, you presented an idea that I can turn into gold." He watched for their reactions. "We consultants at *Torch* can spread even an old-fashioned idea into a wildfire."

"Well, that's wonderful, Mr. Copeland," said Miss Chris. "We think that Elmer is fantastic. We think this also might be a terrific way to educate kids about friendship."

"Educate kids?"

"Well, you know. It could bring up some excellent discussions about mature relationships."

"'Ummm, you said *maturity--*?"

Miss Chris produced her semi-rehearsed thesis. "We're trying to get kids to sacrifice something for others. We love kids around here and we're hoping this little relationship experiment helps both Elmer and the students at Sun City learn how to treat others with love and respect."

Bryson looked confused. The collision of stealth marketing and pure ideals frightened him. "Ooookay...that sounds a little nutty but hear me out first." He opened a leather case and pulled out his gorgeous titanium-framed screen with diamond dust accents. "The way we roll is like this. We embed a psychological reward into the minds of young people through guerilla marketing. We create a flurry of temporary excitement through postings, approval, fake images, manipulated comments, and a host of other strategies."

"Um...I'm not sure this is—"

"Kids these days need to be liked. They want to look and feel like everyone else, but just a step ahead to *appear* original. If they think everyone else wants something, they will go to extraordinary lengths to get it first."

"Well, I'd say that kids have always wanted to be liked…"

"We specialize in the *perception* of approval." Bryson couldn't stop. He had spoken the pitch for so long and now it flowed out in a single stream. "A teenager doesn't even have to practice what he pretends to like, he just has to put it out there, get the digital reactions and BOOM! he'll crave the approval cycle."

"But wait a sec—Mr. Copeland…all we wanted was a few suggestions on how to get the word out—"

"I know you people didn't grow up with this, but I have the tools to connect to teenagers. I know how this works. I mean, not to be rude, but you three—you're a little…" He fumbled for the least offensive phrase. "You three are a little *dated*."

Angelo couldn't take it. Here was a dude who was paid to understand teenagers who had traded eye contact for screens, traded flesh-and-blood relationships for digital manipulation. This guy believed that money equaled power, and that young people had given up on their souls. Team Elm, on the other hand, believed in love. Their alliance was doomed.

Miss Chris felt Angelo's simmering anger and laid a hand on his arm before he could speak. "Mr. Copeland, we appreciate that you've brought some statistical data for us, but we're not really fans of what you're talking about."

Mr. Skinny Jeans rose up. He put away his device and shook his head. "Well, most of my clients are looking to make money. They want an idea to catch fire in order to sell something. You don't actually think social media works in the best interest of its users, do you? If this is an act of mercy, you might need a different sort of marketing model." He rose to leave. "I'm sure this Elmer is a nice boy, but if you think you can actually solve his problems with hugs and shit, we have nothing further to talk about. We don't specialize in reality—only fantasy."

"Thank you for considering our idea," said Miss Chris. "I'm sorry we misunderstood each other's intentions."

———————

Their grand idea had hit the pavement with a thud. Yet Gloria Christenson was still an optimist. A lunatic optimist. She was convinced that *Sun City Matchmaker* could still be a thing.

"Should we ask the drama and art teachers for some help?" asked Angelo the next day. They might know more how to get publicity."

"No good," said Miss Chris. "Remember the year they tried to start up a performance club on campus? They named it the *Future Actors Guild* and they printed up fifty shirts before they looked at the acronym and realized they were screwed. No—the fine arts team ain't the place to look. We need some sharp cookies for this project."

Inspiration needs sugar, so Miss Chris took out her silver box of caramels and they passed them around in silence. After a few minutes, she announced. "Maybe we don't have to trick anybody after all. Did it ever occur to us that some kids might just *want* to be Elmer's friend?"

They sat in silence to think about it. "You're probably right. Let's just tell kids what we're doing and see if enough of them sign up."

"We can call it a 'social experiment' and see what happens," said Miss Chris.

When everyone went home that afternoon, Miss Chris clasped her hands together and prayed for one more miracle, the hope that somewhere God would pluck an unknown human being from his ordinary life and set him down in front of Elmer Whit as a true friend. It just could happen to a guy like him. Just maybe.

————————

The announcement went out on Monday. Over the loud-speaker it went something like this:

Hey, Sun City! This is your principal, Mr. Cardenas. We're doing something really GREAT in your English classes this week. In honor of National Friendship Day, we will be practicing what it means to be a great friend. Our honoree this year is named ELMER WHIT, and one of you is going to get to spend the day with him in two weeks! How do you win? It's so simple! Just write an essay for extra credit and get a paid trip to Coaster City Amusement Land. Let's show our spirit and show Elmer what it means to be a friend!

When the students heard the announcement, it sounded more like this:

Hey, Sun City! This is your overly enthusiastic principal, Mr. Cardenas. We're doing something really lame in your English classes this week. In honor of National Friendship Day, we will be practicing a stupid idea made up by one of our administrators working on a Ph.D. Our honoree this year is that freakishly weird kid ELMER WHIT, and one of you will be forced to spend the day with him in two weeks! How do you win? It's so annoying! Just crank out a desperate essay for extra credit and get a paid trip to Coaster City Amusement

Land. Let's pretend we give a damn and show Elmer what it means to be a friend!

When Elmer heard the announcement, he flipped the hood of his sweatshirt over his face for a moment and scrunched his hands into the fleece. He had agreed to the idea, but now he was scared. Who could blame him? He was the guy who had seen 99 percent of the world treat him like garbage for seventeen years. A guy who had been loved only by a brother and paid professionals. A guy who had never trusted a friend in his life.

"Oh, Elm," Evangelina and her grandmotherly frame stood up and surrounded his hooded figure. "We're going to be right there."

"I know."

"And Elmer, just listen—" Angelo said. "Elmer—think of this as the most fun you'll ever have." He poked him. "It's gonna be so cool—do you hear me?"

Elmer lowered his hands away from the hood, peering out like a Star Wars Jawa in the desert. "Really?"

"Of course."

———

When the students at Sun City first heard the idea, few really cared. But once the leadership class[1] grabbed hold of it? Well, then it *really* tanked. The only way to find a modest pool of candidates was to use that time-tested strategy of extra credit, one of the few commodities that teachers still use.

---

1. Kids can spot marionette puppets and their adult handlers without much trouble.

The kids had one week to submit a 300-word essay in a sealed envelope and placed in the pouch taped to Miss Christensen's classroom door. *Convince the selection committee that you would make a good friend for Elmer Whit.*

During this time, Georgette told Amanda who told Jose who told Justin that Elmer Whit was kind of nice and that maybe he wasn't such a weird kid after all, to which Jacob responded that Elmer was still a freakin' numb-nut, but that in order to get a free ticket to Coaster City you'd have to fake it really good, to which Amanda followed up with a *you're-such-a-jerk* punch on the arm and the admission that she always thought he was nice and since they sat next to each other in sixth grade that maybe she had the best chance to be picked, to which Georgette answered that everything in life is up to fate so you should all just chill out and wait until next week before planning out your whole freakin' life.

In the meantime, Elmer told his mother about the idea. She was predictably uninterested in anything besides his father's eternal, droning, unrelenting failure. She shrugged her shoulders and kept watching *Judge Judy* from her vinyl recliner, swinging her hand in his direction as if to dismiss him from the throne room. Elm had learned to not very much care about his mother's reactions to things, for caring might require dying.

The pouch on Miss Chris's door fattened as the week progressed. Every few days, she would gather that day's essays and lock them in her cabinet. On Friday afternoon Team Elm would read the responses and select the best candidate. When they gathered, they were surprised to find a much larger stack than they had anticipated. A psychologist would have no doubt enjoyed reading the unmistakable case studies of future leaders and losers and psychopaths and beauty queens and poets and criminals and politicians.

High school essays written by a teenager for the purpose of revealing as little as possible about their true selves, is a study in thinly veiled insecurity. As time passed, some scattered essays lay on the center, a portrait of adolescent humanity.

My Friendship Essay
Respectfully Submitted by Jacquelyn Flower

I want to tell you about myself because if I do, then I know you will be super thrilled to have me as your finalist. Being Elm's friend is important, important, important! I think that when someone makes a new friend with somebody different, it makes the entire world better. The normal people befriend the different people, and then other people go "Oh, look at that weird guy who's got a cool friend! Let's go over and talk to him!" and before you know it, everyone begins to understand the layers underneath

You asked why I would make a good friend, and even though I know you will laugh at my answer, just listen to my reasons and you won't find them funny at all. It's a very serious answer. The most important thing in the world is taking care of your hair. Now I know what you're thinking but wait a second. I have a good reason.

A person's hair is like his sacred place. A good hair day can make you feel totally awesome about yourself, and when you do, then you're able to let love's sun rays shine out of you. That's why my life's goal is to open my own hair studio, not a chain or something like that where people are like cattle coming in to get groomed, but a real studio, a place where you can make someone feel awesome about themselves and charge a really decent amount for cut, color, and blow dry, and style.

I saw Elm's hair from the yearbook picture and I think that if I were his friend, it would be like "My Fair Lady," with me being the dude and him being the low-class lady. I think that in the end, I'd like to give Elmer a make-over and I'll teach him how to love himself.

For my final paragraph, I hope that you will consider me to be your final pick. I have everything you're looking for, the looks, the drive, and the intrepidity to go places with Elm by my side!

Friendship rocks!

Why I'm the Man for the Job
Composed by Jonathon D. Forkner, III

As a student of the global community, I present to you my arguments for choosing me as A Friend of Elmer. Due to my overwhelming sense of altruism, my duty to the community, and my desire to achieve greatness in the public square, I am the best choice among your candidates.

As a veteran in the governmental process for quite some time (beginning with the *Itty Bitty Republicans* at Riverview Elementary and culminating with the Sun City Student Council), I have adopted the discipline of benevolence. Elmer Whit is a young person with a great need. I am the man to meet that need.

Furthermore, I feel that we have a duty to the community to protect, defend, and respect the neediest citizens of our community. We will not turn our backs on the lowly or unrefined. In fact, last year I added to my college resume list the role of fundraiser for the SPCA, which rescued thirteen abandoned animals in the Ridge Park neighborhood alone. With Elmer, we should do no less.

In conclusion, my desire to achieve greatness will only be enhanced by the exposure that our selection will bring to my resume. I ask you to consider choosing me as one of your finalist. Both Elm and the public will greatly benefit from the skills I will bring to this worthy endeavor.

The Dark Hole that is My Heart
(a gift from Moonbeam)

It starts small...just a pinprick of sooty blackness
But then the gaping mouth widens and widens with the
corners of its mouth like a vast
   cavern of some cave dying in the Arkansas sunset
Falling
        Falling
              Falling
Like a cave.

Then I see Elm in the distance, like some sort of Savior.
like some sort of bloody redemption
I lick my wounds
And lick
And lick

Til he finds me
Coming to me with a giant band-aid for my soul
And we free each other

Until a new cave yawns
And vomits life's misery into my lap once again

THE MOST IMPORTANT THING
BY DOMINIC COLEY

I AM AN ATHLETE. IF YOU'VE EVER HEARD IT SAID THAT CROSS-COUNTRY RUNNERS AREN'T ATHLETES, THEY WERE SADLY MISTAKEN.

IF BASKETBALL PLAYERS ARE THE GRENADES THAT BLAST ONCE AND ARE GONE, I AM THE LONG TAPER THAT CAN BURN FOR HOURS. IF FOOTBALL PLAYERS ARE THE GAS-GUZZLING HUMMERS ON THE ROAD TO VICTORY, I AM THE ELECTRIC HYBRID WITH A SOCIAL CONSCIENCE. IF BASEBALL PLAYERS ARE AMERICA'S HEROES, I AM AMERICA'S FASTEST SON.

WHAT IS A RUNNER? HE IS SWEAT AND AGONY AND SHEER WILLPOWER. A RUNNER CAN OUTPACE ANY MAN BY DAY AND LOVE ANY WOMAN BY NIGHT.

IF CROSS COUNTRY HAS TAUGHT ME ANYTHING, IT HAS TAUGHT ME HOW MUCH RUNNING LONG DISTANCES SUCK. I WOULD LIKE TO TEACH THESE TRUTHS TO ELM. HE STRIKES ME AS A YOUNG MAN WHO HAS NEVER BELIEVED IN HIMSELF, AND I CAN TEACH HIM THE BENEFITS OF SELF-CONFIDENCE. THERE IS NO NEED TO COMPARE YOURSELF TO ANYONE, AND I AM UNIQUELY EQUIPPED TO SHARE MY STURDY SENSE OF SELF WITH HIM.

LONG DISTANCE RUNNERS ARE PEOPLE WITH VISION. I AM AN
ATHLETE. LET ME RUN FAST WITH ELM.

For Elmer:

I do not know if you will read this. I
heard that someone is trying to find
a good friend for you. When I heard
about it, it made me sad. Even if I don't
make it, I would like to meet you and
tell you that everything will work out
okay in the end.

Elena Cassandra Moon

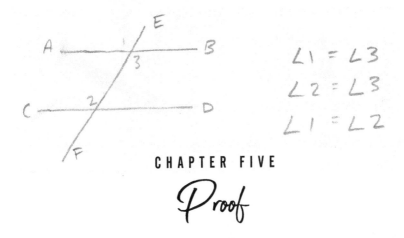

CHAPTER FIVE

Proof

Elena Cassandra Moon was a huge mountain of underestimation. She had grown accustomed to being ignored in favor of the pretty girl *du jour*, but some bright knowledge of her own value, some overwhelming and divine approval, set her upright.

She was a peculiar girl whose simple goodness eclipsed beauty or academic wizardry. Her face was plain and her imagination stunning. When she pulled on her jeans every morning, she never bothered herself with a full-length mirror to check her figure for disqualifications. Her dark hair, like a river at night, swirled around her shoulders. She woke each morning to scrub her face with a cut lemon from the garden and then chose a shirt for its softness and pleasure against her stomach. Her shoes, flat and unassuming, were designed to carry her through her daily adventures rather than tiptoe up to boys and whisper temptations to them. At age seventeen, she was a diligent student of love, not sex, as if she somehow knew the first would require a lifetime of careful study, while the second wouldn't matter much without the first.

She had been born to a mother and father of extraordinary simplicity. Her mother was from Mexico City and her father from Palau, having met in the most cinematic of ways. Elena's father Malachi Moon was a bricklayer who was rescued one afternoon at the age of 24 when a young missionary nurse on a trip to his hometown of Koror attended to his wounds after a construction accident. His first injury required the attention to flesh and blood, and his second required the apprehension of his soul by the mighty Father. Sera, the young angel from heaven, treated both his wounds, and in three years both Malachi and Sera entered into that most spiritual of covenants—a sacred marriage.

And sacred it was. They were stupid and carefree, loving God and each other and a baby girl whom they named Elena Cassandra. When Elena was six, they moved from Palau to the continental United States and began the second two-thirds of their life with little public fanfare.

But Sera knew that something was wrong when the school sent home a letter asking for permission to test their dark-haired little girl. It was not a test for hepatitis or poor vision, but a test for something far more ominous in the world of education: little Elena was not quite right, they said. She was a slow-moving river, full of curiosity and wonder, but sluggish around the academic docks. She might never ace a regular test or attend college, they feared. So let's just do what we can, they said, to keep that stagnant water from growing algae.

With that, mother and father lent her to the school system for a time, but soon realized that their beautiful girl would be just fine either way. Her new teachers taught her tricks and lovely things with paper and pencils, but her parents kept the shallow water moving downstream with nothing but love.

Malachi was not a perfect father, but he overcame his weaknesses (like his intellectual deficiencies or the tendency to hum while Elena asked him questions) through prayer and physical labor. The hard work of hauling stone and brick had given him discipline, and the love of God had given him humility. In this way, Elena might have been the only girl in all of Sun City High School equipped to win Miss Chris's crazy contest. She was a girl who understood love's mysterious ease from a father who barely finished high school but had a Ph.D. in Simple Goodness.

When she heard about the outlandish idea, the idea that someone was trying to find a true friend among a sea of counterfeits, Elena's spirit leaped up inside her. *Why not me?* She reasoned. *I know how to love another human being.*

———————

Nothing gets people worked up more than knowing if they're in or out. From the beginning of time, lists help determine a person's value—party invites, the school play cast list, the honor roll, a list of cheerleaders, student council winners, superior musicians, excellent speakers, gymnasium banners with MVPs, and plaques with VIPs. Miss Chris had posted eight finalists' names on the wall outside the classroom. Monday would be interview day.

Miss Chris woke up that morning with the feeling that everything in her body was rattling around. This afternoon in choosing one final candidate, she hoped that Elmer Whit would begin the preposterous process of healing from the inside out. She was stoked, pumped, and juiced—an impossibility of emotions for a forty-something spinster.

Angelo the janitor, too, woke from his double bed beside his wife of twenty years with the expectation of something remarkable. Evangelina the cafeteria lady popped a few Tums after her early morning coffee and cranked up the volume on her FM truck radio while listening to Los Lobos. She anticipated a grand finale. And finally Elena, who after being kissed half a dozen times by her mother and father, left her house dressed in a simple dark brown shirt and jeans. She had no nervous cramps in her stomach, no fear of the future. When her mother dropped her off, Elena just knew that today would change everything.

When Elmer opened his eyes that morning, he looked up at the ceiling and looked for the shape formed from random plaster—the shape of his father's face that haunted him every morning. It was gone. For six years he had seen a strange outline of that face formed in the shadows of the bumpy plaster, but now he saw nothing but the raggedy, off-white texture of his bare ceiling. He closed his eyes for a moment and then opened them again, expecting to see it: two feet from the corner, six inches from the left. Nothing. He thought of the interviews, but for some reason, he didn't much care. He wasn't nervous, only curious. He had no idea what would come of it.

His dresser was filled with random shirts and pants, the left-overs from a dozen thrift stores. He chose a red shirt today. Red meant excitement. It would make him stand out. He carried his clothes to the bathroom where he showered in the broken tub and counted to ten while he scrubbed his hair full of bubbles. The water poured over his face, taking the foam with it, and he imagined his birthmark dissolving as it swirled down the drain. When he stepped out of the tub and looked in the mirror, it was still there along with his pale chest and too-thin arms. But the red shirt made him feel powerful.

After the final bell that afternoon, Elena and the seven other finalists walked over to the library. Few people really knew her because even though she was in one of the "special classes" just like Elmer, she bore no overt features—like fashion incompetence or awkward social skills—to draw attention to herself. She was just a medium-sized Everygirl with brown hair and olive skin. She would be the least likely to be a public relations stunt; in other words, the most likely to win this contest.

Miss Chris met with Elmer after school in the multi-purpose room of the library to explain the procedure. They would bring in each student, ask a few questions, and then let Elmer decide. As he listened, his mind was somewhere between reality and hope. At least for now, he was hopeful that the candidates who wrote their essays were legitimate. That was good enough.

One by one, Team Elm interviewed students under the fluorescent glow of industrial lights and listened to their answers. Elmer noticed certain things.

Percy didn't look at him.
Allen was a psycho.
Belen fussed with her lip-gloss.
Bennet called him an asylum-dweller.
Hayden picked his nose.
Jordan asked if his birthmark was fake.
Carlo twitched.

But then came Elena. She just was. She walked into the interview room with the quiet beauty of an angel, sat in front of Elmer, stared right into his face, and said, "I've been waiting for you."

"Waiting for me?" he asked.

"Yes."

"Have I met you before?"

"Sort of. We saw each other the first day."

"We did."

"It was nice."

"Yes. It was really nice."

From there, Elmer and Elena spoke freely of Japanese anima-tion and the color of their shoes and the funny curl on the left side of her hair and the origins of his purple birthmark and Miss Chris and fathers and fruit and math and Frisbees. They aban-doned the fake lexicon of adolescence, favoring the language of childhood instead.

Miss Chris observed this unaffected conversation in real time. Even Angelo could not speak a word.

After listening to their easy conversation, Miss Chris finally spoke. "Your essay was really sweet. I'll be honest, the other kids were trying really hard to impress us, but your introduction might have been the only really sincere one we received."

"Thank you." She looked down at her feet.

"Why do you think that you would make a good friend for Elmer?"

Me and Elmer? I don't know him yet, but I know him. I just do. He has something in his eyes that reminds me of...well, *me*. You don't know me or anything, but I know how Elmer feels—feels about things." She paused. "Kids ignore me. I don't know if you know this, but I'm not that smart. I don't think Elmer is that smart either, but his heart is big. I can just tell these things. I think if me and Elmer were friends, we could understand each other. Oh, and I would love for him to meet my mom and dad. He should meet my dad. And my mom—she can cook for us."

Miss Chris looked over at Evangelina. Their eyes, moist with hope, locked in agreement.

"Oh, and it's okay if someone else goes to Coaster City. I figured I'd be Elm's friend either way."

Most girls her age wanted to drive their own cars to school, but Elena was content to meet her mother every day near the green curb beside the tennis courts. Today, like every other day, Mrs. Moon was waiting for her daughter along the curb in the family's old, faded-blue sedan. Elena slipped into the front seat where she and her mother shared their twice-daily kiss on the cheek—once after school and the other before she went to sleep each night. She couldn't wait to tell her mother the news.

"I have something to show you," Elena said as they pulled away from the parking lot.

"What's that?"

"I was picked." Elena took out the instruction sheet and unfolded it in her lap, uncreasing the edges.

"To go to the amusement park with that boy?"

"Yup," she answered. "They picked me."

"Are you kidding me? I *knew* they'd love you!" Mrs. Moon banged on the steering wheel twice. "You are the perfect choice—I just knew it."

"Are you sure?"

"You're perfect!"

Elena waited to say the hard part, the part she couldn't articulate quite yet. "It's just that the other kids were acting so—I don't know. They were acting so weird—like Elmer didn't matter at all. I think they just wanted to get the free trip."

"What about you?"

"I don't know if I even want to go. They want to bring a photographer from the school to take pictures and stuff. That's just weird. I kinda just want to hang out with him."

"Just be yourself. That's all you guys have to do."

What Mrs. Moon had somehow forgotten, twenty years into full-fledged adulthood, is that being "yourself" is the probably the hardest thing in the world, the thing that eludes nearly every young person, the thing that keeps people up at night replaying every word, gesture, and glance that happened the day before, the thing that every human being hopes for during the evolutionary process of growing up. In other words, Mrs. Moon was asking for a miracle when she asked her seventeen-year-old daughter to be herself.

Maybe Elena was the only one who could actually do it.

<hr>

The school buzzed for fifteen minutes when Mr. Cardenas announced the winner of the Coast City friendship trip on Tuesday morning over the loudspeaker. *Who's Elena Moon? Wait—they get a free trip? Is he that crazy-ass kid with the birthmark?*

Several weeks ago, Elmer Whit had simply been the weird dude whom few defended, some abused, and most ignored. But now he wore an aura of *something* around his body, a circle of low-grade celebrity energy. As he passed through the corridors, people gathered and followed, whispered and pointed. Kids who earlier couldn't have told you jack squat about the guy now claimed to know everything about him without having spent a moment in conversation with him. *Elmer's got an older brother, Elmer's got a learning disability, Elmer's a libra, Elmer's not a virgin, Elmer's my homeboy.* The students were vibrating with rumor-energy, the kind of electricity that powers small cities.

Now that being Elmer's friend was associated only with victory, his companionship was unreachable. He still had zero friends but for wildly different reasons than before. A week ago, he was a lonely nobody whom nobody cared about despite unlimited access; today he was a lonely nobody that everybody pretended to know.

But when he saw Elena now on campus, there was no fear. Only a comfortable, steady gaze. They stared at each other like children do when they arrive at preschool and discover a playmate. She didn't see his shoelaces; he didn't see her ordinary clothes. She was stunningly average. He was uncommonly ordinary. They spoke no words to each other but Elena smiled at him as though they had been resting in each other's company for a hundred years.

$$f(x) = \frac{P(x)}{Q(x)}$$

$$A(x)D(x) = B(x)C(x)$$

CHAPTER SIX
Rational Function

When Elena's mother invited Elmer to have dinner with the family, he didn't know what to do with himself. Having lived in a shadowy cave for so many years, he was unaccustomed to the normal gestures of life. *What did it mean to be invited to dinner at someone's home? What was home—and what should one say when he arrives there?* His imagination built Elena's fictional house out of scraps from his past: fleeting images from TV sitcom living rooms, fairy tale dialogue like *How nice to meet you, sir*, and the imagined velvet sofas of rich people. Basically, he had no idea what to do in the house of normal people.

Elena's family heard all about Elmer. *I like him*, Elena said to her mother. *You should meet him.*

He was given her address on a sticky note. *2444 East Empyrean Street*. Elena slipped it to him between classes with the assumption that Elmer knew how to find her family's house. She invited him to come at six o'clock on a Thursday evening "because that's when my dad is clean." She assured him that they would have plenty of food and perhaps a game of cards at the kitchen table. "My mother would love to meet you," she said. "I told her you were a nice person, and she told me that it's hard to find those, so bring him over."

Elmer and Ed and his mother did go to someone's house once before when he was twelve. His mother had been invited to a home-shopping party by a neighbor, one of those awkward capitalist retail schemes that turns hospitality into a profit mill. His mother had dragged them along for the free dinner, and he simply remembers sitting with his brother in the front room, overwhelmed with the smell of cheap candles and overwrought hors d'oeuvres on tiny crystal plates. It was an awful night.

But this was different. Elena's motives seemed overwhelmingly simple: *come over and we'll have pie.* To be invited for the simplest of reasons was beyond his grasp, but he touched the yellow sticky note so many times in the three days leading up to the event, that the gummy surface on the back began to develop a noticeable fuzz.

He went into Miss Chris's room and showed it to her.

"Hey, Elmer," she said. "What's new?"

"Nothing much," he replied.

"Are you getting to know Elena? She's really nice." Miss Chris never made too much eye contact with Elm, sensitive to the masculine temperament. She moved about the room while they talked, straightening chairs and adjusting stacks of papers. It was easier than chatting face-to-face.

Elmer crossed over to her and held out the sticky note. "I wanted to show you something."

"What's this?" she asked.

"Elena asked me to her house for dinner. This is her address."

Miss Chris reached for it and it stuck onto Elm's finger for a split second before giving way. She looked at it carefully. "Well, this is wonderful."

"Should I go?"

"Why wouldn't you go? I think this is a wonderful gesture. It shows you that she wants to share you with her family." Elmer looked frightened. "But do you *want* to go?"

"Sure." He was unconvincing. "But—" He began to pull at his hair, sliding it between his fingers. "But, I don't know what I should do when I get there."

He had never been a dinner guest. *He had never been a dinner guest.* All over the world, in every culture and enclave, people shared meals with one another. It was a rite of passage for all children, no? Didn't everyone, rich or poor, get this kind of education? As Miss Chris stared down at the over-handled square of yellow paper, she recognized the huge gap between the loved and the not-so-much. He was seventeen, and this was Elmer's first-grade education in social etiquette.

"I've got a good idea, Elmer. Angelo is moving some furniture in the building after school tonight, and I'll bet he would have some good pointers to give you about having dinner with Elena and her parents. Would you like that?"

"Okay. But Miss Chris?"

"Yes?"

"Are you sure I should go? I'm not very good at these things."

Miss Chris sat down at the nearest desk and gestured for him to move closer. She looked straight up into his face. "Elmer?"

"Yeah?"

"Do you like Elena?"

Elmer stared at her with eyes of glass. He didn't blink. He didn't swallow.

"It's okay to tell me. Do you like her?"

"If I say yes, will you think it's weird?"

"Of course not. I like her, too."

"I like her," he finally answered. "She looks at me. She is the only one who really looks at me. She talks just the right amount. And her face looks soft."

Miss Chris looked down and smiled. "Well, then, Elmer, I think that a girl like that should have a dinner guest like you. Meet me back here at 2:50."

———————

Angelo took a fat dry erase marker[1] and made two giant circles on the board. "Okay, buddy—here goes the diagram. I was always a visual learner, so it's just easier for me if I do it this way, if that's all right."

The three of them sat in the center of the classroom with the door closed. Elmer and Miss Chris sat side-by-side watching Professor Custodian outline the finer points of boy-meets-parents.

"This circle is your girl's dad." He gestured to the one on the right. "I'm going to write down some of the things he might ask you on Thursday night, okay?"

"She's not my girl."

"Well, you know what I mean." He waved off the lack of confidence and kept going. "And *this* circle—" he pointed to the left side, "—is you." They listened carefully. "Now one of the first things that a father usually asks a boy is something like this." He took his marker and wrote down the first sloppy question: *What do you like to do?* "Now what would you say to that question?"

———————————————

1. Before the dry erase marker was the piece of chalk. Chalk dust made thousands of allergic kids cough and sputter while clapping erasers against the brick sides of school buildings, so in the 1990s educators decided to switch to safer dry erase markers, which contain zylene, methyl isobutyl ketone, and the toxic ingredient n-butyl acetate.

Elmer sat there stunned. "I don't know. I guess I like to walk around the neighborhood and take pieces of bark off of trees."

Angelo's marker hovered in mid-air. "Dude—what kind of a load of crap answer is that?

Miss Chris jumped in. "I think what Angelo is trying to say, Elmer, is that your answer might be kind of confusing to someone. You might like to peel bark off of trees—there's certainly nothing wrong with that—but most people can't really relate to that. Maybe you should think of something more common."

Angelo offered his opinion. "Like maybe you could say you like soccer or maybe drawing or even action movies, or something like that."

"But it isn't true. I don't like those things."

"I know, but we're trying to make a connection to the dad, right?" Angelo looked stumped. "All right—let's try another one." He stuck the marker cap in his mouth and thought hard. "What if he asked this question?" Angelo printed the question *What kind of career are you thinking about for the future?*

"Wait a sec, Angelo," said Miss Chris. "Elmer's only seventeen, you know. That might be too complex a question."

"You're darn right, but dads want to know stuff like this. You have to be ready anyway." He dotted his *i*'s. "So what do you think? What should you say?"

"What *would* I say or what *should* I say?" Elm asked.

"Oh, you're a smart one. Just what's the honest answer?"

Elmer sat and thought about it. "I think I would like to help kids get into roller coasters—like check their seatbelts or latch the iron bars before they take off. Or maybe measure kids to see if they're tall enough to ride stuff." Elmer had seen a movie once about carnival workers and had felt a strange kinship with them.

"You're freaking amazing, dude," said Angelo. He looked at Miss Chris and held out his hands in amazement. "What are we doing here, Glory?"

"Okay, I think maybe this wasn't the right idea here." Miss Chris turned and looked at Elmer. "Listen, son. I think that you should just show up at Elena's house on Thursday and just be yourself. Don't even listen to us. We don't know what we're doing anyway."

"She right, kid," said Angelo. "I'm just an old dope, really." He smiled. "Elena thinks you're great, okay? Forget all this crap… we don't even know if her old man will even care." He walked over to Elmer and put his heavy brown hand on his shoulder. "You wanna know what I told my first girlfriend's dad when she invited me over?"

"What?"

"I told him that I wanted to fix skateboards and sell tortillas."

"That's sweet," said Miss Chris. "I'll bet he loved you."

"Nah. He told his daughter I was a frickin' loser." He shrugged off the memory. "But I didn't care. Listen, E-Man. I never made more money than a janitor's salary my whole life." He grew serious and the room collapsed around his voice. "I been the kinda guy you might not notice around town. But I love people. Shoot, I just love people. That's why I love this job 'cause nobody takes care of kids like I do."

Elmer held out his hand and they clasped each other's palms in a band-of-brothers grip. "You know what? I'm going to Elena's house on Thursday. Her dad's gonna love me."

———

A scooter was hardly the vehicle of choice in which to arrive at Empyrean Street. Balancing a box of Oreos to the handlebars, Elmer slowed in front of the simple boxy house with the numbers *2444*.

He had dressed carefully. After pulling every stitch of consignment store clothing out of every closet in the house, he found one shirt well suited to the occasion. It was made of dark gray cotton with three buttons and a wilted collar. Except for the small embarrassment of a tiny embroidered turtle on the left breast, it was perfect. Accompanying the Polo knockoff was his best pair of pants: dark denim with beige stitching on the butt pockets. On the right man, the ensemble could very well pass as quirky-urban-thrift-store, but on Elm, it was more like white-trash-meets-clearance-table. Happily, Elm—and even Elena, for that matter—would not care about the difference.

The Moon home was simple and tidy. The architecture bore no custom features, but set among a neighborhood of similar floor plans, the house boasted the cleanest yard around. To the left and the right, other homeowners had left bikes, tall grasses, and domestic detritus strewn about the property. Elena's house, on the other hand, showed remarkable pride of ownership. Elmer walked up to the front porch, adjusting the three wildflowers he had taped to the front of the Oreo package.

When he reached the first step, Elena opened the front door and came out dancing on her tiptoes. "Elmer! You're here! And what did you bring?"

"I brought you some cookies," he said. "They have extra cream in the middle." He pushed the package toward her and she fondled the wildflowers on the front.

"Look what you did to it—that's so beautiful." Elena crinkled the package as she brought it to her nose.

He looked around the front porch. "I like your house. It's very clean."

"Yeah, well, my mom was raised to keep everything picked up." Elena was dressed in a blue, lightweight sweater, and her dark brown hair flowed across it like chocolate. "My parents are waiting to meet you. C'mon—I'll bring you inside."

Elmer followed Elena into the front room. It smelled of lemons and old books with a touch of blue toilet cleaner. Mrs. Moon stood in the middle with her arms outstretched. Like Miss Chris, she was one of God's messengers.

"Hello, dear one," she said. "We are so happy to have you here with us for dinner tonight." She reached across the empty space and embraced the gray-shirted stranger with an uncommon love.

"Hi," said Elmer. "Thank you."

"Elmer brought us some cookies, mom. I'll put them in the kitchen for dessert." Elena left the room, leaving Elm and Mrs. Moon to stand by the front door. "Please, come into the living room. My husband Malachi will want to meet you, too."

Elmer followed Mrs. Moon dutifully into the second chamber, a room of tiny, overwhelming details all set in their proper places. At home, Elmer knew nothing of such deliberate placement, as his house was a whirlwind of survival items propped in corners with no forethought. But here, the place where his girl lived and breathed and loved, the rooms were full of precise objects chosen for aesthetic qualities—a crystal decanter, a dried wreath of lilac, a painted farm bucket. For a moment, Elmer wished he were alone to glance around this museum and get his bearings.

He got his wish.

Mrs. Moon excused herself to join Elena in the kitchen, and Elmer was left alone for several minutes propped on the edge of their sofa. He gazed at the room as one gazes at a landscape in a foreign country. Pillows—just for show—and a mirrored tray with tiny glass animals were like archeological artifacts. A chair, covered with a faded, billowy piece of fabric, sat cocked at an angle for conversation. And suddenly, without warning, a longhaired cat sidled up to Elmer with all the insouciance of a farm animal.

"She's Vonda," Elena said, coming into the room. "I've had her since I was five."

"She's pretty," he said.

"Her fur will drive you wild, but she's the nicest thing ever."

Elena sat next to Elmer, and the sofa fell inward toward the center, bringing their thighs perilously close to each other. "Sorry—I didn't mean to sit so close," she said.

"That's okay."

Mr. Moon suddenly filled the space with his body, a bulky presence that shifted the mood abruptly. He made a straight line for Elmer, which frightened the young man to no small degree. "Hello there, Elmer. How are you, young man?"

Elmer and Malachi clasps hands as Elm felt his own palm shrink inside the grip of Elena's father. "Good. I'm good." Malachi pumped his arm several times before letting him go.

"Sera has a few things left to do for dinner, so would you like to come in the backyard with me until it's time to eat?"

Elmer looked at Elena desperately. *Should he go?*

"Go ahead, Elm," said Elena. "I'll go help my mom."

Malachi trotted through the kitchen to the back sliding door while Elmer followed at his heels like a puppy. He liked being led; it saved him the trouble of figuring out what to do. They passed the table, set with melamine dinnerware and stemmed water glasses stuffed with a paper napkin spun into some sort of origami bird shape. The entire house was a kitschy art fair. A kitschy art fair in the Garden of Eden.

Mr. Moon reached for some pruning shears on the back patio, a square of swept cement punctuated by molded plastic lawn chairs and tufts of potted plants. "If you'll grab that bag there—" Mr. Moon gestured to a plastic leaf bag, "—you can help me pick up the scraps."

The two began to talk, side by side. Malachi Moon was a commoner by trade, and this made him infinitely unpretentious. He was not afraid of dirty work, and unlike other professionals who might be tempted to talk about assets and business goals, he preferred to talk about uncomplicated things like World Cup soccer or the beehive under his shed. Working alongside a man who held no grudges, Elmer's stomach began to relax as he opened and closed the lawn bag. He had value in this home, he intuitively reasoned. He was safe here.

Soon, however, Mr. Moon asked the fated question, which Prophet Angelo had written with frightening accuracy on the whiteboard: "So what do you like to do?" he asked casually.

He was screwed. Could he say it? Without even thinking Elmer replied, "Oh, I like to walk around the neighborhood, pulling bark off of trees." *Oh my god*, he thought. *I was warned. I was warned, but I said it anyway.*

With no trace of surprise or condemnation, Malachi simply continued the conversation as though it were the most natural answer in the world. "So you're a budding arborist, eh? I was into trees myself at your age. In fact, arborists make a great living, you know. Some people think they just hack limbs off trees and poke them into a shredder, but the serious guys make an art out of it—they're like math geniuses. You'd be a good arborist, I can tell."

And then, the two continued their orbit around the Moon's house, two men chatting about trees and carnival rides while waiting for the ladies to finish dinner.

"Malachi!" Mrs. Moon hollered from the back door. "Come and eat!"

"We're ready to roll, Missus Moon," Malachi replied, "but we gotta wash our hands."

Instead of using prissy lavender soap and a guest towel, Malachi pulled the hose off the hook on the side of the house and let an arc of water pour over his hands. He gestured toward Elm, and the two of them took turns holding the hose for the other. Malachi even flicked water into Elmer's face—twice.

Coming inside, the four of them took their seats around the table, the parents on the two ends with Elm and Elena sitting across from each other. "Should you pray, dear?" Mr. Moon asked, and then, for the second time that day, she talked to God. Elmer watched the three of them drop their chins, and he followed. Afraid to peek, he listened to Mrs. Moon talk to God as easily as if she were asking him to pass the potatoes.

Mrs. Moon, give him a little grace (God said that morning) and not just love but respect. That's what a young man needs more than anything. Give your wings to your husband for the evening so that he can rise up and give Elmer love and freedom and respect and peace. And while you're at it, said God, if he should happen to drop something, break something, say something, or botch something, love him anyway and fix it together so that he may begin to know that he is mine and no one else's and I made him to love and be loved. If you can, laugh while he's with you, pull out the game board and teach him how to play, teach him how to win, show him how to talk, show him how to love. If you do all these things, his soul will see me, and his heart might be saved from everlasting darkness.

CHAPTER SEVEN
Identity Function

To this day, they still can't figure out what made them do it, but maybe it was fate.

Three weeks of knowing Elena, and Elmer felt re-born. The moments he spent with her poured oxygen into his lungs and light into his path. She never averted her eyes, but rather stared directly at him while he answered her questions. She never confused him, never judged him, never stared at his birthmark except to ask directly, "How come God gave you such a cool birthday present?"

When Elena was near, Elmer forgot himself. When he and Elena were together, Elmer thought of nothing but each word of their conversation in succession—no behind and before, no past and future, but only right now. They were simply beautiful together, an equation whose answer required no effort at all.

At home, Elmer's mother was often too busy with her own self-loathing to notice any subtle differences in her son. But the signs were obvious. A Dollar Store receipt for dental floss. The ancient ironing board moved from one side of the closet to the other. A brief glimpse of push-ups in the living room. Longer showers.

The scheduled trip to Coaster City, just a week away, haunted him for some reason. It felt weirdly staged, like some public relations stunt for his school rather than a genuine reward. He lay in his bed and stared at the popcorn ceiling again as the dawn cast bumpy shadows above his bed. Instead of his father, he saw his brother in the shadows and wondered if the town of Handley had given him hope. *Handley.*

It was better than a roller coaster. His brother had fled to find comfort. Ed had known someone there, and he had left for the only place where he thought he might find escape. To most people it was a side trip to nowhere, a pass-through rather than a destination. But to Elm, who had barely seen past his own city limits, no less Sao Paulo or Las Vegas or Rome, Handley was the edge of the universe, the symbol of emancipation.

He shared his plan with Elena during lunch the next day. They were sitting together against the concrete planter, pulling leaves off the shrubbery in symmetrical order.

"What are you talking about?"

"I mean, we should take the money for the amusement park and go find my brother instead."

"But he lives in *Handley*. That's a long way."

"Only a half day's trip. We could do it." Every two seconds he popped a leaf off its stem and added it to the growing pile on the ground. "Just us, though—no adults."

She leaned in close. "But we're…we're not *grownups* yet. And how would we get there?"

He felt the warm moisture of her breath fall into his ear and his spirit fluttered. Who was this girl anyway, and why should they risk too much in fleeing the world, racing toward God-knows-where without money or a lick of sense between them? Career children don't find success in the big world, do they?

They sat leaf-pulling for a good long time, hearing the vague stupidity of teenagers float across the campus sound waves. Their private world empowered them.

"Let's take a bus. We'll get out of here."

"Oh my god, Elmer. We can't get on a bus. My mother would never let me."

"Okay, then let's ask her first."

Now this was odd. Elmer Whit was certainly not the first boy to come up with the idea of running away from home. With a girl. With no money. To escape the terrors of life. But he was probably the first to tell the girl's mother his plans before they left.

"My mother will be scared. She knows I'm not...she knows I'm not smart."

"Yes, you are," he said. "And I am, too."

This was the first time that Elm said it. *Could it really be true?*

"I believe it, Elmer, but no one else will let us do this." She stared into her eyes. "It's kind of—it's kind of stupid."

This was crushing. He needed Elena to nod and accept and assent with no hesitation, for this would be his freedom, a way to know that he was a man like his brother, a man unlike his father, a man who could make a plan and slay dragons, even if those dragons only sat along the route of a Greyhound bus to Handley.

"It's not stupid, Elena. We can leave for three days—maybe as long as a week. A week of school doesn't matter anymore."

She knew he was right, but this plot, this Revolution, was not in her DNA. It would have to settle in, this freaky plan with no bones or possibilities. "What about money? We don't have any."

"I know how to get the tickets."

"How? I don't have cash—just some birthday money from my family, maybe sixty bucks is all."

"We won't steal, I promise. We can just ask."

"Who's going to give us money for bus tickets? That's crazy."

Elm started to rock back and forth again, crumpling up the wax sandwich paper in his fist as he worked out the details in his half-head. It was all coming together now. His whole life had prepared him for this preposterous journey.

———————

Miss Chris found Elm's letter under her door on Friday morning.

It was written with Elena's purple sparkly gel pen on a piece of yellow legal pad.

It contained the following message:

Dear Miss Chris,

We are leaving. We will be safe and we don't want to steel any money from anyone. Instead of going to coaster city we would like to visit my brother instead. A bus ticket for both will cost $143.52 cents. I'm sorry it is so much but they put some tacks on them. I know you will do this. I will pick up the money tomorrow night under the heavy stone at the bottom of the flag at school so it can be secret.

Love, E and E

p.s. We are telling Mrs. Moon about it, so you and her can talk if you want. We are not going to be gone long so don't panick until at least five days go by. Or maybe seven. Trust us please. p.s. And thank you for doing all this for me. I think Elena is working out real good.

Miss Chris read the letter—read it three times—and went immediately to her desk where she lifted out a long brown envelope. She wrote in big letters E AND E on the front and then wrote a short note on the back. It was five o'clock before she left the bank, and by the time she arrived home, she had picked up the swollen envelope in her hands at least four times. It felt magical and risky and ridiculous and redemptive and she couldn't wait to lift the stone under the flagpole when the sun went down the next day. Of course, Miss Chris wasn't real because real teachers worry about truant officers and kidnapping and liability and losing employment and all that sort of thing.

Elm and Elena had risked it all on the goodwill and under-standing of his teacher. Elena had her doubts, to be sure, but Elm assured her that Miss Chris would come through for them. They would, however, have to figure other things out, like ditch-ing school. Having no background of delinquency served them well; what truant officer would come looking for them? They had practiced anonymity their entire lives. As they saw it, kids skipped school for all kinds of horrible reasons, so why would a "family trip" disqualify them from good citizenship?

They didn't need such a dramatic plan, but it was so much more interesting this way. The money-under-the-stone plot was plagiarized from a lousy B-list action movie, but where's the fun in picking up money from Miss Chris's classroom?

It went like this: Elena would go for a "walk" after dinner, and Elmer simply needed to keep his door closed at home since his mother would not notice whether he had slipped out of the house or remained beneath the bedclothes all day. That Saturday was the slowest the earth had ever spun. At one point, Elmer was certain the world had stopped moving altogether.

They consumed dinner in separate houses—one experienc-ing a home cooked meal of corn tortillas and beef and the other a can of potted meat and powdered mashed potatoes from the broken shelf behind the sink. When the time came to meet at the flagpole, Elena simply announced to her mother, "I'm going to take a walk." Elmer, on the other hand, merely squeaked open the screen door, mounted a juvenile scooter with handlebars, and headed off into the dusk toward the direction of Sun City High School.

Elena arrived first. She saw him coming.

From afar, Elmer was at first a wobbling dark smudge against the horizon. Then she saw his foot, pendulum-like, moving back and forth against the pavement, swooshing his scooter toward her. He was just a child, she thought. But as he moved closer, his body swelled into the shape of a man—a brave, scooter-riding Man-Child.

By the time he approached Elena, he was panting with just enough pace to add suspense to the scene. "We'll walk to the sign first. You'll stay there behind the wall and I'll go in to get the envelope." Elm's role as secret agent gave him new courage. He was light years away from the sex appeal of James Bond, but where there once was none, Elena had given him a smattering of *machismo*.

They walked together to their spot. "Should we have a signal in case someone is coming?"

"Um…okay. What do you think? You got an idea?"

Elena wasn't sure. Her first idea was nonsensical "How about I'll sing a lullaby?"

They thought about this for a moment. Then Elm spoke. "But the person who's coming will know there are people around. Lullabies are too—too obvious?" Elmer didn't want her to feel bad for the lousy idea so he added, "But if we were somewhere else, a lullaby would be great."

"I know. I'll scrape my shoe against the ground. The gravel will make noise. Birds and animals could make that noise."

"Perfect." He was enthusiastic with this plot. Elena smiled.

They walked together to the large sign. The words SUN CITY HIGH SCHOOL were illuminated in crazy fits, the budget having not allowed Angelo to permanently repair the electrical wiring for many months now. In the darkening light, sometimes it said S N ITY HIG COOL and other times it said SI N CIT HIGH S OOL. Elena looked up at it, mouthing out the different phonetic meanings in fascination. She was often distracted by lights and sounds, and this proximity to a light show was making her brain flicker in strange patterns.

Elmer interrupted her reverie. "I'm going in," he announced.

Elena snapped back to central command center and watched as Elm rushed out across the circle drive in front of the school toward the flagpole. She watched him grow smaller in the darkness. He was far away now. She saw him reaching down. He was lifting the rock awkwardly now. So close to freedom. *What was it? Was there something in his hands? Did he have an envelope?*

In an instant, she saw his figure cut through the night air coming toward her. His naturally odd walk had improved with the heroism of his deed, and Elena even thought him pleasing despite his weird shorts, the nerdy hitch in his gait. His hands looked empty—or were they holding something? She couldn't stand it—*did he have the money?*

As he moved to within twenty feet, her spirits fell. He was swinging his arms, grazing only air. Then his hands rose to his head, his elbows bent, as if to say, "I got nothing." But suddenly, with a victor's grin—perhaps the first one she had ever seen on his face—he reached under his shirt and produced a long brown envelope.

He was holding their ticket to freedom.

Under the changing light of the SCHS sign, the two of them fondled the sealed envelope, feeling its puffy contours. Elm turned it over in the light. On the back of the seal was Miss

Chris's unmistakable handwriting: *For the smartest young man I know and Lady Moon, his companion.* Elm handed it to Elena and said, "You can open it."

She slid her finger under the tiny gap in the triangle and felt it give way. They both leaned their heads over the opening and saw a line-up of grey-green bills. Elm reached in and slid one out of the envelope. A twenty. And then another and another and another after that. Eight twenty-dollar bills, some crisp and others dog-eared. Neither one of them had ever held so many bills at once.

A car's headlights broke the pattern of flickering electricity, and Elena dropped behind the bush, pulling Elm down beside her. While they waited, crouched, for the car to pass, Elmer drew the envelope to his nose and inhaled the unfamiliar scent of cash. He made a face. "I really thought it would smell better," he said.

Elena made her own investigation by pulling it to her face. She took a whiff. "You're right. Money stinks. But that's okay. We won't have it for long."

———

Elm's mother, dog paddling in life's deep end, hardly knew that he was leaving. With one son gone and an ex who often snatched the other son on a whim, she heard the plan with limited comprehension. *A road trip to see Ed? Taking a break from school? Get out of here and take a bagel with you. Oh, and here's a twenty-dollar bill. Make it last, you moron.*

Mr. and Mrs. Moon, on the other hand, fought like crazy after the plot was revealed. Malachi was not a foolish man and he resisted the plan like a father holding back the gates of hell. Elena would not travel to unknown lands alone with a young man, he declared, and he and his wife battled back and forth as they would never fight again in their lifetime.

Yet Sera was unmoved. She heard the voice of her daughter and understood the difference between two brands of rebellion. Elena was not giving them the finger, she reasoned. Elena was growing older. She would be eighteen soon. Father and mother, with the sort of calibrated balance that proves a child deserves both, shouted and reasoned with all their faculties until finally settling on a strange compromise. Sera believed Elmer to be good and trustworthy, and Malachi knew his daughter was the same. Sera instructed Elena with odd maternal leniency that she must return safely. When Elmer came to carry her suitcase, she took his face in her hands and said that while they were visiting his brother, under no circumstances would she approve of any naughty business between them. That was the speech. It was powerful in its brevity and seriousness.

So now, with the incomprehensible approval of two mothers, a seventeen-year-old and his soon-to-be-eighteen-year-old female companion were on a highway to Handley, a mid-sized, mid-ambitious, American town. They could have been going somewhere sexy to claim their dignity—Barcelona, Moscow, or New York. The real destination, however, was the city of Otherness. A place that was separate from where they had come. Any place that had a pathway from earth straight to heaven.

A place where love could multiply.

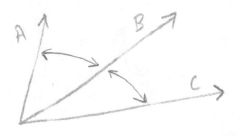

CHAPTER EIGHT

Adjacent Angles

Elena and Elm scooted their butts together in the bus seat and watched their home city fade away from the picture frame of a Greyhound window. The puffs of gray smoke sputtered from time to time from the back of the bus, and Elena choked on the exhaust even though every window was tightly closed.

It was a frightening thing to be rushing alongside the setting sun while moving away from a safe place, so Elena bowed her head and breathed slowly. They had barely considered the insanity of this plan before rushing into it, but it seemed far less chaotic than staying around to face the known world. They would ride the bus through the night and arrive in Handley by early morning.

Elm was less fearful riding the bus, having known about gray clouds and ominous unknowns for many years now. There were about two dozen people traveling with them, all wearing different shades of sadness. Some of them rested their heads against the seat backs and others fixed their gaze on various landmarks as they rushed by. One guy wore a hat with colorful embroidery letters--MAUI ADVENTURES--juxtaposed against the bleak, mid-continent highway. Elm wondered where they all were going, what places had promised to make things better, and whether his own journey would lead to something hopeful.

Elena had brought a bag, a green canvas tote with a black triangle of recycling arrows on the side.[1] When she walked long distances, she could sling it across her chest with the sack hanging beneath one arm. At the bus station, they had agreed that she would carry the return tickets in her bag. Besides that, without the interference of her mother, she had packed three shirts, several changes of underwear in a large plastic bag, two tubes of Chapstick, a map, a toothbrush with a plastic cover, and a Vietnam era military canteen. She had also brought her school ID and a library card from sixth grade.

Elm was equally clueless, and only slightly less practical. His suitcase of choice was his eighth-grade backpack. Its contents were varied and unexpected. He had found one of his brother's old belts, so he had wrapped it in a circle like a snake and secured it with a giant paper clip to keep its shape. This lay in the bottom of the backpack, apparently waiting to hold up another pair of pants which he hadn't bothered to pack in the first place. He had also included in his journeyman's satchel a flashlight, a pack of gum, a plastic baggie of lifesavers with a toothbrush and mini-tube of paste tucked inside, a package of size 30 generic bright-white briefs still in the package, a sleeve of fig cookies, three shirts rolled into sausages and secured with rubber bands, a pair of green flip-flops with rubber toe thongs, and Miss Chris's envelope. His favorite trick, though, was the way he slipped a small comb into his sock for safekeeping.

---

1. During the 2000s, young people became enamored with eco-products. As a result, hundreds of factories produced green fashion merchandise with the help of giant smokestacks and foreign child labor.

The bus, with its faded colors and cheaply cleaned seats, began to take on new dimensions as Elm and Elena vibrated to the engine's heart and soul. Their arms barely touched from time to time, only colliding when the bus bumped over a pothole. The daylight moved from dusk to gray to black-water night.

A moving bus in the dead of night is like REM sleep: its eyelids flutter in quiet repose, but the brain-engine is hard at work. Elmer and Elena's bodies, half-asleep in their awkward and upright positions, wobbled along the highway to the hum of the engine. Elmer's legs woke him up first. They were numb from unfamiliar pressure against the thighs, and the tingling set off an alarm in his body.

He looked over at Elena awash in sleep, whose face was slightly blue from the glowing panel of nightlights that ran along the length of the bus. He thought her beautiful. Her head lay back against the seat at a funny angle, and her hair draped over the cushion like a silky, brown mink. He loved her face. It was bright and hopeful, even in the dark, and its blemishes comforted him. He could not stare long. To stare would be disrespectful in some way although he knew not why.

Instead, Elm turned to watch the inky landscape fly past outside his window. For all he knew, they could be rushing past mountains or prairies; he couldn't tell. But he was leaving something behind. Leaving it all behind for an unknown hope.

"What are you thinking about?" It was an unexpected whisper. Elena pulled her legs up against her chest and grabbed on tight to them before pivoting toward the window to face Elmer. She was fully awake now.

"Not much. Just that I feel happy."

"That's good. Happy and sleepy." She put her forehead against her knees so he could hardly hear her. "Happy and sleepy—that's me," came her muffled voice buried in her legs.

"You know what?" Elmer asked.

"What."

"Our names start with the same letter," he said.

"They do. That's cool. Elmer and Elena."

"Elmer and Elena," he repeated. "It's like in math class." Elmer was trying to think so hard his brain was making popping noises in his head. "We're like…we're like E squared." He was proud of the connection.

"We're like an math equation, then.[2] E times E." Elena laughed at the thought. "That's funny. Neither one of us are good at math." She paused. "But we're a good answer. We multiply."

"I like E squared. It sounds like a big number." They sat in silence for a while longer, thinking about their new discovery. "Can I call us E squared, then?"

"Mmhmm. That's good with me."

Another hour or more passed, in which Elmer and his companion alternated between sleep and wakefulness. Not much was said in the stillness of the journey, but once after waking, Elmer noticed that Elena appeared busy at work, hunched over her lap like a seamstress over a project in a darkened room. When she leaned back, he saw what she had been working on. There, in beautiful black letters, she had etched onto the strap of her traveling bag in permanent ink a capital E with the superscript 2 hovering over its right side.

There was no mistaking it now: Elmer would never again equal zero.

---

2. Math nerds are notoriously finicky about their terms. If you got a C in math, then you don't care whether E^2 is technically an *equation* or an *expression*. But if your average in math class was a 97.23%, then you are going to boycott this book for egregious errors like this.

"Your brother? I don't know him, Elm. What is he like?" They had traveled all night together and now they spoke softly in the dark.

"My brother is cool. But he couldn't take it anymore. He left for somewhere, just took his car one night after saying goodbye to me." Elm bowed his head. "I miss him."

"I never had a brother. Or a sister." Elena caught the bus exhaust in her throat and stumbled on her words. "But I'm not sad."

"No? I'd be sad without my brother."

"How can I be sad for something I never had?" Elena's voice rose at the end of that rhetorical question. "I'm good without a brother or sister, and I would've been good with one. Either way, I'm good."

"I like that." Elm repeated her words. "Either way, I'm good. That means you can't go wrong."

"Nope."

"Where are we?" Elm asked. "Are we in Handley yet?"

"Nope. But close, I figure."

He looked around the interior of the bus and checked out his fellow passengers. Maui hat-guy was wide awake, and two of the old women were fiddling with the contents of their enormous satchels. The driver was the same wax figure in the front, his back looking no different from when he first sealed the front door shut. Several others were asleep, perhaps having spent the entire night hypnotized by the pulsing highway lines out the window and now succumbing to rest.

"Did you sleep at all?" he asked.

"Not much. I miss my mommy." She self-corrected. ". . . my *mother*. She will be worried about me."

"It's okay to call her mommy," reassured Elm. "She knows you are safe with me."

Without a map, one must read signs. Elena perceived that they were close to the Handley bus station since the business markers, though limited, started to show things like *Handley's Family Hardware* and *The Handley Burger*. The city was not large, but in the minds of two barely-adults, the unfamiliar landscape of small businesses and ugly roadside signs made it seem like an urban maze. The light from the recently risen sun cast a peachy glow across the entire district, and Elena watched the buildings swoosh across the windowpane in steady rhythm.

Finally, the bus creaked its way into the open bay of a downtown bus station. The driver pulled to a rolling stop and after the spitting sound of his dying engine, he grabbed the microphone from its holder. His voice, under the influence of a twenty-dollar amplification system, was muffled—even a little spooky.

"Ladies and Gentleman, the local time is now…(he checked the digital read-out)…7:35 a.m. and the current temperature is 67 degrees. I thank you for traveling with us today. Please check your area for any belongings you might have left behind during travel, and I thank you for choosing Greyhound."

Living from one moment to the next had been easy so far, but Elm and Elena now faced the very real possibility that they knew absolutely nothing about their next step. Elmer had been a bit deceitful with Elena's parents when he said that they were visiting his brother since he really had no idea where to find him. They stared at each other for a moment, lost in the finality of this stop.

"You got your stuff, Elena?"

"Yup. Got it all." Elena patted her satchel hanging beneath her arm. "You got everything, too?"

"Right here.

They slipped out of the bus into the growing sunshine. The people with whom they had shared a long journey cared not a bit for this misfit couple on the way to nowhere. The driver swung open the door under the belly of the bus and began to toss various pieces of luggage onto the concrete in a growing pile of shapes and colors. Different people began to slip into the atmosphere, some meeting families, others going to sit on benches in the bus station, and still more walking straight ahead until they were seen no more. Elm and Elena were left standing on the concrete, looking left and right at their destination.

A strange town, especially one as unimpressive as this one, can be overwhelmingly depressing. But for Elm and Elena, it was the very notion of independence that made them rather giddy. The old diner with the red sign might as well have been *Chez Panisse*, and the dumpy used car lot became a limousine service *en route* to a Vegas casino.

"Well, here we are," Elm said.

"Here we are." The weight of Elena's bag tilted her body to touch Elmer's shoulder, and the space around his body warmed.

Standing near them on the concrete was a medium-sized, thirty-something Latino gentleman with kindness about his eyes. He was wearing heavy gray canvas pants, the sort that keep a stiff shape no matter how they move, and a soft chocolate-brown shirt. He looked at Elm and kicked his chin upward in a gesture of acknowledgement. He called out, "Where you headed?"

The two looked at each other as if deferring the question. Finally, Elmer spoke up.

"We came to Handley to find my brother."

THE MULTIPLICATION OF ELMER WHIT

"And we're on a field trip for school," Elena added as an afterthought.

"Awright. Tha's cool." He stood on the sidewalk, simply scraping his shoe on the ground and avoiding too much eye contact.

Suddenly Elmer, who had a sense about these things, made a snap assessment. He would make this stranger a risky ally in their journey. "Um, sir," he said. "We're not really here on a field trip for school."

"No?"

"No. Not really." Elmer looked at Elena, who stared at him with the first signs of doubt. But he continued. "Like she said, we've come from—well, we've come a long way from home to sort of…to sort of learn some new things. We really don't know where my brother is right this minute, so we will need somewhere to go—somewhere to go right now until we find him." Elmer continued, haltingly. "We're here for only three days."

"Three days ain't long."

"No, sir."

He continued. "You know, the library in town is one hell of a beauty. If you need somewhere to go during the day, a place to rest or whatever—that library is a real jewel."

"The library?"

"You betcha. I've spent some time there myself. I ain't much of a student, but I read like a maniac. Just thought you might like a tip."

Thanks, Mr.…Mr.—what is your name, sir?" asked Elena.

"It's Michael Rubio. But you can call me Rube." He lowered his voice and leaned toward Elmer. "That's what happens when you ain't a businessman. People call you by your childhood nickname."

"I like Rube," said Elena.

"Um, Rube, where is this spot?" asked Elmer.

"The library? It's at least a mile from here, so you'll have to walk a little ways. On the corner of First and Cole." The man stretched his arms over his head and leaned first to one side, then the other, before waving his hand toward the north. The three of them instinctively followed his movements, looking wistfully toward the Promised Land. "Well, good luck to you kids. Enjoy your stay in Handley."

The two watched him turn away, and their eyes followed him in silence until he disappeared beyond an old brick building dotted with canvas awnings.

"He was nice," Elena said.

"Yeah," said Elmer. "But you know what? I never liked libraries as a kid. They made me sick." He looked down as though ashamed of his revelation. Even the word *library* evoked memories of long, stupid hours staring at institutional oak furniture. "But this one will be different. You'll be there, and I can leave whenever I want to."

"Oh, Elmer, you're so funny sometimes. And you know what?" She was staring behind him at the concrete near his feet." If you turn around, you'll see something amazing."

Elena's mind could turn on a dime, or in this case, a Hamilton. Elmer looked behind him and straight down. A twenty-dollar bill, rolled up like a cigarette was softly rolling away from Elm's feet, pushed lightly by the breeze. He reached down and grabbed it, and they stared at it, not unlike the night they shared the beauty of finding Miss Chris's envelope. He unrolled it slowly, hardly believing it might be real. But it was—an authentic bill softened by time and now resting in their hands. Twenty dollars. A minor accessory for the rich, a windfall for the homeless.

"Is this somebody's?' Elmer asked. He looked around, puzzled. There were no crowds of people, no one searching for lost bills.

"No one's looking for it," said Elena. "I hate to take it."

"Me neither. But how can we give it back to someone we don't know?"

"We can't. I guess it's ours."

So E-Squared gathered up two new blessings into their travel bags: a weathered twenty-dollar bill added to their modest stash and Mr. Rubio's golden piece of advice.

———————————

Of all the buildings in this unimportant town, the Handley library was its crown jewel. As a member of some Registry of Important Buildings, it was towering and gorgeous, built by ancient settlers long ago who believed that the city, which might never be an intellectual center, should at least look like one. It possessed all the clichés of library lore: boxy stone steps leading to double mahogany doors, a dome with a patina of green metal high above the center, columns alongside the front entrance. They walked up the stone steps and when they touched the metal plate, the double doors opened for them like royal fans parting the air. Two spiral staircases flanked their left and right, leading to a round hallway that curved around the perimeter of the second story.

The top floor housed the children's library and a preschool reading room, decorated by second-string interior designers who felt that pop-art furniture would rescue the room from irrelevance. As a result, the children's library contained old-world bookshelves with Civil War paintings next to red and purple vinyl ottomans scattered throughout the room.[3]

———————————

3. If Dr. Seuss and Thomas Jefferson had been brothers, this would have been their playroom.

The ground floor held various reading rooms, East and West. Green banker's lights curved low over scattered oak tables. The hardwood flooring creaked comfortably under visitors' feet. Periodical rooms, which should have been replaced long ago with digital wonders, still displayed an impressive pulp history: towering shelves of magazines and daily newspapers from around the world. The research room spread out from the high fireplace, now defunct after firefighters deemed it too risky for flames and dusty pages to cohabitate in such close quarters.

Perhaps the most notable fixture of Handley's impressive library, however, was the head librarian herself: Mrs. Geraldine Ottowald. The Big O was middle-aged and ambitious, the kind of woman who might have aspired to be a senator if given enough campaign money, or a network news anchor if given the right face. But having neither advantage, she had settled herself into the position of library overseer twenty years ago and never left. No one knew the library better than she. Every crevice and secret shelf, every carpet stain and window latch were catalogued in Mrs. Ottowald's world. She moved through the library from opening to closing hours like an emperor assessing the plebeian masses.

The residents of Handley knew that Geraldine Ottowald was almost as important as the mayor. Mrs. O. was not a vicious woman, only horribly efficient. For her, and every other workaholic on the planet, productivity and output was the goal. To stand in her way was to invite correction on a good day and scorn on a bad one. So when Elmer and Elena walked into the grand building, their eyes adjusting to the dusky beauty of the place, Mrs. Ottowald sized up the new couple right away. Mistrust, you see, was her specialty.

After spending several hours making their way from the bus stop to the library via Rube's directions, the couple was weary from adventure. While the crevices of the library were the perfect place to explore, the two just wanted to sit in the cool interior of the lobby and simply be. They shared a bench atop the marble tiles, and Elm leaned his head back to rest. Elena, with eyes wide open, absorbed the beauty.

"Good Lord, Elmer. Look at this place," she said.

"I can't," he said. "My eyes stopped working."

"Okay, you just sit there with your eyes closed. I'll tell you what I see." Elena reached over and patted his leg. He twitched imperceptibly.

"Tell me."

She began slowly, a conscientious tour guide narrating a dream. "First, take a deep breath." She modeled the instructions by filling her lungs and holding for a split second. "Do you feel that air? It's just the right temperature, just the right smell." Elmer opened his mouth as if to capture the full effect. The air was, indeed, a soft flutter of old pages, a cool drink of new oxygen.

She exhaled and continued. "If you can imagine a tower, rising up to the sky, see if you can picture the center of the building." She swept her hand up toward the heavens. "Can you see the colors of the ceiling…green and white, like treetops and a cream sky? I can see the tiny little windows made of glass all around in a circle, letting in the light from the outside."

Elmer wanted to peek but didn't. He squeezed his eyes shut so he wouldn't cheat.

"Now imagine that across from us is another bench and then another to the right and left. They're empty. We're the only ones here." Elmer's hands fell to his sides, resting on the bench. "Can you hear the sounds of the place?" she asked. "What can you hear if you listen carefully?"

Elmer, with his eyes still artificially scrunched, sat with all the patience of a sentry. Elena leaned back, too, and their faces slowly softened to the new sounds. Against the silence of the foyer, the noises of the outer rooms suddenly expanded. They heard the *shushing* of children in far-off places, the humming discussions at the checkout counter, and a rolling cart *buh-bumping* along a wooden floor in some distant room. Doors opened and closed while the occasional voice rose up and down the musical scale. Who could have known that this ragged couple, who could've passed for two truants ditching school on a common Wednesday, were here in this place of all places?

Elmer got up first. He stretched his body into a long, narrow tree trunk and reached a branch out for Elena's hand. "Let's look around."

Wandering from wing to wing, they soon discovered that the historic building had unlimited imaginative potential.

The circulation desk was a mysterious labyrinth.
The West Room creaked with history.
The Reference Room was a cavern.
The Children's Room was haunted by forgotten characters.

E^2 wandered in and out of rooms, touching the books, running a curious finger along wooden railings, and smelling the spaces in between. At times they split apart, with Elmer lingering among the computers and Elena wandering into the small, quiet spaces. For an hour, they drifted from room to room, unaware of the other guests, feeling somehow that they were home rather than in an unknown country, wondering if somehow this building would accept a foreign visa. Once or twice the staff asked coolly, "Can I help you find anything?" but Elmer recognized the hidden question: *Who are you and why are you here?* He simply shook his head and moved on.

Elena loved the West Wing best, the fireplace room strewn with heavy tables and lacquered shelves reaching to the ceiling. The ladder on wheels was her favorite accoutrement, a rolling beast, half-contraption, half-plaything, that stretched to the top shelf like a giant in a fairy tale. The shiny sign on the wall read:

PLEASE DO NOT ALLOW CHILDREN TO PLAY ON THE LADDER.

WE WILL ASSIST YOU WITH BOOKS ON THE UPPER SHELVES.

She pressed her fingers into the grooves of the letters and outlined each word.

Elmer, on the other hand, loved the Children's Room best. Sitting among the plastic ottomans and half-pint shelves, he felt as though he could return to a bygone era and re-do his horrid childhood. He smiled at the children there and they smiled back. No sign of judgment or condemnation for his oddities. A few second- glances at his birthmark and nothing more.

Even the picture books felt newly minted. They were propped open in triangles, scattered across the four-foot shelves like little cardboard tents waiting to be slept in. *Where the Wild Things Are, Corduroy, Three Tales of My Father's Dragon, Bedtime for Francis.*[4] Elm saw them for the first time, mesmerized.

Elena touched him on the shoulder from behind. "I love that book," she said.

"You've read it?"

---

4. Some classic children's books steal royalties from much better modern books. For example, Margaret Wise Brown and her inheritors crap on gold toilets simply because she said goodnight to the moon and a publisher took a chance.

"Yeah." She picked up *Corduroy.* "It's good."

Elmer took it from her hands and sniffed it. "I've never seen this book before."

Elena stared at him. "I'm sorry, Elm. I feel bad."

Elm looked at her and then down at the old-fashioned picture of an antiquated bear in green overalls. "That's okay," he said. "I did okay without it."

"You sure did."

Elena took the book from him and flipped through the pages. She smiled to herself as she paused at the pictures. "Oh my gosh," she chuckled. "It's been so long since my mom read this to me." She sunk to the floor, clutching the book. Elm watched her losing herself in the memories of a childhood bed, the callused fingers of a father turning pages.

The two of them escaped to different islands, until Elena broke out of her reverie. She looked up from her reading to see Elmer staring out the window. "I'm sorry, Elm. I didn't mean to get lost in this. Let's get out of here for now." She lowered her voice. "Besides, one of the librarians is coming over to check on us again."

They scooted out of the Children's Room. Elena's green satchel swung from side to side on the way downstairs, and Elmer said nothing as his brain turned the new ideas around and around in circles. At the foot of the stairs, he turned to make his proclamation.

"Hey—" he said. "Hey, we gotta make a plan."

She stiffened and looked straight into his eyes. "What's the plan?"

"We have nowhere else to go. We will spend the night here," he said. "We will spend the night in the Handley Library."

Their first night in the library was both a dream and a nightmare.

The two wanderers left the building for several hours in the late afternoon, making sure to deflect suspicion. They wandered along Handley's unimpressive streets, which were neither seedy nor posh, finding cheap sandwiches and iced tap water at a corner deli and a tree under which to sit and eat. Elm, who for once in his life was so enamored with the present that he could forget the dreams of his future, worked through the details of their plan in fifteen-minute increments. Wherever his logic failed, Elena propped him back up, and he was grateful for it. The final plan was quite simple: they would split up, hide their bags inside the library, and hide themselves separately until the staff left for the night.

At approximately 8:30 pm, they returned to the Handley Library. They walked back into the building one at a time, mingling with separate groups in order to camouflage their illegal purpose. Their first task? Stashing their stuff. The afternoon reconnaissance mission had exposed several secret places, at least for the short term. Elm stuffed his old backpack into an unlocked cabinet at the base of a research shelf while Elena slid her neo-hippie bag behind a stack of outdated *National Geographics* in the West Reading Room.

They had thirty minutes to slide like ghosts among the late-night visitors. That was all.

When the intercom crackled and buzzed with the announcement that *All guests must now exit the building*, Elmer had briefly panicked. He and Elena had rehearsed the stealth mission at least five times, but now the buzz around his brain was failing him. Old ladies checking out large print mysteries and community college students with laptops began to file out the front entrance to the proper goodbyes of the staff. But Elmer and Elena crouched behind different bookcases, always on the move, feeling their breath coming in shorter spurts.

At 9:15 pm, the Big O and her staff began wandering into every corner of every room shortly after closing, making it nearly impossible for Elm and Elena to elude them. They split ranks. Elm had curled up into a ball behind a shelf, hoping that no employee would find him. Everything was resting on his level head—a quality Elm had rarely tested.

While he was tightly packed into the shadows, he heard Mr. Capshaw the circulation assistant moving through the shelves, presumably looking for a book out of place or a discarded gum wrapper. *Would he discover a living body breathing in the corners?* Elmer judged the movements of his steps, assessing that his enemy's serpentine path would eventually pass by his hiding spot. It would never work staying still, so when he got his chance, Elmer unfolded himself, zipped along the edges of the shelves, and repositioned his body in another corner, the one that Mr. Capshaw had already checked. He hugged his knees on the floor, perfectly motionless, believing the pounding surge of blood through his neck and chest was sure to give him away.

Where was Elena? They knew that from 9:00 to 9:30 they would have to hide separately. The success of this entire plan rested on their ability to independently outsmart the staff. *Had she been caught?* If either he or Elena choked on the pressure of the moment, their dream would die prematurely. While Elmer listened to the noises with every cell in his body, one panel of lights on the ceiling made a humming sound and died suddenly, leaving him with a creeping fear of abandonment. Darkness was familiar, but that very familiarity was not comforting, only laced with panic. He presumed that the lights would begin to die, one by one, until all that was left was books and darkness. *Why hadn't he figured on this inevitable shut-down? Why was his head so fuzzy and useless to him?*

Mr. Capshaw continued his trail through the East wing, until finally Elmer realized he was alone. He heard the employees in a distant room, thumping stacks of books around and adjusting their car keys. One worker, perhaps the younger one, laughed once or twice, and he thought he heard the staff talk about a television program. It would be 9:20 now for sure, maybe 9:25. He would have to be patient before looking for Elena. They could make no mistakes.

At about the same time that Elmer had positioned himself in the East wing, Elena had hidden herself beneath the portable book cart in the Children's Room upstairs. She was certain that the college student in charge of checking the children's area would be a less meticulous closer than Mrs. Ottowald. But she had misjudged the nightly routine. The Big O was the final set of eyes, the ultimate finisher. Elena had stayed motionless inside the large metal skirt surrounding the cart. Through the small slit in the book cart, Elena could see Mrs. Ottowald moving through the room, picking up a dropped library card and wiping a vinyl cushion with her sleeve. *When would she be finished?*

Then, in a moment of horrifying anticipation, she saw the Big O's shoes clunking directly toward the cart. The cart normally rolled by means of metal wheels on casters, but the brakes had been set, so Elena had figured her hiding place to be stationary. Even so, perhaps the movement of Elena's body as she had slipped underneath jostled the cart out of its regular position. To a normal person, three inches of misalignment would mean nothing, but to the Maker of All Things Right, three inches off line meant madness. It must be fixed.

Mrs. Ottowald muscled the cart into its proper position, throwing the hidden Elena off balance. Her shoulder rammed against the metal skirt, making a noise like a soft thunder-*bonk*. Holy crap. Elena was doomed.

The Big O moved the cart again, judging its position, but by this time, Elena had centered herself in order to give some margin to the madwoman's adjustment. Then, in a frightening investigation, Mrs. Ottowald bent over and peered directly into the open slit of the cart. Elena didn't breathe. She looked directly into the eyes of her enemy, a watery blue eyeball behind an eyeglass, blinking for several seconds into the dark crevice. Afraid that the moisture of her eyeball might catch the outside light, Elena lightly and slowly shut her own eyes, preventing any giveaway glint or sparkle. She counted to three, hearing nothing.

When she opened her eyes again, she saw a pair of black squarish shoes, tiny now, pattering away from the cart. All was safe. The next thing she knew, the lights hummed off overhead, and she, like Elmer some twenty feet below her, was sitting in complete darkness.

———————

Their hands found each other first.

At approximately 9:37, the entire staff had left the building, leaving Elmer to begin breathing normally again. He unfolded his crouched legs and stood up, noticing that several small security lights continued to glow in corners of the lower floor. The library became a different place under these circumstances; he was now a sleeping king in a castle with a ghostly taper burning beside his canopied bed.

Elmer was afraid to call out to her. Only ten minutes had passed since he heard the outer door latch shut, and he could not risk a miscalculation. *How much longer should he wait?*

He slipped from East wing to West, gliding along on his quiet old shoes across the floorboards. He felt for the first spiral staircase until he found the worn wooden railing, still warm from the day. Elena would be waiting for him on the second floor, and it seemed only right for him to be the one to pursue her, to comfort her in the dark. After all, he had been the one to draw her into this madness in the first place, had he not?

He pulled himself up, one step at a time, sliding his hand along the rail, feeling the tiny, pitted marks along the curving banister. Then he felt her presence in the dark. No sound, no ghostly fear of the unknown, only the overwhelming sense of her body descending the staircase. When their hands met, neither one was startled. His fingers felt the bones of her hand, delicate and fluttering. Whose hands were these, these hands that had not touched before? Whose hands were these, new hands in a new land?

Their index fingers curled together for a brief second and then Elena drew back. "They're gone," he whispered.

Elmer could barely see her. She was several feet taller than him, standing upon steps higher than his. He slipped his hand to her back and led her down to the step next to him.

"We'll go downstairs," he said.

They found their way beneath the dome of the building where the moonlight seeped into the atmosphere. Elena reached the bench in the center of the lobby first and sat down quietly, exhausted from the day's escape. Elmer sat beside her, saying nothing for a long time.

"Are you tired?" she asked him.

"Yup," he said. "But happy,"

"We did it. Can you believe we did it?" Her face looked exultant in the shadows.

"We have a place to stay tonight. At least tonight." Elm didn't want to think about tomorrow yet. They had planned for several days of escape, and it had just started. Don't think of tomorrow, he thought. Just now. *Was it only this morning they sat here with their eyes closed, listening to the sounds?*

The church bell from the distant square bonged ten strokes, the last of the peals till morning. They listened to its repeated sound, a faint, even gothic, echo from far away. When it ended, it seemed as though a nanny had summoned them to bed. Elm got up and put his hands on his hips. He made two turns, looking around the lobby as if wondering where they should go next.

"Where will we sleep?" Elena asked.

"I don't think I can sleep yet," he said. "I think I need to keep watch."

Elena's confidence had been spent; she was fading now. "I don't think I can stay up all night. I didn't sleep much on the bus."

"I will help you find a place," Elm said.

First, they looked for a spot for Elena in the East Reading Room. There were chairs in there, chairs with cushions, and Elm tried to push several together to make a comfortable bed. But even so, the gap between them made an uncomfortable divide in the makeshift mattress, so they quickly abandoned that idea.

They went to each spot, one by one, looking for a resting place.

The circulation area was too cluttered.
The West Room was too dark.
The Reference Room was too cold.
The Children's Room was too drafty.

Finally, they settled on one of the study rooms on the second floor, a private alcove, like a sky box in an MLB arena with windows looking out to the stars. At no bigger than eight feet by four feet with a latching door, the tiny room boasted a spot on the floor behind the desk into which they had dragged a host of cushions from the Children's Room. While Elena waited outside, Elm busied himself with making her bed, fluffing the cushions and surrounding it with chairs. When he was done, he realized that she had no blanket.

"You need a blanket," he announced.

"No, I'm okay, Elmer. I don't need one."

"You need a blanket," he repeated. "I will make you one."

He went to the backpack he had stashed in the men's bathroom and brought back his two shirts rolled like sausages with rubber bands. Elena watched him unroll them on the floor. "They are too small," he said. "But I have an idea."

While she sat cross-legged on the floor, Elm went to the circulation desk and brought back a stapler. He carefully lined up both shirts on the carpet, putting the bottom seams together, with one hem overlapping the other. He then stapled them together, like some bootleg quilt designed by an accountant. "There," he said proudly, "is your blanket."

Elena laughed at Elmer's sincere industry. He was not embarrassed by his offering, but instead held it up to her with confidence. "Here you go. You will sleep better with it."

Elena went into the study room, now her guest bedroom, and lay down on the cushions. "Can you get my bag, Elmer? I don't want to leave it in the bathroom."

Elmer scurried to the first-floor restrooms and reached the women's door. He hesitated for a moment. He had never been inside a women's restroom before and it embarrassed him. *What would he find there?* He knew he needed to simply retrieve Elena's satchel, but for some reason he felt naughty. He took a deep breath and pushed open the door, almost holding his breath as if he might inhale some forbidden air by accident. It was completely dark. There would be no finding Elena's bag in the pitch black.

He went back to the nearest bookshelf and chose the heaviest volume he could find. When he returned, he propped open the door with his makeshift doorstop. He could barely make out the outlines of the place, but he observed the notable absence of urinals on the wall and the strange presence of a "sanitary products" machine instead. While still unconsciously holding his breath, he pushed aside the frilled curtain beneath the sinks and found Elena's canvas bag stuffed in the corner. He grabbed it in a rescue gesture and tore out of there like a bat out of hell.

When he brought it to her, Elena had already settled into her bed, lying on her side with one arm tucked under her head.

"Here's your bag," he said. She rose up and took it from him. She placed it beside the bed. "You will be cold," he said.

He took the homemade T-shirt-quilt from the desk and snapped it open like a blanket, small though it was. He waited for her to lie down and then he spread it out over her shoulder and side, gently smoothing out the wrinkles. He made sure the metal staples were not touching her skin.

"Thank you," she said. "I will be warm now."

Elmer stood at the door, like a guard. "I will come to you in the morning—way before anyone comes in to open the place." They had rehearsed their plan during the day, but Elmer wanted to remind her of their strategy. "We will take our spots on the first and second floors and wait until it's safe to appear."

"Okay," she answered.

"You can go to sleep now," Elm said. "I'll take care of everything."

"Good night, Elmer."

"Good night." He turned his back to shut the door slightly.

"Hey wait a sec—" she said. "Hey, Elmer?"

"Yeah?"

"Do you want to hear my mother's lullaby?"

Elmer sank to the floor and sat cross-legged. Elena began to sing, just off-key, just awkward enough to fill the room with real life rather than fantasy, just good enough to hang in the air with the likes of medieval church bells.

The moon is high
The dark has come
You are ready to sleep, bayi
You are the beautiful one
Like malam, you are dark and sweet
Rest now, my sayang

And with the sounds of her voice swirling through the building, he would have no homesickness, a young man who quite possibly for the first time was feeling the cocoon of home in the strange and quiet midnight shadows of the Handley library.

———

Few things feel as strange as waking up in a dream and discovering that parts of it are real. When Elm awoke in the half-light of morning, he imagined he was head wrestling—yes, head wrestling—with a beast of unknown origins. They had sparred and pushed each other to the brink of defeat, two creatures with their lives at stake. His neck was aching with the pressure of this strange combat when suddenly he realized that the beast was merely the very hard edge of the bench upon which he was sleeping.

His eyes were startled by the transformation of the library in early morning. He would have to adjust to its new mood. *Was it five in the morning? Maybe six?* Lying horizontally, he noticed that all the books on every shelf looked stacked top to bottom instead of right to left. He corrected the perspective as he swung his legs to the floor and sat up. *Dude. Aw, dude, you're an idiot.* Only an idiot would sleep this way, he thought. His neck was shot from three hours of ninety-degree angles and the anxiety of posing as night watchman. The inside of his mouth was a slippery, foul mess, and his face felt oily.

"Good morning," came an angel's voice from the heavens.

It was Elena, standing on the upper balcony, looking down into the rotunda to greet him. She smiled and gave a little wave.

"Oh, hey," he said.

She was adorable and clean. She had changed her shirt and pulled her dark brown hair back from her face with a headband. There she was like a little seraph hovering over him in the sky.

Elmer had been self-conscious his entire life, but never had he felt embarrassed in this way before. In the past, he wanted to dissolve, but this morning, for the first time ever, he wished to look handsome and vigilant. He was certain he was neither. This would have to be remedied.

Elena made her way down the spiral staircase as Elmer remembered the comb clinging to the inside of his sock. He slipped it out quickly and raked it over his head. He reached up and felt the side of his hair spring back into a fountain-like spray. *Why this?* The hair was cursed. "I sort of took a shower in the bathroom this morning. I didn't want to wake you yet." Elena announced.

"A shower?"

"Yeah. I let the water run hot for a long time. I used the paper towels and the powdered soap from the sink." She laughed. "It was pretty funny. There were no lights yet, so I opened the door enough to see."

"You're smart. You're turning this place into a hotel."

"A free hotel, you mean."

"Even better."

Elena pulled out a granola bar from her bag. "I also brought you breakfast." She noticed his hair and added, "Your hair is funny this morning."

"I'll fix it," he said.

"You don't have to. I like it."

Elmer leaned forward and put his face in his hands, feeling his slippery forehead with the tips of his fingers. He wished she wouldn't stand so close to him. Not yet.

"Do you think I have time to take a "shower"?" he asked. He curved his two fingers around the word for effect.

"I'm sure," she answered. "The employees wouldn't come back this early."

Elmer stood up suddenly, as if she reminded him the entire scheme was close to collapsing. "We have to make sure everything is back exactly the way it was last night at closing time." He felt suddenly nervous, anxious to protect and succeed.

"I already put my bed stuff away. And the doorstop."

"Good. Good job, Elena."

Elmer left Elena on the lower floor and took the stairs, two at a time with his hands upon the railing, to the second story restrooms. His stomach was aching with hunger, and his neck was still pulsing. On his way to the men's room, he grabbed another giant volume, *The History of Man*, and set it flat on the floor to let in a sliver of natural light.

Once inside the shadowy bathroom, the water poured from the faucet. New faucets use nozzle screens that aerate the stream, but the library's eighty-year old fixtures emptied its water like Moses' miracle in the wilderness. Elm plunged his hands under the flow, and it was first cold and blue. Soon, the water changed to lukewarm, then hot. Elmer unwound the paper towel roll onto his hand and soaked it under the soothing water before bringing the dripping mass to his face and neck. He could barely see his purple birthmark and hated it slightly less. He then worked the soap powder into his skin and scrubbed his face and arms with the gritty paste. It was still dark, but Elm was learning through feeling, the way that all young men do who haven't a clue about dark places.

Next, he dried himself with more towels and placed all the waste on the counter to be eliminated later. To leave it in the trash bin would be to leave irrevocable clues. All traces of life must, of course, be erased. After that, Elmer reached into his bag and felt for the toothbrush, the final addition to his packing that now seemed indispensable. He moved up and down his teeth, swirling the bristles from side to side and stopping to rinse at least twice.

As the final act, Elmer cupped his hands together to create a bowl and poured water onto his crazy cowlick. Most of it ran off the surface like a duck's feathers, but some seeped down toward his scalp and dribbled off his sideburns and into his eyebrows. He pushed the comb through his hair again and again, until the cockeyed sprouting settled down. He could not see much in the mirror, only that the silhouette was finally head-shaped, as opposed to the shadow puppet of a two-feathered peacock. Elmer gathered his things and took one more look at the shape in the mirror. He cocked his thumb like a trigger finger and pointed at his face with a click of his tongue against the back of this teeth.

Elmer was hardly angelic. From the outside he and Elena were still an awkward mess, two runaways from the island of misfit toys whose hair and skin and gait and speech rendered them useless in the teenage hierarchy. They were fringe people. But love has a way of expanding the boundaries of things, and with each passing hour, the edges were starting to look more beautiful than the center.

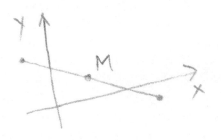

CHAPTER NINE

Midpoint

It's one thing to have homelessness thrust upon you, and quite another to embrace it willingly. Elmer had never been without a bed or a meal before, and despite the dark and sometimes vile days of his childhood, he had never felt the cold panic of a vagrant's life. Elena was even more removed from such fears, for her loving parents had readily supplied her with clean sheets, vegetables, and even a curling iron. Here in Handley, Elm and Elena floated somewhere in the space between resident and alien. In a small way they were homeless—if by homeless one means without permanent shelter. Yet in the larger more important way, they were fully homeowners, having created an emotional shelter under which they could take cover.

That morning, Elmer and Elena spent several more hours in the library, sneaking out while the staff opened for business and then returning with nonchalant purpose. But when hunger moves into the body, fantasy moves out. Food would be their next challenge. They would have to play it cool.

The sun scalded their eyes after spending so much time huddled among the shelves and tables indoors. In the bright light, Elm thought Elena looked incandescent. And Elmer? Elena thought him impish and adorable with his goofy hair.

"Where should we eat?"

"How much money we got?"

He swung his backpack around and fiddled with the outer pockets until pulling out a pile of bills. "Looks like we got enough for both of us. But we gotta space it out—gotta be careful with what we have."

They began to walk. It is a strange thing to move from dark shadows to light, from small spaces to large ones. Elena, aware of her hurried steps, hung back slightly to allow for Elmer's shallower strides. She was not comfortable walking ahead of him, allowing him to trail in her wake, so instead she slid her hand through the loop of his arm and clicked into place—his equal.

The library anchored a large corner of the city, and within several blocks were rows of businesses. Not slick, commercial affairs, mind you, but time-warp mom-and-pop shops, the perfect freeze frame of another era. A small hardware store. A place to buy dark-colored work shoes with orthopedic soles. An old-school beauty parlor with pink swivel chairs and ball lights shining in vertical strips. Among these establishments, Elm and Elena began to walk, saying very little, feeling the contractions of hunger.

Suddenly, a sign. Not a heavenly one, but a small wooden sign propped open like a tent on the sidewalk: *Handley Senior Society Pancake Breakfast!* It was well past breakfast by now, and Elm saw a squatty old woman with floppy floral sleeves pulling the sign off the concrete across the street. She was dragging it across the sidewalk, humming some odd tune. Perhaps by the power of suggestion, his pace quickened almost imperceptibly, and he could smell the remains of those pancakes shifting in the wind. He looked at Elena and pulled her hand out from the circle of his arm.

"Stay right here," he said.

Elena stopped and leaned against the empty brick wall, the space between *Jo-Jo's Gems* and *Handley Real Estate,* while Elm took large leaps across the street to reach the old woman who was now pulling the sign through the door. *What would he say to her?*

Elena slid down the wall to wait, squatting on the backs of her heels. She would watch for signs of success. She saw the old woman turn, startled at first at the sight of Elmer and his dark coat and backpack. He was surely a young punk come to make mischief. *Or was he?* Elena could not figure out what Elmer was saying to her but watched him as he pointed back at her. Elm and the old woman gave her a little wave, and Elena lifted her hand in response, offering a huge smile.

The woman patted him on the shoulder while Elmer helped her lift the sign and bring it into the storefront. *Where was he going?* Moments later, Elmer sprinted back across the street like a child.

"C'mon—she's going to give us the leftovers from breakfast," he shouted, waving me across like a crossing guard. "It's cool. C'mon."

Elena drew her bag against her and met Elm halfway across the street where he took her arm and led her to the old building where the wonders of pancake batter and cold sausages awaited.

The door opened and they found not one, but four old women fussing around the room. The wooden floor was dotted with old round tables, most of them still covered with the remains of this morning's fellowship. The woman with the flowered sleeves spoke first, extending her hand toward Elena. "Come in, sugar. We've got plenty of leftovers for you and your friend here."

"Oh, we were just gonna have to dump that extra batter down the drain, good golly," said a second grandmother, an equally squatty hostess with gorgeous crepe paper eyes the color of blue mist. "Get on over here and have a seat."

She patted the crumbs off a metal folding chair and scurried to clear the old dishes. A silk daisy in a corny plastic vase stood artificially straight in the center of the table as Elm and Elena took their seats.

Elm had never seen four ladies so happy to serve. Perhaps they had grown weary of Hardy and Lawrence and Candy-Bob, old men who came every week to talk about their arch supports and prostates, or maybe they were eager to hear new voices echo against the walls of their fellowship hall, or maybe they missed being useful, or maybe it was simpler than that. Maybe they were just freaking *nice*.

Whatever the reason, these four ladies—Hannah, Lupe, Emma, and Vonnie—had discovered, for at least an hour, their purpose for living: pancakes and strangers.

The pancakes came. Elmer's first stack came in an ultra-straight column, delivered by Lupe who was followed by Vonnie and her plastic maple syrup jug. Elena's plate arrived via Hannah, who had dressed it up with two orange slices and a daisy on top ("Don't eat that now, sugar—it's just a pretty thing") along with four ribbons of bacon. The young folk ate and ate under the careful watch of their hostesses who shared the most specific details of Handley life, not the least of which included the location of Candy-Bob's mistress's gravesite and the best place to buy toilet paper on the cheap.

The women learned that Elmer and Elena were on an "educational journey" from another town and that they would only be staying for a few more days, which somehow reminded Emma of that long summer in 1952 when she toured the Grand Canyon with her grandfather and began collecting glass animals—specifically donkeys, who by their very nature are rare and coveted in the antique world. Apparently old people love to share details.

Finally, pushing back his plate, Elmer asked, "Here—here's some money." He began reaching toward his backpack to pull out some bills.

"Oh my gracious, child—what are you talking about? We woulda had to pitch all this in the trash today if you hadn't come around." She patted his arm. "Just keep your money."

Elena spoke up. "I think we would really like to help you do your dishes, ma'am." She looked at Elmer who nodded. "Yes… yes, we would really like to do your dishes for you."

"Oh no, we couldn't ask you to—we couldn't really—"

"No, we really would like to," said Elmer.

"Well, all right then. We'll show you where to put the dishes."

The six dishwashers went to work, clearing the white chunky coffee mugs with pink lipstick smudges and the plastic water glasses with crushed ice-turned-slush. Elm and Elena swept the floors and wiped down the checkered plastic tablecloths before propping all the silk daisies back to their unnatural poses. After the fellowship hall of the Handley Senior Society returned to splendor, the runaways gave neck hugs to their one-day grand-mas and shut the door behind them.

———————

And that's how it would be, meal by meal, like manna from heaven. Elmer and Elena's meals arrived on schedule through-out the day and always paid for in either good will or cold cash. After the pancakes came the roast beef sandwiches next door to the beauty salon and an ice-cold water fountain with all-you-can-drink privileges. After lunch, a bubble gum machine turned just-so magically clunk-clunked a handful into Elena's palm, and the two worked those stale pieces between their jaws for thirty minutes in the park blowing bubbles the size of fists.

It wasn't just food that rained down. Their collection of useful objects grew hour upon hour, from the discovery of almost-new hair shears lying atop the trash can outside the barber shop to the pair of sunglasses left on a city bench. Small things grew into great blessings: the clouds clearing out to make room for the sun, or the trash can set at just the right angle for a perfect hook shot from the left.

The most amazing acquisition, however, came the most unexpectedly. It was the granddaddy of all gifts, the kind of miracle that you couldn't even write in a book. If you didn't know that Elmer had endured a lifetime of sorrow so far, you would almost be jealous of his good fortune. Even Elena could hardly believe their great luck.

Elmer found a car.

Well, he didn't quite *find* a car as much as it was given to him. And he didn't actually own it outright, as in getting a pink slip in his name or anything. And it wasn't even a car, but more like a working mechanical beast with seats and a steering wheel. But it was a *car*, I tell you, the holy grail of every teenage boy who has ever gotten his driver's license.

Which brings us to the next strange detail, the small fact that neither Elmer nor Elena had ever driven a car before, no less gotten a driver's license.

But first, an explanation.

The car was hideous. It was an oxidized-red Chevy Chevette (almost pink now), made in that vintage automotive year 1979. The metal stripping on the left side was bent, missing its middle section. Of its four doors, only three were seated properly in the frame when closed, with the passenger side slightly ajar—enough to slip your index finger into the crack. Inside, the brown dashboard with silver duct tape hid God-knows-what damage underneath. Its hatch bore the design markers of postmodern angst: an oddly geometric shape, like early Star Trek architecture. Its original front bucket seats were hiding beneath two fuzzy, matted seat covers the color of plumber's putty. The back seat? Well, no one bothered to look back there since 1987, presumably because there might be unsavory evidence of past debauchery or maybe the aftermath of a Depeche Mode concert.[1]

In short, the car was a monstrosity.

Elmer, however, took three seconds to fall in love.

It might help to know how he acquired the object of his affection. You see, while blowing bubbles in the park behind the Handley Senior Society Fellowship Hall, Elmer and Elena saw Pancake Hannah loading kitchen equipment into her husband's truck. Hannah waved again from a distance, her flowered sleeves wobbling back and forth and her husband tottering around the place looking busy.

Several minutes later, the couple crossed the grass to where Elmer was scratching E^2 into the bark of a tree with his ankle comb. Elena saw them first.

"Hey, Elmer, here comes Hannah and another old man."

The couple was cuter than you can imagine, the kind you picture in the movies attending their Golden Anniversary party wearing matching shirts. Elmer began to chat, finding out that

---

1. As an industrial-pop icon, Depeche Mode had become the world's most notable purveyor of electronica music in the world, having risen to stardom in the 1980s. As a reaction to the disco fluff and soft rock, DM might have been the forerunner of emo music, a hybrid of dark, gothic compositions. Apparently, driving a Chevette made one very, very depressed.

the old man, Mr. Dahlin, was a retired auto mechanic, the owner of Handley's oldest junkyard. *Would they need a vehicle during their stay? Would it help to have a loaner car for the duration of their visit to Handley?* Had Mr. Dahlin been thirty years younger, he would have factored in the pesky details like insurance and liability, but the elderly have a lovely way of ignoring the future and living in the present, making him the ideal giver of ridiculously dangerous gifts.

Mr. Dahlin had just acquired the car. It was parked on the back end of his lot, having been brought there only yesterday by a woman whose thirty-two-year-old son finally moved out of the house to make his own way. It had been his car, she said, and he no longer needed nor wanted it. She collected her tax-deductible receipt in exchange for the keys to the 1979 Chevette.

"My wife started calling it *Old Dahlin,*" he told them. "She named it after me. If you say it right, it sounds like 'Old Darling' with a Southern accent." Elm mouthed the name to himself. *Old Dahlin.* His first car.

And now, Elmer found himself with a girl on his arm, following Mr. Dahlin the retired mechanic to the back of a junkyard to collect his reward. Elmer and the car were the perfect match: two throwaways who were born again—one, just getting the odometer started, and the other on its final adventure. When Elmer felt the keys in his hand, he finally believed in miracles.

"What do I do first?" he asked. He was almost hypnotized by the experience of sitting in a driver's seat.

"You need to turn the key."

It was just past three o'clock. The Dahlins had entrusted Elmer with the keys to the Chevette an hour earlier. Elmer said nothing during the old man's cheery monologue, pretending to understand the mysterious language of rear-wheel-drive chassis, old-tech four-cylinders, and 52 horsepower. They had discussed the car's imperfections, like its bald tires and ancient carburetor, while Elena had waited in the grass, watching.

Now they were sitting in the front seat of the monstrous thing. "Like this?" They listened for the sound. He turned the key and the creature gargled to life. Elmer, who was already trembling for joy, hardly felt the tremors, but when the interior shimmied, Elena placed her hand on the dash to steady herself. They sat under the spell of the Chevy's black magic for several minutes, just feeling its occult powers.

"Now what?"

"Umm—I'm not sure," Elena said. "It's not like my mom's car."

Elmer examined the dash instruments, but saw nothing that made sense, much like the math worksheets under which he had labored for years at school. But this was different. The car actually mattered.

Elena pointed to the transmission handle. "You have to move that," she said. "You have to put the car into gear—into drive." They both examined the letters D, R, N—a thrilling secret code.

"Is that all? Just move the handle?"

"Wait. Do you know the foot pedals?" Elena asked.

Elmer felt the pedals with the soles of his shoes. He pumped the right and the left, vertical and horizontal. Age had loosened their mechanisms like Mr. Dahlin's octogenarian bones. The car had wasted its youth, trading tight connections for the pedals of a homemade go-kart. But for all Elmer knew, he was manhandling the accelerator of a Lamborghini.

"You have to put your foot on the brake when you put it in gear. I don't know for sure." They stared at each other. "Go ahead and try it."

The moment hung in the air, frozen. Elm licked his lips and pressed his eyes shut. Elena clasped her hands together as if in prayer. Then, in a swift, beautiful motion, Elmer whisked the transmission into drive, feeling the old beast jolt out of the junkyard.

It was a monster.

The first thirty seconds were a nightmare. The car hobbled and jerked through the dirt openings leading out of the yard. Small clouds of dust rose alongside their flanks and a stray dog fled yelping into the alley. Elena's eyes were fixed on the hood of the car and both hands gripped the duct tape along the dashboard as Elmer and the car duked it out. Perhaps God had cleared the area ahead of time to ensure that no one would be killed in this divine joyride.

The little Chevette began to adjust to its driver. After two or three awkward turns down side streets and downtown neighborhoods, Elmer began to feel the car's strange fits and surges. He gripped the steering wheel at noon and six o'clock, gunned the gas pedal in rock band rhythms, refused to use a turn signal, drove his left front wheel along an imaginary center line—in other words, defied every driver's education manual ever written.

They would never forget the sound. The grind of the perverted engine shouted over the whistle of air leaking through Elena's passenger door while the potholed pavement cursed the tires as they sped by. A mile in, Elena wiggled the ancient FM radio knobs until the spotty notes of some eighties punk song hissed and crackled its way into the composition. The resulting cacophony was the perfect soundtrack to the world's wackiest rendezvous.

It was the best case of recklessness ever recorded.

It was the coolest adrenaline rush apart from love.

It was masculinity at its most ironic.

It was the ugliest joyride in American fiction.

But it was also part of Elmer's salvation—a romp into the back roads of the promised land where the Reject actually gets the girl, the freedom, and the thrill of a late afternoon spin along a dusty road in a dream car. Ahead of them the sun began to fall into the horizon, and Handley was the most beautiful place he had ever seen.

That is, until he turned to look at Elena.

Elena's childlike wonder at the world, a world which might seem uninspired to others, excited Elmer. Through her eyes, an ordinary world was rendered extraordinary. She saw beauty. She made beauty. She *was* beauty, for heaven's sake.

In the meantime, Elena was watching Elmer, too, seeing his incomparable gratitude for the smallest things. There was no entitlement in his spirit, no twisted arrogance that can grow out of a life of privilege or excess. Having lived in an environment of gross negligence, having endured the mismanagement of father, mother, and peers, Elmer now entered his second life. Born again, he was spending his life like a new convert: wearing the halo of salvation.

"It's like a miracle," Elena shouted over the noise.

"What?"

"A miracle."

"The car?" he asked.

"This! Today—it feels like we're in heaven."

Elmer, with the bravado of a bike-riding child who lets go of the handlebars for the first time, took his right hand off the wheel, gunned the accelerator, and reached over to take Elena's hand. It was smooth and pale, her small bird-like bones falling easily into his palm. His left hand might be steering *Old Dahlin*, but in his right hand was all the power.

$$P(A \cap B) = P(A) \, P\!\left(\frac{B}{A}\right)$$

$$P(AB) = P(A) \, P\!\left(\frac{B}{A}\right)$$

CHAPTER TEN

Probability

The second night at the Handley Library was markedly different from the first. When Elmer and Elena finally arrived at six o'clock in the evening, their clothes covered with adventure dust, the library felt strangely familiar. The double doors creaked open and they were home again.

Earlier that evening, Elmer had parked Old Dahlin three blocks from the library. With no skill at all, he had wiggled and accelerated and maneuvered that car for twenty minutes trying to get it flush against the curb. Elena helped him from the sidewalk. *A little more this way but wait—you're too far!* The two had looked back at the car every minute as they walked away, half wondering if when they turned around it would be gone. Old Dahlin's headlights stared back, relaxed.

Now back at the library, Elmer and Elena parted ways. They never doubted that they would spend the second night in a building that now seemed to belong to them. While they had come to discover Elmer's brother in this town, he had now been forgotten in the urgency of daily survival. Elmer took his undercover place in the second-floor children's room. He surrounded himself with picture books, watching kids move among the shelves and purple vinyl ottomans in unpredictable patterns. The less he moved around, the less attention he received.

Elena, in the meantime, settled into a cushioned wing chair facing the window in the West Reading Room and laid her head against its side. She drifted into a quiet half-sleep, letting the breeze from today's joy ride slowly subside in her imagination. *Wind speed love joy freedom.* Once, a library volunteer with a red badge peeked around Elena's chair to check if the girl was all right only to find her with a book open, reading intently. They smiled at each other. The timing had been just right, for Elena could not comprehend the book at all but having interpreted the approaching footsteps as possible danger, she managed to fake it with impeccable timing.

For several hours the two sat alone, on separate floors, waiting for the night to come. The contrast between night and day was extravagant. The outrageous good fortune of finding the sun, pancakes, and Old Dahlin had pushed Elmer's adrenaline to the outer limits. Now he settled into the familiar refuge of bookcases and fluorescent lighting. In the same way, Elena's childish joy at bubble gum and mechanical engineering traded places with the gentle peace of fading sunlight at the old framed window. The daytime was an adventure tale; nighttime, poetry.

At around eight o'clock, the windows turned gray and the banker's lights glowed green. Elena took the stairs to the children's room to find Elmer and arrange the evening's conspiracy. They would have one hour in which to plot a second night's sleep. She adjusted her green shoulder bag, heavier now with the afternoon's found treasures. *Where was Elm?*

With the evening stretching into night, the children's room had emptied out, presumably so the little folk could get home to brush their teeth before their bedtime stories. Elmer was nowhere. The reading areas were clean and stacked, the side tables cleared of books. Nothing was askew, not even the chairs around the mini-table in the center of the room. Elena walked up and down the shelves, looking into corners finding nothing—nothing but the ghosts of storytellers.

"Can I help you?"

Elena was startled for the first time all day. "Umm, no thank you," she replied. It was Mrs. Ottowald[1], the tyrant herself come to purge her castle of strays and miscreants.

"Are you looking for someone?"

"Uh, no, ma'am. I'm just seeing if…I'm just seeing if I left my book here."

"What book was it?" Mrs. O's eyes flickered suspiciously across Elena's clothes and bag. She was big and scary and wore her glasses around her neck with a blue strand of beads.

"It's okay. It's not here—no big deal really."

Elena wanted nothing more than to move out of Mrs. Ottowald's sight, to flee the scene. The head librarian pushed further. "Are you a visitor to Handley?"

Elena answered as casually and truthfully as she could. "I am here on a school visit. I'm here for just another few days."

"I see. Well, welcome to Handley." She was brusque but polite. It was all Elena could ask for.

As Mrs. Ottowald walked away, the immediate crisis passed but only temporarily, for Elm was still missing. Elmer was the synapse between thrill and fear, between glorious adrenaline and dreadful panic. Without him, Elena was a single digit.

Afraid of Mrs. Ottowald's suspicion, Elena left the top floor and traveled again to the circular staircase surrounding the foyer.

---

1. It is a well-known fact that in literature, librarians are either a Christ archetype or Satan—nothing in between.

The place had emptied out of the regulars, leaving behind the last-minute visitors. Still no Elmer. *Would he be in the bathroom? Would he have left the library without telling her?* Elena was a level-headed girl, not given to spooky predictions. She would wait patiently. She would rest until the answer came.

Elena's footsteps annoyed the old wooden steps around and around the curve of the stairs. They made a protest, the beautiful noise of ancient architecture. Just as she arrived at the landing, the front doors swung open and Elmer marched in from the black outdoors with a bright smile. His body drew in a surge of fresh air.

"Elm!" she whispered from the stairs, almost in scolding. "I was freaked *out*. Where did you go?"

He glanced around for spies and, seeing no one, held up a white bag. "I got us dinner. We have to eat, right?" For Elmer was the hunter-gatherer now, the Man, the finder of good things. Perhaps it was the hunger that spoke to her. Perhaps it was love. But in that moment, she stared into his face for the first time. He was not the boy who had stepped onto her porch with cookies, but a young man of infinite possibilities. She clapped her hand over her heart in gratitude and whispered the words *thank you*.

"You know what to do next?" he whispered back.

Elena nodded and spun around to make the climb back up the stairs, understanding that to be discovered tonight was to be ruined; they must again make no mistakes.

"This is amazing, Elm" Elena held the stick with both hands and moved across it horizontally with her mouth. She had not eaten lamb before and if she had, it would not have tasted this good. "Armenian you said?"

"Yeah. He was the nicest guy. Told me we'd love it."

The two had set up their impromptu restaurant in the light of the emergency exit sign on the first floor. It was 9:35 p.m., ten minutes after Mrs. Ottowald had finally locked up the place. The second night's library closing was infinitely easier than the first with both castaways rehearsing their technique and feeling the rhythms of secrecy. Elm's pulse, racing dangerously high only twenty-four hours ago, had settled into a more comfortable pace now. They had spread out sheets of paper towels from the bathroom for their dinner place settings. Hummocks of rice pilaf swelled in little paper boats while the remaining lamb kebabs lay wrapped in tin foil. It was one of the first real purchases that Elmer had made with his cash, and it lay in front of them like a well-chosen feast.

Here in Handley, neither time nor obligation dictated their next move, only impulse and feeling. Soon they would take their odd little sink-water showers, sleep in their royal quarters beneath T-shirt blankets, and wait for another morning. Elmer leaned against the ancient plaster and wiped his mouth with a napkin. Of all the spatial coordinates in the world, why would his body occupy this one space at this precise time with this particular girl? There was no articulation of such philosophy in Elmer's mind, only Curiosity and Wonder who had rented out the vacant space.

Elena spoke. "Mrs. Ottowald almost caught me tonight, you know."

"She did?"

"Yeah. She asked me what I was doing and if I was visiting here. I told her I was on a school visit." Elena scooped up the rice with her plastic fork and laughed. "You know what?

"What?"

"I *am* on a school visit. I'm learning how to be a grown up." She let the words settle in the air before saying it again. "I'm learning to be a grown up."

Elmer sat back and thought about that. *Learning to be a grown up. What does it mean to be a grown up? Does it mean you can talk dirty, or wear size eleven shoes, or drive a car—or does it mean you can finally take care of someone? I am a grown up*, he thought. *And my father is not.* The vocabulary words were first grade; the concept was genius. *I'm taking care of someone,* he thought. *That makes me a grownup.*

"I'm going to take my shower," Elmer announced. Do you want to stay here?"

"I'll use the bathroom downstairs at the same time." She scrounged through her bag, looking for the last clean clothing items she could find. "You know, we're going to have to wash our clothes pretty soon." She looked down at the grains of soft rice that she had dragged across her shirt. "I look pretty messed up, don't I." She looked up at Elm, whose shaggy pieces of hair stood up in strange places. "You look funny, too." She said it with no trace of criticism, just an endearing observation of fact.

"That's good," he said. "We're both messed up." They smiled at each other and she slapped the side of his head, trying to get his hair to lie down. He slapped back, catching her hand in his. He held it for a moment. "You're crazy." He felt her soft hand, so willowy and smooth.

She looked down, embarrassed. "Excuse me? *I'm* crazy? Who goes to the special class at Sun City?"

She stopped when she said it. Elmer had not believed her capable of cruelty, not ever—the girl who was divine and holy and otherworldly, the girl who only spoke light and life. *Was she a real girl? Could she use his faults as a weapon when she wanted to?*

She spoke up quickly. "I—I'm sorry, Elmer. I didn't mean it that way."

Elmer said nothing.

Then, feeling the cold rush of air between them, he gathered his things. "I'm going to the shower now."

"No." Women recognize pain faster than men, so Elena rushed to soothe the wounds she inflicted. "No, I have to give you a haircut first."

"What?"

"A haircut." She reached into her bag and drew out the rust-flecked shears they had discovered in the street earlier in the afternoon. "Remember these?" She grabbed the two handles and *snip-snipped* in the air with a grin on her face.

So this was her strategy, he thought. Change the mood, change the subject, change the air, through diversion. It just might work.

"Do you cut hair?" He was still hurt.

"What's there to know?"

"I dunno. The girls at the *Shear Beauty* have special frames hanging on the wall. They must know something different than you."

"My mom's cut my hair since I was a little girl. I watched her every time. It's not that hard." She slid a chair in place under the nearest emergency light and patted the seat. "C'mon, let's go."

Elmer, under Elena's magic spell, moved to the seat with no free will of his own. She held the blades like one who rules the universe—not maniacally, mind you—but longing to make all things right.

There is a physical intimacy within grooming that hearkens back to primitive times, even animal kingdoms. The proximity of two bodies (one grooming while the other reclines) is obvious, and Elmer felt the awkward presence of Elena's torso behind his head. The light was poor, but she could see enough of his hair to determine the ragged patches. She moved her fingers through it in circles, feeling for the thicker spots, finding the valleys, cowlicks, and hill countries.

Elmer sat, possessed by his own senses. If he should lean back just a few inches, he would find her stomach there and be content to lean against her forever. He felt her fingers moving in patterns, stirring up the blood in his head. It was delicious and really, really frightening. He had forgotten why he was in the chair, forgotten why he was floating into new atmospheres, forgotten why he couldn't move, until he heard the first *snip-shweet*.

"There it goes," she said. "Look down."

A loose tuft flopped into the crook of Elm's arm, a lock of trust. He couldn't move to shake it free. He just stared at it until more began to fall upon his body like autumn leaves off a blown tree.

"Do you like how it looks?" he asked.

"I can't tell yet." Her fingers paused. "But I like *you*, so it won't matter."

The words fell across his shoulders, weightier than the locks of hair. *I like you so it won't matter.* He could smell her, the faint cloud of cheap powered soap and Old Dahlin's exhaust living in the fibers of her shirt.

Elena stopped for a moment and the air was still again. Then Elmer felt her index finger on his face, resting on the dead center of the odd little birthmark spreading across his jaw and disappearing beneath his chin. She dragged her finger across slowly it as though feeling for its pulse.

"Elm?"

"Yeah."

"Does your birthmark ever bother you?"

"Sometimes."

"Do you wish you didn't have it?"

"I don't know. I don't think about it much."

"It's okay if you do." She traced its shape with her finger. "You know what? It sort of looks like a map. A country on a map."

She waited, as if trying to sort out her next thought. "You know, some people wear all their weirdness on the outside. That's me and you."

Elmer turned to look at her.

"Do you think I'm different?"

"Of course! But so am I. We're just *odd*." She flicked a lock of hair off his head and it twirled into space. "But other people wear their strangeness on the inside where it's so much harder. They look fine on the outside, but the inside is weird."

"I think I understand."

"You and me?" She fluffed his hair. "Our insides are so *normal*. It's just that God put all our weird stuff on the outside."

Neither one said a word for a long time after that. Those sentences floated in the air like the lingering sound waves in an echo chamber. Elena snipped and tugged and fluffed and snipped again until the scene came to rest as softly as the last lock of hair fell to the floor. Elmer's hair had lost its ragged, childish edges. He looked like a man.

"There."

"Are you done?"

"Yes."

"Is it good?"

"Yes."

"Can I see?"

Elena came around to the front of the chair and put out both hands to his. He grabbed them and she pulled him to his feet. "You look like…You look like you're in college now."

He reached his hand to the back of his head and tugged at his newly shorn hair. "You think so?"

"Like a college professor, really. Just as handsome as any of them." She stepped back to admire her work. "Yup, just as handsome as they come. And really smart."

Then, in the middle of their gorgeous flirtation, the impossible happened.

With no warning, a mighty sound ripped through the quiet air. Elmer and Elena, frozen like the men of Pompeii upon hearing the volcano erupting, suspended their arms in shock. It was the unmistakable sound of an intruder. Someone had opened the back door of the Handley Library.

"My god, Elmer," Elena whispered. "*Who is that?*"

"Holy *crap*. Someone's here." Elmer's flight instinct ignited, and he began to shove their dinner trash into Elena's bag. "We've got to move it."

Elena pressed her hands against her cheeks for a moment, unable to move, while Elmer grabbed everything he could see. They heard the sound of a heavy door banging shut downstairs followed by a cough, a whistle, and a long, grinding *sshhleeet*, like the sound of a large object being dragged across a concrete floor.

"I'm so freaked out, Elm," Elena whispered. Her breathing started to come in little pants.

"Let's *go*," he said.

Elmer pulled Elena to the nearest bookcase, leaving the chair and remnants of dinner behind. This was no time for precision, just escape. They were on the second floor and the unknown creature was on the first. This distance might be their salvation.

The two crouched behind the ceiling-high shelves until the cramps in their legs forced them to fall to their knees. The presence of another person in the library made the atmosphere haunted and unreal as they listened to the terrifying movements on the lower floor. Strange combinations of sounds—melodies and grunts, banging and hums—floated up to where they hid among the shelves.

Elena leaned her mouth toward Elm's ear and whispered, "Who do you think is here? It's almost midnight."

"Do you think someone is stealing stuff?" he answered.

"How? The doors have alarms, right?"

"I don't know—but it sounds like more than one person."

They waited behind the shelves for minutes-converted-to-hours until the lights on the upper floor suddenly buzzed and hummed, drenching the furniture with a fluorescent glare. No longer shadowed in darkness, Elena could see every patch of Elm's newly-shorn hair, and her own hands, she noticed, were flecked with Armenian sauce and hair clippings. *Oh my god*, she thoughts. *We will be discovered.*

As they squinted at each other in the bright light of disclosure (shirt stains and raised purple birthmark and tangled hair making them look every bit the freaks they were), the intruder called out.

"Come out and show yourselves."

Elmer swallowed and blinked. They said nothing.

"I *said* come out and show yourselves. It's kind of stupid to make me wait."

No answer.

They heard the man's voice speak under his breath: *for heaven's sake, let's get this over with.* Then, another command: "You're gonna feel really stupid when I have to walk the shelves lookin' for you."

Elmer gripped the edge of the shelf while Elena pressed her face into the back of Elm's shirt. He could feel her breath warming a small patch of skin on his back, making the fabric moist.

The terror was almost over. The man was coming for them, searching shelf by shelf.

When the monster stood in front of them at last, he announced proudly, "Well, golly Miss Molly, what do we have here? It's the bus kids on a field trip."

"Rube?" Elena blinked fast and her relief poured out of her lungs like a waterfall over a cliff. She recognized the kind man who had given them directions to the library when they first arrived. "You were at the bus stop!"

"And I told you to check *out* the library. I didn't mean to check *in*." Mr. Rubio rubbed his eyes and ran his hands across his hair and to the back of his neck. He was cleanly shaven, still wearing the canvas pants, but with a line-up of hardware dangling from the belt loops. He wore a black box pager on his belt and looked at them with an intangible kindness. Elmer began to breathe again but felt his heart still clonking around in his chest.

"Okay, so I'm gonna get my work done around here, and in about fifteen minutes, you're gonna come downstairs and tell me a little more about why you're here breaking the law. We'll have a nice conversation and figure out what we should do with you."

With that, Mr. Rubio turned and headed for the stairwell just as he came, whistling some off-key tune as he disappeared into the stairwell.

When he was gone, they sunk to the floor, recovering, before Elena spoke. "Oh my god, oh my god, he's gonna call the police and my mom will regret that she ever let me come. What does this *look* like? Elmer, what does this look like? We're like living together in a *library*, for god's sake." The absurdity of it rained down hard.

"Don't freak, Elena. We're not doing anything that wrong. We didn't steal anything. We're not hurting anything or anybody. Rube is cool. Let's go down and talk to him."

She nodded her head up and down fast and wiped her nose with her sleeve before rising up from her crossed legs like a scissor-lift. Without a word, they cleaned up the hair cuttings and packed their bags as though they knew that both would be set out on the curb before long.

When they got downstairs, Mr. Rubio was polishing the circulation desk with a green cloth and the entire place smelled like an orange grove. Unruffled, he simply waited until he was finished rubbing the length of the counter before he finally spoke.

"So, let's go into the East Room."

The two followed behind, saying nothing.

He motioned to the two chairs on one side of a table, not unlike a lawyer's meeting with new clients. Once he settled into his chair, he simply asked, "So tell me the truth. Where did you come from? And why are you sitting here in the Handley Library scamming the city for free lodging?"

Elmer leaned forward earnestly and stretched his legs out, wanting to know the answer himself, wanting to say the right thing that would make this whole preposterous plan make sense somehow. "I…" he looked at Elena. "…we needed to escape."

"Escape? From what?"

Elena offered her version. "Our teacher wanted to help Elm find a true friend—kind of like a lesson for our school or something—but it was so weird with so many people wanting to get attention. We were supposed to go on a trip for school, but we decided we'd rather escape—" she flashed a look at Elmer. "—so we came here. Elm's brother came here first. But we don't know where he is."

"You came here? *Handley* is your great escape?" Rubio laughed with a giant, warm voice. "Good God, I guess you can get an education anywhere." He leaned back and grinned.

Elena offered quickly, "We're not completely crazy. My mom knows we're here."

He eyed her with suspicion. "No mama I know would let her daughter hop on a bus with—" he looked at Elmer, "—with a young man."

"Elmer's different." They didn't look at each other. She just said it as a matter-of-fact. "He's not that kind of boy."

Rubio shook his head and smiled before clapping his hands in strange delight and leaning back in his chair. "Hoo-ee! It's the oldest cliché in the world."

"What do you mean?"

"Running away. Finding yourself. Getting a thrill. That's so old school. Everyone tries that trick. You need a better education that that, my friends."

"What do you mean?"

"I mean it's craziness, thinking that everything you need to know is in the doing."

"The *doing*?"

"Yeah, the *doing*. Like you're gonna learn everything you need on the street or something. We're sitting in here in a freakin' *library* for a reason, my friends. You think I only learned by doing? Reading ain't for smart people, it's for curious people. And curious people are the only ones who figure stuff out and keep getting better. How am I supposed to know things outside of Handley if I don't read?" He stared at them. "You wanna figure stuff out for yourself, too?"

"I guess that's why we're in Handley, right? To figure stuff out." Elmer said.

"So's how about I school you. Right here in the library."

"School us? Like teach us lessons or something?" Elena was confused. Rubio was a teacher of massively ironic proportions. What kind of education comes from a small-town night janitor with keys and a screwdriver swinging from his belt? Was he going to teach them how to dust, tighten windows, or change the oil in Old Dahlin?

Rubio was smart enough to read her immaturity and secure enough to ignore them. "Yeah, chickee. Me and you and the dog named Blue over here are gonna learn us some history. Listen, I'll make you a deal. I won't bust you for breaking into city property, and you'll sit in my own personal class for the next few nights."

This was appealing, to be sure. Elmer knew in his gut that Rubio was legitimate, an ordinary guy with love in his soul who happened to be the latest in a string of improbable miracles on the way to the Emerald City. Rubio had made the library a safe house. What class Rubio had planned was beyond Elmer's imagination, but he would have to trust—at least for a little while.

Elena leaned over and whispered in Elmer's ear, "I think it's okay. Let's sign up for Rube's class."

"So what makes a person bad?" Elena asked.

All three were dog tired. An hour had passed, and it was close to 1:30 in the morning. They were sprawled out at the table, and Rubio had launched into an adult-sized discussion of good and evil, the core of everything big and important and frightening in the world. GOOD and EVIL, he said, would be their first lesson.

"Sometimes it's just plain meanness. I dunno how it gets into them, but it does. When I was twelve, I remember a boy who just *had* to hurt you. It was like if he didn't hurt somebody every day, then he would die. It was his food. Three meals of meanness a day. You ever know someone like that?"

Elena nodded her head first, then Elm. He spoke up soberly. "I know people like that. Lots of them," he answered. "One of them used to live in my house."

"I gotta tell you—I used to think if you were nice enough you could change somebody. Sometimes it happens, but not regular. Cause you ain't dunkin' that person in goodness—you just splashing him a little with it." Elmer stared, fascinated by Rubio's theory. He kept talking. "Now, if you ever find a real mean dude? The best bet is just taking him out of wherever he is and putting him in a big tank of niceness. Let him sit and marinate in it for a good long time. The younger he is, the less time it takes to soak in. If he's an old bastard, you might have to put him underwater for the rest of his natural life. Even then. No guarantees."

"I think bad people should go to prison," offered Elena.

"Ah, and that's the trouble with meanness."

"What do you mean?"

"You take somebody who's been swimming in meanness his whole life and then you dunk him an even bigger ocean of it. Now how's he supposed to find some dry land? Make's no sense to me."

"I still think you have to lock some people up," Elmer said.

"You're right about that. But not everybody. You gotta find out why they're bad first." Rubio's lesson was making Elm's head hurt.

"So how do you dunk somebody in niceness?" Elena asked.

Rube tapped his finger on the table before wagging it in front of Elena. "Ah...now *that's* a question for you. The best kindness tanks are right at home, with fathers who let God into the house and talk about him in front of the kids. The dads don't steal even a penny, don't trash-talk their mommas and wives, and they peel off love like twenty-dollar bills in a rich man's wallet. The mammas don't run off neither. They feed their kids right and talk softly and change the sheets every week. It's not that hard, really."

"So, it's your family that makes you good?" Elena asked.

Before Rubio could answer, Elmer sputtered, "That's not fair," His own father fluttered down in his memory like a demon spirit. His own mother choked him as he said it. "You're saying that bad parents made bad kids. You're saying that inside all the lousy houses right now there are boys just like me waiting to turn into their fathers. Mean. Stupid. Angry." Elmer was now getting agitated. "You're saying that boys with bad fathers don't have a chance. You're saying that we don't have a chance." Elm grew even more intense. "You're saying that if a father hurts his son, it's all over. It's like you're telling me that kids with shit for parents have no hope at all. WHAT YOU'RE REALLY SAYING IS THAT I DON'T HAVE A CHANCE! ELMER WHIT DOESN'T HAVE A CHANCE—IS THAT WHAT YOU'RE SAYING?"

Elmer, who rarely varied his decibels, surprised even himself with his outburst. The fear of his own destiny oozed out of him like warm pus from a new wound.

Rubio, who had only partially told the truth when he claimed that books could educate better than experience, knew this fear himself. He knew that social determinism in all its violent, frightening possibility can stalk you for years, even decades.

"I'm not gonna answer you yet, young man," Rubio said. "It's too important and I can't pop out the answer like *th*at." He snapped his fingers for effect, and watched Elmer wipe the sweat off his forehead. "But I'm giving you some homework on your way to figuring it out."

"Homework?"

"You gotta have homework in school, right?" Rubio asked.

"I guess."

"You like homework?"

"Serious?"

"Of course. Do you like it?"

"Okay, no."

"Well, have you ever heard of The Ottoman Empire? Rwanda? How about Tibet? Syria? Darfur?"

Rubio's words were foreign and strange and suddenly everything wrong in Elmer's brain lit up like a switchboard. Rubio was using Big Talk," the phrase Elm used to categorize academic language all through the years of school. He was allergic to Big Talk; it made him break out in emotional hives, the red welts of insecurity and failure that characterized his life in special education.

"Not really."

"You don't know about evil until you start reading. You think it's about guns and power and bad government? Or do you think evil is an insider crime like beating kids and shooting up heroin? Is Evil part of the Devil's domain or does it live inside you and me? Evil is huge but Good is even bigger, and they both live in this world. And if you think your own pain is the worst there is, then you gotta get an education before you feel sorry for yourself."

Elena sat in stiff silence, watching her friend suffer under the weight of his ignorance. She was ignorant, too, but her tunnel vision was a different sort. His rose out of personal suffering; hers, from relentless optimism. Both world views would require some extraordinary expansion.

"So tonight, you sleep upstairs in the library and I go home. When you sneak out in the morning before opening, you will find three books by the front door. Live with them all day long—read what you can, ask each other questions, and bust out of your little world for a while. Class starts again tomorrow at midnight."

The two wanderers were cautious. "Hey, Mr. Rubio?" Elena said. "Why are you being so nice to us? Is there a reason you aren't going to tell on us?"

"Maybe I'm just one of the good ones. People don't believe in our existence, but we're real." He winked and smiled.

And then, like some blue-collar sprite, Rubio floated off to the back exit where they heard him securing the doors for the night, dragging his trash can behind him.

As the nighttime clouds parted, letting the moon slip into the tiny study room where Elena slept, Elmer curled up outside her door, wondering how Rubio would manage to place their textbooks by the double doors by morning. He could only guess it was the same sleight of hand that managed to leave a navy blue blanket folded neatly by their belongings at half past two.

$$9(x^2 - 2) = 9x - 18$$

CHAPTER ELEVEN

Simplification

"I can't read this, Elena. It's too hard."

In the hazy light of a cloudy afternoon, Old Dahlin sat under a tree two miles out of the city limits. Elena had taken the front seat and Elmer the back. The windows were open. The air was humid and their clothes were rank from days of half-showers, library carpets, and *eau de Chevette*. Both were becoming accustomed to the stink of homelessness, so it seemed hardly noticeable when the moist breeze would halt.

"I don't understand this," Elmer repeated. Two books lay open on the seat, one titled *The Roots of Genocide: When Good People Do Nothing* and the other *The History of Evil: Mankind's Global Legacy*. He was sitting across the back, legs propped across two seats, trying to follow Rubio's instructions. It wasn't working. He ate the cracker packets leftover from yesterday's lunch, brushing the crumbs off his shirt.

"Wait a sec, I think I got this part," said Elena, flipping through the pages of the third volume, a massive anthology of heroes who had distinguished themselves as peacemakers. "Listen to this," she said as she read a passage with the halting confidence of a fourth grader:

Rose Mapendo, whose last name means love in her African language, gave birth to twins in the most horrible of places—a refugee camp. She asked God to forgive her captors and named her boys after the commanders in charge of killing her family. This simple act of forgiveness led to not only her salvation, but also the founding of an international aid organization.

"And there's lots of other people in here, too." Elena knew she could not pronounce their names, so she flopped her book over the seat and pointed to names: *Romeo Dallaire, Irena Sendler, Rigoberta Menchu, Mairead Corrigan.*

Elmer looked at them, mysterious markings in black ink, the cryptic Big Talk that made him shrink back. "I can't read them, Elena. Don't even try to make me."

"I'm not trying to make you read them. I can't say their names either."

It was infinitely easier the day before, when their only job was survival, but now Rubio's instructions had brought new challenges. Intellectual grappling was a strange new practice. Who needed to think deep thoughts when every square inch of brain power for the past five years was spent on averting the wicked schemes of Sun City High School? Where had been the luxury of literacy when swarms of students were massacring Elmer's self-worth in weekday battles, or Elm's mother was sweeping out her son's dignity with the daily trash?

Elena was the opposite. Her childhood love cocoon, nurtured by the warmth of her mother and father, had left her undamaged but naïve. Could she face the truths of the world's evil without losing her grace and innocence?

Both their brains felt cramped and awkward; the black and white pages were enemies, not allies. Why had Mr. Rubio chosen books? Couldn't they attend the movies—listen to songs? Books meant trouble. Books were oxygen-poor mountain ranges that they had not been trained to traverse. Books equaled pain.

But Mr. Rubio had left them with little choice. They would have to adapt to his requirements if they wanted to continue their journey. So in the confines of an ancient car, they turned pages. And turned pages. And turned some more.

———————

In the interior of Old Dahlin came the longest, deepest sleep so far. At about three o'clock, after four hours of brain-busting deciphering, E2 fell into a nap so vast that every brain wave flickered and went dark. The previous two nights at the library, which had been punctuated by fits and starts, offered little quality sleep, but now as late afternoon ran into the watercolor edges of early evening, the boy and girl lay at peace inside the ugly car.

Elmer's face, if anyone had been present to see it, changed forms as the sun patterns ran across it. Time lapse photography would have shown his skin moving from pink to gray as the light shifted through the back-seat window. The tilt of his head, usually to the subconscious left in order to hide his birthmark, now fully exposed the strange, purple continent. Its distinctive shape was somehow less ghastly in the fading light. It was almost beautiful. His long legs crumpled into the small space, but his arms were loose and free to tumble over the edge of the seat and flop to the floor, fingertips resting softly on the grimy floor mat.

While Elmer slept in an air-tight chamber of peaceful nothingness, Elena's mind fell to dreaming in the front seat. Her face reflected the angels' movements in her subconscious, even though scientists might say it was only an REM phenomenon.

Her knees buckled up and leaned to the right, coming to rest on the steering wheel, while her head leaned back against the green bag stuffed against the door handle. While she slept, her heart danced around with Rose and the Canadian rebel Romeo and little Anne Frank and Desmond Tutu, teachers all. She learned some steps in the books today, halting and awkward, but for heaven's sake, she was dancing. She was learning their moves, listening to God's voice, saturated with goodness.

When the alarm woke them up hours later—a speeding Dodge with a loud horn heading out of town—they unfolded their limbs with slow and articulated movements. Their limbs were slightly stiff, an easy compensation for the gorgeous healing sleep that left them deliriously relaxed. Elena hugged the broken headrest on the passenger side and peered over into Elmer's bed as she sighed in half-sleep. "Oh my god, Elmer, we've been asleep *forever.*"

"Forever. Yeah." Elmer's brain synapses were still yawning. He was hot and moist, covered with nap-sweat. "What time is it?"

"Don't know," she said. Elena pushed open the creaky passenger door and swung her legs out. The evening wind swirled into the space, blowing out the sleep. "We did good, Elmer. We read almost six chapters," she said while thumbing through the books.

"Did we?" Elmer was still confused.

"Remember Betty?"

"Betty?"

"The lady from Ireland we read about. And Tutu."

"Too?"

"No, *Tutu*—the priest. We have lots to tell Mr. Rubio tonight. You know he'll ask if we read anything today."

"Yeah. You did good, Elena." He looked at her directly. "*We* did good."

They were growing accustomed to each other's mannerisms and moods. Elmer opened his own car door—with the squawk of a bad hinge—and stepped into the early evening. He had pulled Old Dahlin into a patch of shade hours ago and now the tree under which they rested made new shadows on the two-lane road. He reached both arms to the sky and pulled his entire body upward, shaking out the awkward kinks in his body. A house sat a half mile in the distance. An old barn, even closer.

Elena stood beside him and they looked toward the direction of town before staring at each other. Elmer was decidedly homely in an utterly adorable way. His sockless feet wiggled down into his old shoes, and he plunged his hands in his pockets. His new haircut was priceless: hipster-meets-lawnmower.

Elena looked like the favorite doll that every child keeps forever, a slightly rumpled version of a perfect toy. She pulled her hair away from her face and twisted it up in a loose knot. One perfectly shaped pimple dotted the center of her forehead, more like a carefully placed Indian *bindi* than a sign of imperfection. No flaw could disqualify her in Elmer's eyes; no weakness turned him away.

"How long should we stay here?" he asked.

"I don't know. What do you think?"

"Are you hungry?"

"Yeah."

Elmer reached into his pocket and wiggled the car key in front of her face. "Let's go find some more surprises."

Elmer waited until Elena sat in the passenger seat and then shut the door for her. He walked around the front of the car to the driver's side, catching a peek at himself in the side mirror. Not bad, he thought. As they drove back to Handley, the car pitching and jerking under Elm's awkward skill, they reviewed their homework.

"What do you think Mr. Rubio's gonna ask us at tonight's meeting?" Elena said loudly against the wind roaring into the car's interior.

"I don't know," Elmer shouted back. "What do you think?"

"I think we should remember the names of some of those people who tried to make peace with their enemies," said Elena.

"I don't think that's what he's gonna ask us. I think he wants us to know about the wars," replied Elm. "The wars are the most important part of those books."

"The wars? I can't remember all of them."

"Yeah, but without the wars, there wouldn't be the heroes."

Without the wars, there wouldn't be the heroes. Their conversation had illuminated the primary difference between the way the loved and unloved see the entire world. When you are loved, you see yourself reflected in the peacemakers, hardly bothering with the ugly details that necessitated such peace. But when you are unloved, the darkness of man's heart rises up with such familiarity that it becomes the primary thing. They had read the same book and found a very different thesis. He recognized a world of evil waiting to be redeemed; she recognized a world of peacemakers waiting to be celebrated.

"I guess we should just wait and see," she said.

"I guess so."

The risk of being discovered on this third night was too great, so E2 spent most of the evening several blocks away from the library, watching the sun go down first before reading underneath the brightest streetlight on the city's west side. They knew the librarians were eagle-eyed. They would not ignore three consecutive days of unusual visits by the teenage strangers. So instead of roaming casually about the place until shortly before closing, they decided they would walk toward the back entrance late into the night at the time when Mr. Rubio was scheduled to return for his nightly chores.

It was a big risk. *What if he did not come at all? What if Mr. Rubio's intentions weren't pure after all?* If they did not find shelter in the library by the witching hour, they would have to sleep outdoors the entire night and become a target for roaming policemen or street hooligans. Worse yet, it would mean they would've been duped, which is far more distressing than sleeping in a car.

They waited for their teacher. Sitting against the wheels of the car, Elmer looked through the index of one of their books, looking painstakingly for clues about which he knew very little. He had always hated to read, hated the slow-moving letters that tripped his mind and made his brain feel clumsy and awkward. Elena was only slightly more focused, looking only at the names and places in bold print. Yet for all their painful study, they had to take Mr. Rubio seriously, for he held the keys to their survival. They believed him when he made his deal last night. They would have to sit under his teaching—good or bad.

Dinner had been another small miracle. Three college-aged boys, gluttonous upon ordering two large pizzas at the corner diner, scarfed down one-and-a-third pies, leaving a healthy portion nearly untouched. Elmer had left Elena in the car to hunt for food and after watching the trio's movements through the restaurant window for ten minutes, determined it was safe to retrieve the abandoned pizza where it rested on the garbage can, safely protected by its cardboard box.

He carried the beautiful acquisition back to the car like a waiter holding a silver tray. "Got us something good," he said.

"You like pizza, right?" And with three pieces each, they enjoyed another meal on heaven's tab.

Now back in the neighborhood of the majestic library, they watched the people begin to trickle out of the library far in the distance. First one group, then another. It was nearly nine o'clock, but Mr. Rubio was not scheduled to arrive until close to eleven. Could they possibly spend two more hours waiting for him to arrive? Elena was slightly cold and she missed the warmth of the library. Her clothes were itchy and they smelled bad. She was miserable.

For all Elmer's genetic misfortunes, his intuition had never failed. He sensed Elena's distress. "We've got two hours. Let's go find a shower," he said.

"Where are we going to find a shower?"

"Come with me."

He slid his backpack onto his shoulders and locked the door of the car. Elena swung her bag across her chest and sunk her hands into her pockets, following Elmer's lead.

They walked at least five blocks. The stars were hidden behind a heavy cover of clouds. Sometimes talking was necessary, but tonight the silence between them felt right. They fell into a military gait, first his right foot outstretched, then hers. Before long, they were *right-left-righting* down the thoroughfare, content to walk in step with no words between them. *Where were they going?*

Then, as they turned a corner facing east, Elmer stopped and pointed straight ahead. With only the faint glow of remaining sun backlighting the silhouette, the shape of Handley High School stood out, beautiful in the shadows.

High schools, by their very nature, are architectural mysteries and psychological triggers. Anyone who has attended a high school knows its power. They are monuments to education, markers of fear, reminders of lost innocence. To Elmer, a high school meant nausea and cold rejection. Let's not forget that the smell of even one school cafeteria has the power to send some students into professional grade panic.

Here stood another building, less personal of course, but just as symbolic. Elmer set his feet firmly and announced, "Stay right here." Elmer left his bag beside her and ran off toward the side of the building, leaving Elena alone in the dark.

Almost immediately, Elena grew frightened. *Baby girl sweet daughter of mine you are almost grown and free a beautiful reminder of God's love and grace go go go and find your way in the world but come back and share it all share your joys and fears and we will always always be with you.* Elena's mother passed through her daughter's consciousness until she couldn't help but crave her voice, to hear the approval of a job sincerely begun and nearly completed. She glanced to her right and left. A relic of days gone by, a telephone booth stood out on the corner about a hundred yards away, and Elena decided right then that she could not rest until she heard her mother's voice.

She crouched down and unzipped her bag, reaching for the envelope that contained their money, passing over the return bus tickets and miscellaneous artifacts. So far, both of them had agreed on every purchase. Would it be wrong to take part of the money now without consultation? She felt for quarters and dimes in the deep crevices of the bag, collecting a small sum cupped in her palm. She looked and saw at least a dollar in change. This would work, if only for a brief conversation.

Elmer was nowhere; the street corner was empty. Elena gathered the bags and trotted toward the public telephone, heart accelerating. She rolled each coin into the slot, hearing it clatter into its belly. She pressed the eleven magic numbers, each one making a different musical tone. Leaning into the phone booth, she heard the monotone ring. Then another. A third.

"Hello?"

"Momma?"

"Elena, darling? OH MY GOD! OH MY GOD, ELLIE! You precious girl—where are you?" Sera shrieked and fussed through the handset.

"I—we…are in Handley. I am fine, momma."

"I know that, you silly thing, but I—I mean I miss you so much and we can hardly stand it having you gone but I know you are well and when you come home we will have so many stories to share together and—"

"Wait! I don't have much time on the phone, but I wanted to tell you I love you." Both paused much longer than they had time for. "I don't want you to worry. We only have a few more days and then we'll be home." She could hear her mother's breathing through the line. "Mom—I need to go; we have everything we need, so don't worry." And then she added, "I'm staying clean."

"I know that," her mother said, reading in between the lines. "I know that. How is Elmer's brother--?"

"I love you. I will tell you everything in a few days." And with that, the corporate beep from Bell Midwest Telephone toppled their conversation for good.

Elena hung up the phone, hearing the final digestion of coins. Her mother had sounded lovely and confident, and the brief intersection with home filled her with a hollow nausea. She waited several long minutes more for Elmer to arrive, who by now was breathless with anticipation of his plan.

He came out of the alley and moved toward her. "C'mon. It's safe!"

"Where are we going," asked Elena as Elmer whisked their things into his arms and grabbed her elbow in the direction of the side building. They rushed past the institutional shrubbery and formal signs around to the back, where a large chain link fence surrounded the physical education complex.

"There it is," Elmer said. "There's our shower."

A huge industrial swimming pool barely glistened in the dark acreage behind Handley High School. Elena looked at him with frightening curiosity, as if to say *you really are crazy.*

"There's a place where we can hop over—right above that box thing over there. I already tried it," he said.

"I can't take a bath in a *swimming pool*, Elmer. I don't have a suit—not even a towel—and you know it probably has a security alarm."

"Look at this." They walked fifty feet to the storage shed where a clipboard swung on a nail above the door. On it was a custodian's spreadsheet of tasks and times, each one checked off in pencil. Next to today's date was written in messy handwriting: *PM shift: 11. Check for towels on deck. Shut off main valve. Check gate lock.* "See? They won't come for another hour or more."

Elena had given in to all of Elmer's plans, but this one was ridiculous. True, the back lot of Handley High School did seem exceptionally remote, and it did appear that the night help would not arrive for some time, but her well-developed conscience could not abide the rebellion of fence-hopping. At the same time, the sink showers at the library had its limitations. The smooth-as-glass water of the swimming pool whispered fresh promises, and Elmer looked at her, pleadingly. She might be able to do it. But one serious obstacle could not be overcome.

"Elmer, I don't have a swimsuit."

He looked down at his feet, embarrassed by the notion. "Neither do I."

"What can we do?"

"I will help you over the fence. Then I will stand guard over here." He scratched his head. "You can just swim in your underwear and I'll turn my head away."

Elena laughed. "That's funny the way you say it. We're not kids, you know."

He looked at her puzzled, as though she hadn't understood. "That's why I'll turn my head away."

Elena stared at him. "All right. I'll do it. But it will have to be quick. When I'm done, you can take your turn."

The two moved quickly to the water pump which afforded them several feet of help. Elmer went first and then reached out his hand to steady Elena as she climbed up toward the top of the fence. The metal notches hurt her hands, but she was determined. She slowly lifted the ball of her foot to the top edge while Elmer steadied her back. And then, suddenly, in one swift Ninja-esque move, she leapt to the concrete on the other side with a heavy thud, barely on balance.

"Okay, now I'll go stand over here until you're done." On the other side of the fence, Elmer walked over to their pile of things and faced the foliage like a dutiful child.

Elena, feeling the rush of fear, removed her clothes with lightning speed, knowing that if she did not strip in under thirty seconds she would lose her nerve completely. She wiggled down to her unmentionables in record time. Her clothes lay in a heap at her ankles.

Suddenly she was in.

It was the coldest bath she ever felt.

It was the most modest case of indecent exposure on public record.

It was the summit of bravery.

It was the scariest plunge into dark waters.

It was the holiest of baptisms.

But when she was done, she was certain that no descent into the unknown would ever frighten her again.

At first the mysterious water felt haunted, but the sensation of three days' grime being swept into the deep end was so beautiful and so clean and so restorative that if there were any ghosts, she wouldn't have noticed.

As she plunged beneath the surface in complete silence, Elmer, who had been standing fifty feet away could not help but turn his face to witness the spectacle. He could see almost nothing in the water, just the torpedo shape of her body moving beneath. By the time she rose to the surface with her white shoulders like a marble statue in a European fountain, he was at the fence clutching the links with his fingers.

Unaware of Elm completely, Elena swam for one minute more in and out of the water, her dark hair trailing behind her like the decorative markings of some exotic deepwater fish. Elmer watched her swim, knowing she was beautiful. Not merely because her body was sex-worthy, but because he loved her.

Underwater, Elena felt safe and free, but getting out would require a strange courage. She whispered over to Elm standing at the fence. "What should I do about a towel?"

"There are some old ones over there." He pointed to the deck facing the back wall.

"Can you get one for me?" Only her eyes peeked over the pool's concrete edge.

Elmer climbed up and over the fence with practiced dexterity and grabbed one of the discarded towels in the corner. He walked over to the pool and looked down into the water at Elena's submerged body. He didn't see some mermaid or goddess—just the wavy layers of barely visible skin and water. He wanted to see all of her, but it wasn't the right time.

"I'll stand here and hold it up for you."

"Can you close your eyes? I'm sort of embarrassed."

She hoisted herself up to the deck and fell into the crusty towel as Elmer wrapped her from neck to knees. "Sorry the towel doesn't feel very good," he said. "It's all we have."

"I know." She was feeling anxious about the time. "Your turn." She walked away to give Elmer privacy. *Being naked is not like it is in the movies*, she thought. *In real life, you're fragile.*

Elmer became noise. She heard the rustling of clothes and splash of water, but did not see it take place. While Elmer took his turn scrubbing the filth off his skin, she peeled off her wet underclothes behind the shed, and slipped into the only semi-clean garments left in her bag. Even with the closet smell of her wadded-up clothes, she had been made new by the water. The night air whistled through her wet hair and she was cold.

After dressing, she was compelled to look at Elmer, as he had been compelled to look at her. She was a bit ashamed of the curiosity but glanced inside the fence to see him pulling himself out of the shallow end. He was dripping like a family dog after a bath, and he flung the extra water out of his hair accordingly. He was wearing his white briefs, looking so silly and vulnerable that she snorted a hidden laugh. He heard.

"Are you laughing at me?" He wasn't accusing.

"No, not laughing. Just happy."

"Where's *my* towel?" he whispered. "I'm standing here freezing, you know."

"You can have mine," and she flung the damp offering over the fence where it landed at his feet. Elmer picked it off the wet concrete and dabbed it over his skin, not eager to wrap the soggy thing around his entire body. He trotted quickly to the fence, still in his tightie-whities, embarrassed.

"We need to get out of here, Elena. We're running out of time." Elmer pulled his old clothes over his wet body, and the pants dragged along his skin. "I'll put my cleaner clothes on later," he whispered loudly, "—let's get out of here."

Zippers down, pool water dripping, tripping over fences, with bags bouncing, they plunged into the black alley that led to the front of the school. "C'mon," he called as he ran, reaching out his hand to grasp hers. Had there been security cameras, the digital record would've captured the image of two fleeing, soggy criminals in a mad dash for safety. "Two more blocks!" They stumbled past the closed businesses with neon signs barely lighting the sidewalk until they could see the Chevette still parked near the library.

"Let's stop here," panted Elena, trying to breathe. "I need to rest a minute."

"C'mon, you can do it. Let's just make it to the car. You can finish getting dressed in there." Elmer nudged her a little. "You can do it."

When they arrived at Old Dahlin, glowing oxidized-orange under the streetlight, Elmer unlocked the back door and gestured for her to enter. "Wait. You go first," she said. She glanced at his filthy pants, drooping low. "You need it more than I do."

Elmer smiled and climbed inside the back seat, leaving the door open just a crack. In the meantime, Elena smoothed out her wet hair with a comb and hung her damp clothes neatly over the back bumper. She rearranged her bag and shook out the dust and crumbs from the past 24 hours. She looked into the two-inch square mirror, seeing just enough of her face to know she was clean. She felt born again.

When Elmer stepped out of the back seat, he was practically beaming. He had put on his last clean shirt and ruffled his new haircut. His feet were bare and gleaming white against the dark pavement.

"Now I'm all ready for my second day of school," he announced.

———

"And what did you remember reading about places like Darfur or Tibet?" Mr. Rubio asked.

The two sat across from their teacher in the East Reading Room and looked at each other. It was just after midnight and Mr. Rubio was grilling them on their first day of homework. The library was plunged in darkness except for the glow of red emergency exit signs.

Elena spoke first, hesitant about her answer. "Well, it was pretty complicated."

"Ah," Mr. Rubio said, banging the table with his hands. "Now *that's* the first step toward what I'm after."

"How was *that* the right answer?" Elmer asked.

"Everybody likes to simplify things. To make answers easy. People like to put big, ugly things in a single sentence for a test or a protest march or a sign. But the more you read about the world, the more you know it's not simple."

Elmer looked confused. "But can you tell us why there's been so much fighting in a place like, say, *Darfur?*" He pronounced it with hesitation. There's got to be an answer."

"Well, just because it's complicated doesn't mean there aren't bad guys. In Darfur you had the Janjaweed—a horrible, violent army, I tell you." Rubio shook his head as he explained.

"You couldn't tell if they were under the government's control or a crazy leader. They would slaughter people—just go right in knock off the farmers and tribal people because for a long, long time different groups were pissed off at each other. It went on for years and years."

"How many people died?" Elena asked.

"Don't know. Could be 70,000—could be 300,000. Could be only one. But if you're the one—or your father is the one—does it really matter?"

"Why did everyone hate each other?" Elmer asked.

"Let's back up a minute. Listen, if somebody does something really mean to you, are you gonna hate them?"

"Probably."

"That's because there's this one guy, see, who did something to you, right? That kinda makes sense."

"Yeah."

"But what if that one guy made you so mad that when you saw someone *else* hanging out with him, you hated him, too—just because he was part of that group."

Elena stopped him. "But you can't hate the other guy. He didn't even do anything to you!"

"That's right. But you still remember that horrible way you were treated. And you're afraid it might happen again." Mr. Rubio stopped for a moment and cleaned out some junk from under his thumbnail. Elmer watched him carefully. "Listen, it's easier to hate a chunk of people than just one. If a daddy says to his kid, 'Hey see that guy over there? He looks like this or that and if you see one of them, you go the other way because they're really bad,' then if you're the little kid, you're gonna believe your daddy, even if you never talked to one of them guys."

"But that still doesn't explain why wars start," said Elmer.

"You're right about that. Being pissed off at one or two guys doesn't start a war. But being pissed off, plus desperation, plus having no homeland, plus starvation, plus revenge stirred up over lots of time equals war."

"Actually, it doesn't even sound like addition," said Elena.

"No?"

"It sounds like multiplication. Anger times anger. It's called an exponent, I think."

"My god," laughed Mr. Rubio. "Were you in smart classes at your high school?"

Elmer looked at Elena and they started to laugh. She put her head down on the table and shook it back and forth. "Oh, Mr. Rubio, you don't know us at all, do you?"

"What? You ain't a smarty-pants?"

"What she means is that we're both...well—we're both in special classes at school. We're dummies."

"Get outta here," he said. "You're two of the brightest bulbs in the fluorescent light panel up there." He pointed to the ceiling for effect. "You ain't *special* kids. You just special, kids." He chuckled at the beauty of what he just did there. Then he pointed at them. "I'll bet you're wondering why I'm telling you this stuff."

"Why?" Elmer said.

"It's because no one's talking about it. And it starts with people your age. I don't mean talking about the book stuff—you'll learn some of these facts in school. But knowing *about* things isn't the same as knowing things. If all the kids in the world would understand why shit happens, they can see it coming down the chute—they can evaluate it and figure out what's true and what's not. They won't just act with their gut but with their mind, too." He stopped. "Anger skips the mind and goes right to the gut. You can't think when you're in pain."

"You're right."

"So in a place like Darfur, where there's this deadly mix of skin colors and being pissed off and having no say in what happens and knowing you either have to kill or be killed—well, you gotta see the violence coming. And the governments sometimes do see it coming, but they don't do anything about it until after the fact, or until somebody makes a movie about it or something, or they start to fall off their thrones, or the money runs out, or other governments find out about it."

"And a place like Tibbit? Stuff like this happened there, too?" Elena asked.

"Not Tibbit—you mean Ti-BET? Holy crap, yeah. You got different religions flying around, China and Tibet holding up six-year-old kids and saying they're baby gods, everybody wanting to be in charge and nobody knowing how to do it right. You've got this little piece of land with history and pride and everybody wants some of the action. And in the middle of it, somebody's always starving, I tell you. In the meantime, little kids are being shown pictures of all the bad people and pretty soon you can hardly see the facts anymore. Like I said, anger goes right past the noggin' and straight to the gut. And if you ain't got dinner on top of it, the gut will always win out. The reasonable thing will always lose."

"We read about other places, too," said Elena. "Palestine. And a place I can't say right." She flipped through the book and pointed to the word *Kyrgyzstan*. "—and Irish people had trouble—"

"—and the Armenians, and the Croats, and the Jews and the Native Americans and you can keep listing them 'til your tongue dries out, sister, cause we just can't figure out how to love people yet."

Elmer was thinking, thinking so hard that his head was pulsing with ideas. "I know about this." He tapped his finger on the table.

"Have you already studied this before?" Mr. Rubio asked.

"No, I mean I know about this."

"What do you know?"

"I know that I am different. And that makes some people hate me."

"Who hates you, Elmer?"

"The kids at my school hate me."

"I don't think it's the same thing." But Rubio knew what was happening in Elmer's brain, knew that he was breaking through, knew that he was making the connection. He would let him continue.

"But it kinda is. My face. My face is different." He reached up to stroke the side of his face as if to demonstrate the truth of his claim. "And I'm in a special class," he said as he curled his fingers in the air, "and that makes me part of group that no one understands."

"I understand you, Elmer," said Elena.

"But you're different, too. You asked questions and started to know me. Other people? They don't know *me*. They only know my face. And my class. That makes me hated for some reason. And my father," he added. "My father hates me, too."

"But, Elmer…But he doesn't know better. He's cracked. He's completely crazy and you told me he drinks, so that changes everything."

"But in some of these countries, it's the same way. Some people are just cracked, some people hate you for looking different, and other people hate you because they hate their own life."

Mr. Rubio was nodding his head. "But here's the real deal. Reasons don't turn evil into good. Reasons are just reasons. They don't let you off the hook or make things right."

"I know," said Elm, "but it makes me feel better just knowing."

"That's true," Rubio said. "That's true. Knowing is a good start." He stood up and walked past the old fireplace to the dark window where the city slept in the dead of night. He gazed outside at its human mysteries. "But you can't just know," he said. "You can't just *know*, child. You also have to *be*."

Elena, cradling her head in the hollow of her crossed arms, listened quietly. Elmer slowly stacked the three books, one on top of the other, and straightened them once, twice. What was this thing growing inside of him, this meandering, organic vine of understanding, these green and glossy leaves birthed from a truthful soil? What was this desire, this hope, that he might not only know but *be*—be light and life and forgiveness and beauty and joy and power? Like staring at a new plant under time-lapse photography, Elmer watched his soul uncurl and blossom in record time, a multiplying expansion of cells and tissues with roots going deep and leaves spreading out to the ends of The World, or at the very least, the ends of his world.

Rubio saw it breaking through. He continued. "Have you also read about those who changed everything?"

Elena said, "Yes."

"Yes," added Elmer. "They lived around danger. "Some died. All of them did things that the other people were too scared to do."

"That's right," said Rubio.

All three were quiet.

"And what about you? Have you ever been scared?" he asked.

Elmer reached into his memory, pulling out an iron key, black and cold. He walked to his head and found the locked door. He turned the key over in his hand, wondering if it would slide into the opening. And if it would enter the lock, what was behind the door? Elena's hand rested on his and together they slipped the key into the lock. When the door opened, the fear poured out like wall of water released into the corridor, drowning him in ice water too fierce and cold for human survival.

This is fear, he thought. This drowns men's goodness and waters hatred. He stared at Rubio as his voice rose.

"What causes hatred?" he asked.

"Fear," said Rubio.

"WHAT CAUSES HATRED?"

"Fear," he answered again.

"And what makes fear disappear?" he cried.

While Rubio paused in the weight of this question, Elena stood to her feet and whispered.

"Only love."

$$a_1 \longrightarrow 3$$
$$a_2 \longrightarrow 3+4=7$$
$$a_3 \longrightarrow 3+4+4=11$$
$$a_4 \longrightarrow 3+4+4+4=15$$

CHAPTER TWELVE

Sequence

Elena lay on her back across a park bench, knowing the time was growing short. They had been gone from home only a mere three days, but the intensity of her experiences had multiplied the hours into months. She missed her home, ached for her mother and father and cat and bed sheets and the smell of food cooking on the stove. She needed the cream from her refrigerator and the tiny silver hairbrush from her great aunt and the sunlight streaming through the leaves into her bedroom.

They would be leaving soon.

After last night's astonishing discoveries, Mr. Rubio had given them a final task: take what you know about good and evil and do something with it. Don't just learn it and sit cross legged in the knowledge, but take it and use it and—*for God's sake*—make it mean something for someone else. Rube expected a final exam, something he could see and measure, before he would release them without reporting their truancy to the authorities. They had until nine o'clock tonight to bring their final product to the library steps.

"Do you really think Rube would turn us in?" Elmer asked.

"Yeah, I do."

"But he likes us."

"That's why he would do it. We've come too far now."

"I guess so." Elmer paused for a while, tearing a blade of grass into two strips. "What are we going to do for the final test?"

"I'm thinking,"

"We have to do something before tonight. And our bus leaves tomorrow anyway, so we can't mess around."

"I know. But we can't rush through it." She sat up. "What do you think?"

"I dunno. It can't be stupid. It can't be like a school test or a worksheet or report or anything like that."

"I know."

"What do you think he's looking for?"

"Maybe a plan."

"A plan?"

"Yeah, like a plan to do something."

A plan to do something. Simple enough. Plans require thinking. Plans require knowledge. "But I don't think he just wants just a written plan—I think he wants us to do it, too," said Elmer.

"Do it?"

"The plan. Whatever we decide we should do. It's not enough to think it, remember? He said we had to *be.* Just knowing something is not enough."

For the next hour, they sat and fidgeted and yawned and rolled in the grass and slapped at mosquitoes and stared at the sky and poked each other and ate raisins and used the public bathroom. And then suddenly, Elmer stood to his feet and announced: "We will write one."

"Write one? Write what?"

"A Friendship—what's that called? A Friendship Man-Fest-O."

"A what?"

"Like those peace treaties we read about in our books. A Fest-O or whatever it's called."

"Like a *manifesto*?"

"Yeah. *That.*"

Elena thought about it. "I like it. I like it a lot. But instead of writing it for countries, we need to write it for little kids. Little kids are still figuring things out. They're not frozen yet."

"A Friendship Manifesto." Elmer said it with authority. "We can write down a list of things that friends need to do—then we'll make copies for little kids."

"Rube will love that."

"He can help us pass them out."

"But you can't just give strangers a list," said Elena. "We'd have to find out where kids are and then show them."

"We can give the manifesto to schools—elementary schools."

"Yeah, we'll give them to the principals."

"Nah—bad idea," she retracted. "They would have to get it approved and then they would type it and make photocopies and then they'd make the kids take tests on it and then the kids wouldn't care about it anymore. We have to put it in the kids' hands ourselves—let the kids see it first. No adults in the way this time."

"Can't hurt."

"I say we go to the library and look at some different manifestos that people wrote and then write our own. We can finish by nine o'clock tonight. I know we can."

———

"Holy crap, Elena!" said Elmer. "Look at this!" He pointed to a title on page 42 of a huge, dusty book: *The Declaration of the*

Rights of Man and the Citizen.[1] "I have no idea what this means. It was written in 1789—" before he added, "—in France."

"I can't figure this one out either," she said, dragging her finger across *The Industrial Society and its Future* by Theodore Kaczynski. And this one that says *The Fascist Manifesto*.

"We can't write a manifesto," said Elmer slumping down into his chair. "I can't figure any of this out." They had traipsed into the library an hour earlier, asking the reference desk for all the books they could find on "manifestos." And this was the dismal, soul-crushing result.

"Let's face it, E," she said. "We can't read very well."

"Do we even know what a manifesto really is? Let's find a definition." Elmer left the room and came back with an Oxford Dictionary. "*M...Man...Manifesto,*" he said rippling through the pages. "A public declaration of principles."

"We've got the right idea. We're trying to write a list, right? Of stuff that friends should do? Something like that? And we want it to be public, right?"

"Maybe it's more like a 'Declaration' than a 'Manifesto'." Elmer looked at the examples in the first book. "Here's the Declaration of Independence. That's a good one."

"We're not very good at writing, Elm. I think it's okay to borrow some of their words and add our own. It will sound more official that way."

With their primitive intellectual engines grinding their gears, E2 worked and fussed and scrawled out their Mani-ration (or was it a Declara-festo?) for three hours, taking necessary breaks of water, children's books, snacks on the outside marble steps,

---

1. If you haven't studied this yet, you will. The French Revolution can be summed up easily: regular people hate kings.

and random scratching. The legitimacy of their task, bolstered by the rising stack of books in the East Wing Reading Room and the request for paper and pencils, made the library staff less suspicious of the young vagrants.

Elmer was sweating from all the pressure, and Elena's brow began to form the faint ridges that would one day crease her forehead for good. But over time the two writers, constipated by years of special education and intellectual delay, finally pushed out their infinitely sincere Friendship Manifesto, a document as meaningful and substantive as any that Thomas Jefferson labored over in 1776.

They stared at it, a formal document written informally in pencil and covered with eraser smudges—a testimony to both bad handwriting and the power of revision.

"It's beautiful," Elena declared.

"Oh yeah," said Elmer, wiping the corner of it with his elbow.

"We will have to type it. All Manifestos are typed."

Elmer thought about this. "At least the new ones."

"Let's have our last dinner in Handley first. Then we'll make it official."

———

Finales are usually great spectacles. People like endings to be important, like war victories. Or dessert. But sometimes endings are common and not that exciting at all.

Such was the case of Elmer and Elena's last dinner in Handley, a meal shared on the front hood of Old Dahlin, two blocks east of Handley's notorious junk yard. They had broken their last twenty-dollar bill on a plastic plate of fettuccine alfredo, a hunk of bread, and two lemon-lime sodas. The broken gumball machine had given up three more ancient marbles of blue, green, and yellow, which they would save for the trip home.

The humidity of spring had poured into town that day, lubricating every surface, living and dead. The air was not hot but thick, and Elmer wiped his face with his sleeve in between twirls of pasta.

"I have something to tell you, Elmer."

"What?"

"I talked to my mother yesterday."

"Your mother?"

"Yeah. On the phone. You were gone looking for the pool at Handley High School, and I was so—I was so lonely for my mother all of a sudden."

"That's okay. I'm not mad or anything." Elmer touched her on the arm. "I think it's good."

"I spent some of our money. I should have told you about it—or even asked first."

"What did she say?" he asked.

"She was happy to hear from me—we didn't talk for long. My dad wasn't there…but she sounded so good." Elena looked at him. "I miss her."

He grabbed her fork and curled a perfect bite around its plastic tines. "Here you go," he said as he lifted it to her mouth. After she swallowed, he said, "I don't miss my mom."

"I know. That's okay."

"She doesn't know me."

This was foreign territory. A mother and father who were disengaged from their son—this was beyond Elena's comprehension. But so were wars and genocides and selfish empires. Large and small, evil has its power, she thought.

"I think you should call her," she said.

"My mother? She thinks I'm with my brother."

"I don't care. I think you should call her."

Elmer drew the soda in one long pull through his straw. "All right. Let's go. I'll do it."

Even with the car's hideous paint job, Elmer was careful to sweep the hood clean with his arm. They neatly gathered their garbage and tucked it into the brown *Leo's Pasta* bag before taking their places in the front seat. She buckled both their seat belts—flimsy lap belts that gave out an anemic little *click*—and Elmer headed for town again.

"We're going to have to find gas before we give this back to Mr. Dahlin and Hannah." Elm felt the engine inhale as he turned the key. He knew its workings now, understood its old bones.

Elena leaned in to observe the gauge. Almost empty. "Do we have enough money?"

"Only five bucks or so. But we can't bring it back empty."

Reaching into her bag for loose change, Elena drew out a few dimes and—surprise!—a quarter. "You can use this for your phone call, Elmer. We'll have enough."

The heavy air rotated through the car's interior, and they drove in silence to the front entrance of Handley High School where Elmer cozied the car up to the curb and turned off the engine. It was a Sunday when all government buildings cope with abandonment issues. The phone booth, looking entirely different during the daytime, was just where she left it.

"I'll wait here," she said. "You go call."

He hesitated. She leaned against his arm with her shoulder. Then she opened his hand and dropped the coins into his palm before squeezing his fist shut. He replied, "All right. I'll do it."

With determination and a little bit of woman-push behind him, he walked to the phone booth, hiding his face from the world as he buried his head into the private space. Elena watched him from the car. *What would he say? What would his mother think? Would she even care where he was?* He put the coins into the slot and she saw him punch the numbers in slow succession. Leaning his back against the phone, he turned to look at Elena with a small nod. *It was ringing.* His lips moved. He was talking to her. *What were they saying?* She could see his explanation, making out small phrases and conversational body language.

Suddenly, his face shifted, the kind of transformation when soldiers see the enemy on the horizon in a war movie. He was stunned, silent, lips frozen. He reached up and dragged his fingers through his hair before clonking his forehead against the side panel. His feet were shifting, right and then left, left and then right, all the while only listening while Elena, with the intuition of a mother, opened the car door and moved to his side.

"I will come...I said I will come. Tell him I will be home tomorrow. No, I won't wait," he said before cutting off the line with his index finger. Elena waited. She had learned to be patient for the answers.

The confusion was as heavy as the air, and he whispered to her, "My father is dying."

―――――――――

The phone call changed everything.

Elmer collapsed onto the hood of the car and poured out the truth to Elena in the simplest terms he could find.

Carl Whit's leg was nearly gone. The blood loss had rendered him close to dead.

The longer version was more colorful. He had taken a demolition job in a nearby town. Piss-drunk and stupid, he had fallen into the path of a rotational hydraulic shear which divinely subtracted a good part of the man who was already a negative integer. His mother, who for a decade had hated this man, was now retracting her curses against him, hysterical with grief at this news. The object of her hatred might just die, and with it her reason for living.

As for Elmer, he now felt the hot breath of death on his neck, knowing that he must chase it down before it had the chance to take his father down. He had hated the man for most of his life, but like the peacemakers in Handley's books, Elmer now believed in the power of forgiveness. Carl Whit was Elmer's personal war criminal, and for him to die without appearing before a tribunal—well, that would haunt him forever. He must forfeit the bus ticket and get home *now*—but just how he did not know.

"Let's take Old Dahlin home," announced Elena.

Elmer was doubled over, sick with grief. "We can't just take it—we can't steal Hannah's car."

"I don't mean *steal* it, Elmer. I mean we go to them and *ask* for it. We tell them the truth."

"Oh god, why is this happening—why now?" he moaned. "They can't give us this car, and even if they did, it won't make it 500 miles to home. It's a piece of junk." As if to apologize, Elmer stroked the door as he said it.

"Listen to me. This whole trip has been one big ridiculous miracle anyway—let's see if we can take the car and get you home. If we drive all night, we'll get there in the morning. And then you can see your dad quicker than you thought."

Elmer sat in the puddle of decisions, wet and confused. "Besides that, what about our manifesto? What will Rube think if we don't show up?"

"We did our work, right? We can leave it for him—somehow we can leave it for him," said Elena.

"But it wasn't enough to just write something, Elena. We were supposed to *do* something with it, remember? We can't just write it and forget."

"But we have to get home—now. You know that."

Elmer slid down the side of the car and squatted on the asphalt road. "Maybe we can do both."

"Both? What are you thinking, Elmer?"

He creaked open the door and took out the car key. "First, we gotta find out if Old Dahlin can go the distance. Get in. Let's go talk to Hannah."

The ten square blocks of old town Handley were now as familiar as their own neighborhood. Crushed under the weight of his father's accident, Elmer could hardly speak on the way to the Dahlins' car lot. Elena tucked her knees up on the dash and closed her eyes. *Would they find a way to leave for home tonight?*

As Elmer pulled the car into the old back lot behind their house, Mr. Dahlin was putting away his tools in the ancient shed. He grinned when he saw them and gave an old man wave. "Elmer!" he shouted out. "How's the baby running?"

The couple got out of the car and came to stand in front of Mr. Dahlin who by now had summoned the missus to join him in the backyard. Hannah came out of the back door and tottered over to them wearing high heels and an apron. "You sweetie pies," she said, "come on inside and set awhile."

"It's okay, Mrs. Dahlin," said Elena, aware of the time and gravity of their impending request. "We just came to ask you and your husband a question."

"Well, you can't ask a proper question out here in the junk-yard. Come on in and ask away." Hannah led them like two puppies into her house, a cluttered, fussy two-bedroom cottage built just about the same year as Mrs. Dahlin herself. "Come sit in my living room. I'll get us some sweet tea."

Sitting under the glow of ancient beaded lamp shades, Elmer looked out of place with his wild hair and dirty pants. Elena was barely better. Her brown hair—usually sleek at home—was suffering the effects of do-the-best-you-can hygiene. Had Hannah's eyes been ten years younger, she might have regretted offering these vagrants a place on her sofa.

Mr. Dahlin settled into his chair and spoke up first. "So, how did ya' like the old Chevette? It's a piece of work, I know, but it's still got some life in it, no?"

"Oh, it was great," said Elmer. "In fact, that's why we're here."

"Are you headed home tomorrow?" asked Hannah.

"Well—" Elmer looked at Elena and they shifted awkwardly on the sofa.

Elena batted first. "We…I mean, Elmer got a pretty bad phone call from his mother today. His father was in an accident. She needs him to come home immediately."

"Oh my goodness, child," said Hannah. "You must be sick about that." She shook her head. "Boys need their daddies— even when they're almost grown."

"Of course, you gotta get home," said Mr. Dahlin, nodding.

"That's sort of the problem," said Elmer. "We really can't wait for our bus trip home."

Everyone was silent for several seconds.

"I think I know what you are saying, son." Mr. Dahlin rose from his seat. "You sit right there a minute."

He disappeared into the hallway and emerged with a photograph. It was a picture of a handsome young soldier holding a baby boy. "See this? This is my son. And *that*—" he said pointing to the child emphatically, "is my grandson."

Hannah got up and went into the kitchen while Mr. Dahlin kept talking. "My son was killed a battle. Fighting for good.

Always fighting for good, that boy. When he was gone, we had to help our grandson's mamma raise him right."

Elmer and Elena couldn't shake their gaze from the photograph. "You must miss him," said Elena softly.

"You never get over it. And now you must be with your daddy, son. It don't matter what he ever did to you—you need to get in that car and go to him tonight." Mr. Dahlin wiped his eyes. "You still got the key?"

"Yes, sir."

They heard Hannah call out from the kitchen. "Don't you go anywheres now…You just wait a second."

"We don't know how to thank you," said Elena as they waited to Mrs. Dahlin to return.

Mr. Dahlin lowered his voice. "You know, you're driving that car illegal now. I'm giving you a car that's gonna cross some state lines with no insurance. I'll give you the pink slip to put in your glove box, but by golly you're on your own, son. Don't you tell nobody that Mr. Dahlin gave you a criminal record." He almost laughed when he said it. "When you're my age and you've lost the most important thing ever, you stop thinking and just *feel*." He put his hand on Elmer's shoulder. "And this feels right to me."

Hannah emerged from the kitchen holding the handles of two brown grocery bags in each hand. "When you drive through the night you need lots of food. There's everything I got that's fit to travel. You got a map in there, too. And some pink napkins with hearts on them." She looked at Elmer quizzically. "I never asked this, but are you two sweeties?"

Elena stared at the carpet, not knowing what to say. It was the unspeakable question. No one had forced an answer before. E2 was just a beautiful expression that required no explanation.

"Elena is mine and I am hers," said Elmer.

"Oh," she replied. "Then you'll like the napkins."

As the sun went down, God's messengers went to work. The night would be long and the labor great. Ten waited to hear the good news, ten made bright by the clarion call of hope. The winds would be contained and the water would be held back, for gospel truth always penetrates the darkness, always prevails against every wicked scheme.

Make straight the way of peace, he said. Make smooth the way of love. Nail the message onto every door. And when you are done, the celebrations can begin

---

"How long will it take?"

"I'm not sure. Let's figure it out."

Elmer spread Mrs. Dahlin's map onto the sidewalk in front of the glorious library as the day slipped into dusk. He dragged his finger from Handley to his knee, where he anchored the map against the rising wind. Elena stood behind him and she swung her arm across his shoulder to trace the line from north to south herself. "It doesn't look that hard. Just a straight line, really."

"It will take us all night."

So far, driving Old Dahlin had been a pleasure, just a surprise joy ride from point A to B in a circumference no bigger than a child's imaginary kingdom. But pulling out onto the long desolate highway in a clunker as old as Moses was an unknown terror as great as any Elm had felt. They would have to travel in the dead of night—just the two of them—with the ghosts of urban legends scraping their fingernails across the roof of their car.

The map appeared to show great sterile swaths of land between here and there, land that had passed beneath the wheels of their Greyhound bus unnoticed four days ago. But then he heard the voice of his mother wheezing out her grief on the phone. *He is dying, Elmer. Come home and see him before he goes.* To stay in the safety of the library even one more night would be to remain a child.

He would have to breathe in and out. He would have to do this impossible thing and become a man.

But first, the manifesto.

"We can't wait until nine o'clock, Elena. We will have to leave this for Rubio." Elmer reached into his bag and pulled out the handwritten copy. "We didn't type it."

They looked down at the document. It was crinkled and childlike with stunted handwriting and an awkward upward scrawl. The title stretched out across the top in big fat letters, and the sentences alternated between Elmer's tiny painstaking script and Elena's loopy, sprawling mess. No one had seen its message yet. This had been part of their journey, he thought. He couldn't leave without making good on their promise to Mr. Rubio.

"We can leave it on the library door for him. The back door."

"No. Mrs. O will see it."

"He's coming at nine. She won't be gone yet."

"I say we put in right on the front door of the library—right where everyone can see."

"Won't someone take it down?"

"Maybe. But we'll know we did the right thing. We followed through."

Elena squeezed her eyes shut. This was too hard now. The journey had been beautiful, but now it was just hard. "Elmer?"

"Yeah?"

"I think we need to do more with this."

"More?"

"Like we talked about before. We should show this to kids."

"We—I—we have to get home. We don't have time to do more than this. My father…" He waited, unable to finish his sentence.

Light burst into Elena's eyes and she took Elmer by the shoulders. "Wait right here."

Grabbing the manifesto and her green bag, Elena ran up the steps into the library, leaving Elmer to wonder what she could possibly be doing on the eve of their departure. Alone, he squatted down to look at the map again. The snaky line reminded him of his brother Ed who had fled the opposite direction two years ago. The sounds of his brother's bootleg guitar mixed in his head with the chords of rage so often heard outside his bedroom door. *War and peace*, he thought. *The only two sure things in this life.*

When Elena returned, the stack of papers in her hand held the answers to their questions. She had photocopied their Friendship Manifesto—ten smooth, white copies for distributing God-knows-where. She fanned them out like playing cards and smiled. "Rube would be proud. These are for the children," she said.

"Which children?"

"The ones from here to home."

"How will we find them?"

"God will show us."

———

Michael Rubio had arrived at the library early that night to complete his mission. It was half past eight when he noticed two things as he walked up the steps to the library. The first was an agitated breeze, a premonition of the night's coming storm, and the second was the sound of a sheet of paper flapping against the big door of the entrance. Several people were clustered around it, reading silently. He walked up behind them and looked at the paper, its edges rising and falling with the wind.

The Friendship Manifesto by E2

In case you don't know this, friendship isn't easy. It's hard. We hold these truths to be self-evident, that people should love each other, and with the support of this Declaration and with a firm reliance on the protection of divine Providence, we ask friends to pledge to each other their Lives, their Fortunes and their sacred Honor.

1. Two friends are like two nice countries. They trade things and don't use weapons.

2. A friend says things about you to other people that make you seem better than you might be, but not worse.

3. You can tell good friends by the way they sit next to each other. They don't mind their leg touching your leg. Even boys.

4. A real friend doesn't mind when you find another friend. It means everybody gets more love.

5. Two good people usually make good friends. Two bad people won't work at all. If it's a mix, the bad one might just need some more time. Two years is about right. After that, the good one

can leave without feeling too bad but even then it hurts.

6. Your friend will write your worst parts in chalk and your best parts with a permanent marker.

7. A friend lets you cry without trying to fix you.

8. If you're doing something bad, a friend doesn't say "I understand." He will try to stop you.

9. You don't need a hundred friends. A couple of good ones are all you need.

10. Friends don't kiss each other. Never. If they do, then its not called friendship anymore but something different, and you'll have to look at another list.

Magnificent, he thought. Then, next to the sheet of paper he spied a yellow sticky note. On it was written:

Mr. Rubio. We hope you like our final exam. We had to leave. Elmer's dad is sick. But we are takeing the manifesto with us. We will spread the good news. —E2

As if knowing that the papers were sacred, no one in the crowd had touched either one. Mr. Rubio excused himself and pulled the yellow note from the door, folding it once, twice, before putting it in his pocket. He pressed the duct tape firmly against the door, anchoring the Manifesto even tighter to the entrance. The group of people scattered one by one, leaving him alone on the white stone steps. He squatted down to sit, watching the trees begin to bend, feeling the shift in the air—the warnings of unrest in the universe.

He took the library keys off his belt one by one and set them down on the steps beside him. Next, he removed the tools: a small knife, a dusting chamois, a black box pager. He lined them up neatly in a row and stood up to leave. As the first drops of rain began to fall, he moved to the sidewalk, his quickening stride moving him from present to past. He grew smaller and smaller until he was nothing but a tiny dot on the streets of Handley.

$$\bar{v} = \frac{\Delta x}{\Delta t}$$

CHAPTER THIRTEEN

Velocity

The interstate highway began as a thick ribbon and then unraveled into a tiny whisper of thread as it disappeared over the horizon. The weight and ballast of the bus had faked them into thinking the road to Handley was smooth and easy. Sitting atop Old Dahlin's ancient suspension, they now felt every bump and texture in the concrete. Groves of trees came and went like whooshing tufts of green, and as Handley faded into the past, fewer buildings interrupted the vast expanse of land.

The windows of the car were slightly open, as they were from the beginning. With a broken mechanism, the panes of clouded glass moved deep into the pocket of the doors and then three-quarters up, but never further. This would be a problem, as dusk and storm prepared to collide. The falling light cast a gray-green glow on the road and prairies, and molecules of water joined together until the air could barely contain it.

On this night, rain would be bad.

A storm was coming; there was no doubt about it. Elmer, uneasy in his driver's seat, felt the chaos in his bones. Elena sat upright, saying very little, with the copies of their manifesto in her lap. The moist wind swirled into the front seat, and with the help of the side windows, moved like a spinning cone of air. The papers on her lap thrashed about until finally she tucked them on the floorboard under her bare feet.

Mr. Rubio's request was made shortly before departure. Between Handley and home, they would find ten school doors on which to hang their manifesto. It was Sunday night when campuses are dozing off before Monday morning's alarm, so most schools would be quiet and accessible for a middle-of-the-night raid. Either Elmer or Elena would attempt a quick dash to the cafeteria door while the other planned to wait in the getaway car. Cafeterias, they reasoned, were better places to post their message than administrative offices. (Food is a better magnet for the soul anyway, is it not?) But if it were the type of building like a fortress, with limited entrances and an interior cafeteria, then they would tape their message on whatever door they could find. Perhaps some child would find it first before the adults would try to clear the door of unauthorized graffiti. This was Elena's hope.

Elmer's thoughts were less bright. His father's life-and-death struggle stood at the end of this journey as a monolith, a travel landmark more significant than the nation's capital or Mount Rushmore or the Grand Canyon[1]. While they passed other cars on their happy road trips to who-knows-where, Elmer was traveling to a destination of reconciliation, or even—if he dared to imagine it—a finale of grief. Elmer could think of little else. *Would his father be dead when he arrived? What would he say if he*

---

1. Children all over America understand the Family Road Trip, a rite of passage that includes traveling long distances in order to see important landmarks. The length of the trip should be proportional to the quality of the destination. Sometimes the inverse is true; in other words, traveling twenty hours in a minivan with your bratty sister might only result in seeing the cast on Aunt Emily's broken leg.

were still alive? The journey home was longer than the journey to Handley and infinitely harder. Of that he was certain.

"The storm will be here soon," said Elena as if foreshadowing his thoughts. She reached her hand out of the open window, feeling the thick, rushing air knock her arm about. A wide, charcoal smudge hovered in the distance, a giant cloud waiting to break open.

"It's getting dark. Really fast."

"Shouldn't we try to find our first school?" she asked.

"I don't know. Let's ask when we get to a town." They were barely twenty miles out of the city and Elmer wondered if there even existed ten schools in the space they traveled.

They drove in quiet watching the landforms change. The flat prairies began to swell into small hills and as time went on, the steady drone of engine noises hypnotized them both. They fell into the road trip hypnosis that career truck drivers know so well. A few times Elena shifted in her seat and poked Elmer in the arm just to know he was conscious, but as a driving newbie, Elmer was still somewhat freaked out about sitting behind any wheel. His eyes were glued open. He stared and stared and stared some more.

As he entered into an altered state of consciousness, out the front windshield he pictured his father standing in the doorway of his house. His jeans were, as usual, encrusted with dirt and his hair stood up in front. He was always quiet at first before the tempest swelled into great billowing clouds of anger. Carl Whit was one of those giant storms that some call an act of God. But how can a natural disaster strike during God's watch? How can such things as brokenness and despair be divinely ordered? In Elmer's imagination he saw the man blow and spit and pour out his wrath against the windshield, beating it with his fists, his face pressing against the glass in distorted, horrified expressions. His father's mouth grew wider and wider as it looked to swallow the car whole. His arms encircled the vehicle, growing longer and longer until they joined hands under the chassis, and his body swelled, snuffing out the remaining light leaving nothing but darkness. Elmer pushed himself back against the seat, feeling the power of his father's memory take over. It was brutal and horrifying, the remnants of unspeakable pain.

Then, Elena's hand on his arm.

Reality tossed the figure loose from the car, bringing in a smattering of grayish light. As Elmer looked out the windshield, he now could only see a severed leg in the road. It was his father's. The dark object was unholy. *Was it true? Was his father's leg really taken from him as his mother had feared?*

Elena gripped his forearm a bit tighter. She saw his expression and shook his arm, harder this time. "What's going on in your head right now?" she asked. Elmer pressed the back of his hands into his eye sockets and shook off the panic. His breathing was quick and uneven. His father's memory, like a flush of panic, had rattled his pulse and left a moist stain where his back pressed against the seat.

"Look ahead," Elena announced. Not an unholy limb sent to haunt him, but a green traffic sign lay ahead, bearing the first marker of civilization. *Barfield 18 miles*. Elmer peeled his damp fingers off the steering wheel and repositioned them. *I'm okay*, he thought. *I'm okay. Elena is here.* He reached over with his right hand to verify that she existed in the flesh.

Elena unfolded the clumsy map and scanned the surface. "Where's Barfield," she muttered. Barfield was a speck of a thing, a tiny smudge in the world. "Yup. There it is. Doesn't look too big to me. But even a small town has an elementary school, right?" She was not discouraged.

"It's got to. Every kid has to go to school. We'll stop in Barfield and ask somebody."

Soon Elena noticed the markers on the side of the freeway. Who would have known that Barfield would be so thrilling as to require a mileage countdown? *18...17...16...*Every pole that passed squeezed a little adrenaline out of her, and by the time they reached marker number nine, she began to sing the number out loud in anticipation like a child. "NINE! It's NINE and oh so fine...EIGHT, it's EIGHT and that's really great..."

Apparently, Barfield liked to flaunt its sex appeal around exit number three. "Let's get off here," he announced, swerving the car toward the right and rolling toward the gaudy orange gasoline sign on the side of the road. Old Dahlin sputtered to the parking lot and rolled into a spot along the side of the building.

Elena was feeling spooked now. Barfield felt rude, desolate. By comparison, Handley was cozy. This was a place even lonelier than the open road, for it actually aspired to something but failed. They parked along the wall, smelling their old engine's rusty stink as it rested its weary body. *Would it even start again now that it had stopped?* "I'll go ask where the nearest school is," said Elmer.

"I'm coming with you. I don't want to stay alone."

The Barfield Mini-Mart was the ugly stepsister of the grocery store, the illegitimate child in the retail family tree. After they entered, the floor stuck briefly to the bottom of Elena's shoe with each step, making a sucking sound as they approached the counter. Racks of brightly colored snacks masquerading as food cluttered the aisles, each one with a lime green price sticker. Industrial tanks of flavored cappuccino and hot chocolate stood beside the mini cement mixer rotating blue and red frozen slush. Two workers, maybe nineteen or twenty years old, roamed the sacred space behind the counter, one poking at the dark brown

197

corn dogs in the brightly lit incubation chamber and the other hovering over the cash register, suspicious. Elena could hear the laugh track of some 1980s sitcom buzzing out of a tiny television with antenna ears. No one else was around.

"Can I help you?" It didn't seem like the cashier really wanted to help, but hey, it was in the training manual.

Elmer walked over to the counter, dragging his fingers through his hair. He was certain he looked like a mess. "This is a funny question, but is there a school around here?"

The cashier stared at Elm's birthmark. "A school? What kind of school?" The second worker looked up from the orange heat lamp but said nothing.

Elena spoke up. "An elementary school."

The cashier reached over to turn down the television. Then he walked over to Elmer. "Well, there's the one I went to."

"You went to school in Barfield?" asked Elena.

"Hell, yeah. Everybody went there. It's the only one."

"Is it close to here?"

"'Bout two miles." He waved his hand toward the overpass. "You go down this road and then turn left at the concrete company."

Elmer and Elena looked at each other and then back at the cashier. "Thanks." They turned to leave.

"You gonna buy anything?"

"Nope. Sorry 'bout that." They kept walking to the exit, but Elena gave a little wave to the cashier before the door closed behind them.

When they got back in the car, Elena suddenly started to cry. "It's so sad, Elmer—it's just so sad."

"What's wrong? What's so sad?" Elmer turned on the ignition and waited for her to answer. They sat together for a long moment before she said anything.

"He's never left Barfield," she sniffled. "He's been in this town all this time with nothing at all."

Perhaps it was this moment when Elmer finally got his proof. Proof that Elena was the kindest, most compassionate person he had ever met. No one else would care about that man, that zero-person behind a zero-counter in a zero-town. But Elena did. "It's not so bad," Elmer said. "He's got a job. And a friend there." The absurdity was sinking in. "And he's got free refills of Mountain Dew." He knew it was ridiculous, but it made Elena finally smile.

She smeared her face with the back of her hand and took a deep breath. "It just makes me so sad. There's people like that all over the world right now. Just doing nothing. Going nowhere."

"Not us, baby. Not us."

It was the first time he called her that. *Baby*. That was a word reserved for flirts and married people and lovers and songwriters. Not a word for geeky Elmer. She liked it.

"Don't let me ever work in a place like that, Elmer. Drag me away from there and tell me I can't do it."

"Okay, I will." He creaked the gears into reverse. "It's getting dark. Let's go to the school."

They rumbled over the desolate overpass and toward the cashier's directions. Elena saw the cement company building first. "There it is! Turn left right here."

Old Dahlin clunked onto the two-lane road. Houses were scattered here and there, porch lights just starting to flicker on. Most yards were dusty with little patches of green grass comforting the neighborhood in tiny doses. They rolled past old cars and decrepit Radio Flyers, noticing the shrubs vibrating in the wind. No one was outside their houses tonight except a woman in a flapping cotton nightdress who, while at her mailbox, looked up at the ugly Chevette intruder as it rumbled past. Elena looked up at her and waved, as if by instinct, but the woman only watched them drive by.

The wooden sign was positioned at an angle on the corner. *Barfield Elementary: Home of the Blue Jays.* The teachers at Barfield fought a good fight against the dreary landscape. The windows were splattered with die cut sunbeams and rainbows made of crepe paper, and along the fence flapped spirited homemade banners promoting *Hugs Not Drugs!* and *Jays are Number One.* A tiny garden. A parking lot for bicycles. An old school bell swinging from a wooden platform. No one knew about this school except for the hundred families who called it theirs. To them, it was the town's sunshine, even if that sunshine was only made of crepe paper.

"Where's the cafeteria?"

They pulled into the main lot, a small square of parking spaces for the faculty and staff. "I think it's right there," said Elena pointing to the blue double doors on the right. The long line of windows betrayed the rectangular tables inside.

"You wanna go by yourself?" Elmer asked.

"Yeah. Stay here but don't turn off the car," she answered.

Re-tying her shoes, Elena prepared to sprint. She reached back for the duct tape and peeled off one of her photocopies from the stack on the floorboard. In a cinematic gesture, she kissed the paper briefly and turned to look at Elmer. "Here I go."

Elmer watched her through the front windshield which was now speckled with bug carcasses and freeway dross. She ran to the blue doors, fighting the strong wind, ducking her head under the overhang. Several plops of rain warped Elm's view, but he saw her through the shimmery prism. She arrived at the double doors, focused and determined.

Paper up.

Tape across all four sides.

Girl running.

Elena was back in less than 45 seconds.

"That was crazy," she said as she swept into the car's interior bringing the rainwater with her. She slammed the door. "Let's go."

As the Chevette pulled out of the parking lot, Elena looked back to see the white manifesto outlined in blue electrical tape, clear as day, under the eaves. The school door grew smaller and smaller until finally she could see nothing but the architectural lines of the school building.

"Our first one," said Elm. "Rube would be proud. We're doing it."

"Who do you think will find it first?" she wondered.

"I dunno. What do you think?"

"I think it will be a little girl. She will be in third grade and she will read it to her friends. And then she will hang it up at home and put it in a gold frame by her bed and read it every night."

"That's a nice thought, Elena," said Elmer. "I think you're right."

The rain was growing fierce. Old Dahlin was a leaky bucket full of holes and they would have to find a way to contain it. Elmer wiped his arm across his face as the water *spit spit spit* across his cheeks. It did not occur to them that the car might not make it home.

"But really. Who do you think will find it?" Elena asked.

"The paper? I dunno. A kid, I hope." It was getting louder outside and Elmer's voice rose to conquer it.

"What will they think? Do you think they'll think it's a joke?"

"Some might. But some might really like it. They might think about it."

The rain began to assert itself even more. It was clear that driving under these conditions with broken windows would be impossible before too long. "Let's stop before the highway. We need plastic bags," Elena shouted over the rain. "Go back to the store."

With only two turns, Elmer was able to navigate back to the gas station where the parking lot was still desolate and forgotten. This time, he pulled under the peeling orange structure stretching over the gas pumps. The sound of the rain battering the car roof stopped abruptly as they rolled under cover. "I'll get some bags," he said. "Wait for me."

When he walked into the store again, the cashier was gone, but Mr. Corndog was sitting in his place. "Back so soon?"

"We need some plastic bags. For the rain. Our window is broken," announced Elmer, who while dripping inside the doorway, looked like a desperate man.

"You have to buy something to get a bag," he said.

"Can you just give us some used ones? Something old?"

"Nope."

Elmer wasn't sure what to do. Up to this point, most of their angels had been accommodating. He looked around the place, trying to see what he could buy.

The beef jerky was too pricey.
The magazines too smutty.
The coffee blacker than night.
The Big Gulps monstrous.
The rain ponchos too ugly.

Wait. Rain ponchos? Since when did mini-marts sell rain ponchos? This was perfect.

"How much are the rain ponchos?"

"I dunno. Did you look?"

Okay, this guy was trouble, thought Elmer. Not nice, angry at the world, a Sun City High School prick without the fancy letterman's jacket. Elmer looked for the green price sticker. The poncho packages were clipped in overlapping order on a piece of cardboard, ten in a row with not one missing. The company that made them had presumably shipped them to the store several years ago and not one person on Highway 129 had needed a rain poncho to seal up an old Chevette during a storm. Amazing. A dollar ninety-nine and not one single sale.

"You gonna buy one?"

"I don't know yet." Elmer waited. "Listen, we're trying to get home fast. We don't have much money. Do you think we could just get some old bags?" He was trying.

"I don't give free stuff to ugly people."

Wow.

Elmer was stunned. The old feelings were rising inside of him, the years of exploitation and pain. Rube's lessons about forgiveness and pain were meaningless in the real world. This guy was threatening to turn off the lights in Elmer's brain. Elmer was feeling himself falling into darkness again.

Elena, coming from behind, had heard it all. She touched Elm on the shoulder and whispered into his ear, "Let me try." She walked up to the young man and, leaning in, put her hands flat on the counter. "Hi," she said.

"Hey."

"Is your manager here?"

"That's me."

"How old are you?"

"Nineteen."

"That's cool. I don't think I could be a manager at nineteen. I'm only seventeen and I can't even finish my algebra homework on time."

"I hated algebra."

"Most people do. But that's okay. It's probably good for us."

"Whatever you say."

Elmer stayed back and watched their conversation. *How could she love people, even the unlovable ones?*

"We are on a road trip," she continued. "Doing something kind of crazy."

"What's that?"

"Do you have a little sister—or maybe a cousin or something?"

"Yeah. My stepsister is ten."

"I have something for her." Elena reached under her shirt and pulled out a folded piece of paper. "My friend and I are going around telling kids how to be a good friend. Do you think you could give this to her?" She opened up the paper and laid it down in front of him. lk

He didn't touch it. He looked at it, cautiously. "You guys are crazy."

"I know." She watched his eyes scan the paper. "Tell me which one you like best."

"Which what?

"Which number."

Elmer watched from a distance, seeing the cashier mouth the words as his eyes moved down the paper. He put his hand to the back of his neck. He didn't want to do this. "I don't know—maybe this one." He pointed to number eight. "One of my buddies smokes dope and I when I told him to quit, he told me to get lost."

He stared out the front store window.

"So I quit hanging out with him." He tucked his long hair behind his ear. "Yeah, so now we're enemies."

"You did the right thing," she said.

"Maybe, but it don't mean nothing."

"Sure it does. Doing the right thing means everything."

He finally looked at her eyes and saw a miracle there. No one ever talked to him like this. She was transparent, beautiful. A messenger of light.

"Keep this, okay, and give it to your stepbrother. Good night." She turned around and walked toward the door where Elmer was waiting in silence.

"Hey," the cashier called out. "Wait a sec." He reached under the counter and peeled off a half inch stack of slippery plastic bags. "Come and get this." When she returned to the counter, he pulled seven rain ponchos off the cardboard display and set them in the center of the bags. "Here's something for your trip."

Storms are wild things. They are untamed beasts of wind and water that beat and thrash at the earth, given permission to spank the mountains and prairies for things they've never done. The storm that passed over Highway 129 punished the land without due process, and the tiny orange car trembled through the tempest barely hanging on. If one were to see the drama unfold from above, he would see a lonely stretch of road lashed by horizontal winds and blinding rain as a tiny creature fought desperately to keep going.

The interior of Old Dahlin was no less terrifying. The make-shift plastic sheeting they had rigged over the open windows with duct tape made a horrible noise like the broken sail of a pirate ship flapping against the hull. They soon discovered that the rusted chassis had open wounds which allowed rainwater to spit upward from the pavement. It soaked the floor mats from underneath and Elena's bare feet squished into the puddles until she finally sat cross-legged. The decrepit windshield wipers labored as they swept across the glass, *schweet, schweet, schweet*, with pitted rubber barely clearing the torrent of water from Elmer's vision. In the daytime, such a trip would have been risky at best. But once night came, the storm would become a beast of sound and feeling only, a worse terror with no vision to guide its adversary.

No sane driver would have attempted the crossing in these conditions, but then again, E^2 was a crazy expression. Both of them could barely move, every nerve and muscle tensed. Every so often, one of them would shout above the wild noises.

"Are you all right?"

"No!" the other shouted.

Elmer was driving by feeling, inching along the road in painfully slow increments. In clear weather, the headlights might bathe a quarter mile in light, but now they could only illuminate several feet of sweeping rain made horizontal by the wind. Only twice did another car pass in the other direction, two lights appearing out of nowhere and cascading a sheet of water across the side of the car. The left side of Elmer's body was drenched; the right side, damp. Elena saw a shiver pass through him.

As Elena looked out over the hood of the car, she thought she saw her father's face. It was a kind face, full of love. In the gray light she imagined him gesturing to her, asking her to come toward him. He spread his arms open wide and smiled at her, tossing his chin upward as if to say *c'mon here, baby girl. I'll take care of you. Was he actually here on the highway with her? Was he protecting her from harm?* His arms grew longer and longer until he reached his fingers beneath the body of the car and linked them together, tucking the entire vehicle in his embrace. His face said *I love you* through the glass. She closed her eyes and imagined her kitchen table, daddy sitting at the head with one hand on her mother's arm. She could breathe again, full of peace.

"Elena?" Elmer reached over and laid a hand on her arm.

She opened her eyes. "I'm all right," she whispered.

Then, noticing Elmer's shivering body, she announced, "Let me make you a cover."

She reached into the back seat and took one of the plastic bags that Mr. Cashier had given them in Barfield. They had left an hour ago, and the storm had been picking up strength ever since. The rain ponchos were hoisted across both windows, so now it was up to Elena to use the plastic bags for Plan B. She blew one open and turned the closed end up. Reaching for her scissors, the ones that cut Elm's hair only two days ago, she snipped a medium sized hole across the seam. "There!" she said, as she slipped it over Elm's head and shimmied it down over his shoulders.

She had forgotten about his arms. He looked like a freaking Pez dispenser.

"Sorry," she shouted. She pulled it off again and cut two smaller holes for his arms.

"You wear it first. You need one, too," he said.

She slipped into her plastic shirt-poncho-raincoat and quickly made another one for Elm. She helped him into it and the two sat like Niagara Falls tourists on the deck of *Maid of the Mist*.

"I think we should listen to the radio—see if there is anything about the weather," he yelled above the bluster.

The radio crackled and buzzed as the knob turned from right to left. At these coordinates of space, would any signal reach them? Finally, she found one distant satellite signal, enough to capture a news report in splotchy decibels.

The National Weather Service...the severe thunderstorm east of...large hail in parts...funnel...spotted near the town of... extremely dangerous...cover...

They strained to hear it. Broken pieces of the newscaster's voice crackled over the speakers until one final pop silenced the radio for good. Nothing. Not even static.

"Funnel?"

Elena knew only one funnel and it wasn't good. Tornado.

The hostile earth was gathering its weapons and preparing to strike. In the middle of a vast open space with only the protection of rusted metal and rain ponchos, Elmer and Elena wondered if they had tested the limits of their independence. A rainstorm they could survive, but a funnel cloud? This was not an abstraction like fear or insecurity or disrespect, but a real monster with velocity and torque and power. Tornadoes have been known to pick up lumber and skewer fences. They have a reputation for terror. Dorothy and Toto needed therapy after their ordeal, and don't forget that during the spring of 1974, thousands of people across thirteen Southern states respected twisters once and for all. Storm chasers were professionals, but Elmer was a rank amateur.

And now here they were, helpless, with night falling fast.

"We're going to have to stop." Elmer knew that he had crossed into real danger. "The first place we can stop, we will."

Elena tried to read the map for signs of the nearest town, but her head felt woozy from the pitch and movement of Old Dahlin's struggle. The air was thick and uncomfortable. The sounds were making her head hurt. Far ahead on the horizon, she could see the faint sliver of light fighting through the clouds. She wasn't thinking clearly, for she was convinced that if she would become sick—with fear, car sickness, or even the flu—she would simply open the door and fall out into the abyss, splashing through puddles as she fell down, down, down. It seemed that in the confusion the storm had taken over.

Elmer thought of his momentary flashback. His father had been reaching for him, trying to snuff him out, and now the twister and his father became one. The force and power. The propensity for darkness. The drill bit chewing into flesh.

And then, Elmer and Elena saw the very thing that few of us will ever see, an image so intense and terrifying that to experience it even once is to see it every stormy night in your dreams until the day you die. A swirling, pencil-thin funnel cloud reached down from the sky and pierced the distant ground, its circumference expanding as it ate the prairie in bites. Its outline, hardly visible against the falling light but growing more immense as it rolled across the land from left to right, was swollen with dirt and dust. Even a mile away in the dim light, Elmer could see the land spewing bits of flesh where the point of the funnel cloud drilled deep into the soil. He was completely and totally hypnotized, driving unconsciously as his eyes were locked onto the power of the tornado.

Elena, whose breath came in quick little puffs, finally shrieked, "Stop, stop, stop—Elmer, we have to take cover! Anywhere!"

They saw their salvation ahead, a concrete overpass. It was one of those lonely structures one finds on the way to here and there—the place where someone who discovers he's been going the wrong way can change his mind. "Oh my god, oh my god," he moaned, as he maneuvered the car toward the bridge. "We have to make it," he begged. "We have to make it there."

"Hurry—oh, my god, hurry!" she yelled above the insane flapping of plastic and the roar of the approaching cyclone.

The car, now going no more than twenty miles an hour, slipped ghost-like under the concrete bridge where the noise grew dense and muffled. Not a single headlight in either direction interrupted the vast expanse of space—simply the monster which had now moved a quarter mile closer. Elmer cut the engine and they felt Old Dahlin shudder. "Get out, get out!" he shouted. "We have to get to the top before it gets here!"

Elena creaked open her passenger door and they felt the rush of cool, wet wind slap across their cheeks and arms. She scrambled out of the car and Elmer leaped over the passenger seat following right behind. By now the entire world became The Noise. It was louder and more terrifying than any noise they ever imagined. Elena went first, scrambling up the slippery embankment to the sharp angle where the concrete and the grassy hill converged. She could see the tiny triangle of safety.

"Further!" he yelled. "Go further to the smallest spot!" He pushed her from behind, seeing her flying plastic cape whipping around her head. Elena got there first. She wedged her body in the crevice and Elmer tucked in beside her, pulling her close to him with his left arm. Looking out from their nook, they could see the whirling beast approaching closer, closer. The temperature dropped for just a moment as cold air whipped through the crevices. The Noise became everything in the universe for five long seconds and they clung to each other like. The cyclone chewed up everything loose it could find, thwarted briefly by steel and concrete. It surged one last time. The fear passed over them, and The Noise beat inside of Elmer's chest as Elena buried her face into his neck.

When it left, they were changed.

The passover had taken five or six seconds of the day, but stole a lifetime of peace. No more poems about beautiful storms or gentle rains. Every gust of wind or peal of thunder from now on, no matter how innocent, would hold the power of life and death.

When The Great Noise subsided, the couple looked into each other's eyes with their arms still wrapped tightly around each other. Elmer looked at the water on her face, wondering if they were her tears or his. He reached up and swept a finger across her cheek like a windshield wiper and then, just like that, he put his mouth over hers.

She felt her own mouth disappear. Only warmth remained. She had no vision, only feeling. When he finally pulled back, he leaned against the concrete and looked at the empty mud nests of the cliff swallows. The moisture on his lips evaporated.

They said nothing to each other but leaned over to watch the funnel cloud dissipate into the past. A minute passed, and the rain stopped, spitting little drops over the side of the overpass. The air settled into smaller gusts.

Elmer looked down at Old Dahlin, now parked at an awkward angle with the back passenger window smashed into pieces. The broken glass lay like black onyx on the light pavement. They scooted down the concrete slope on their butts and stood to look at the war zone, a freakish, shadowy display of debris. Chunks of wood, shingles, tree branches, and twisted metal lay scattered across the highway. The road was no longer divided from the shoulder with a neat black line, but now looked like finger-smudged mistakes along an oil painting.

Elena reached to open the passenger door, and it swung open with a grinding creak. Bits of glass fell on the road. The eight remaining manifestos had blown throughout the cab like twenty-dollar bills in a game show turbine, and they saw them scattered about the interior. Elena looked at Elmer, who had said nothing since the cyclone passed, and picked up one of the papers. She squinted at it, then pushed it into Elmer's chest.

"Gotta change number ten."

He smiled. "Yup."

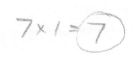

CHAPTER FOURTEEN

Prime

The storm had defined their journey.

No single event since their first meeting so completely wrapped itself around them. Not the library, not the car, not even Rube himself. It had taken two hours before they could even speak about it.

"What do you remember?" asked Elmer finally.

"Everything," she said. "And nothing."

It was totally dark now as they shuddered down the highway toward home. Elmer had picked out the largest pieces of glass from the back seat and floorboards and chucked them in silence into the prairie grass. The gas gauge had crept up to half a tank after Elena spotted a gasoline can abandoned fifty yards ahead of the overpass. They removed the shredded plastic sheeting from the windows. Now only the calm night air whooshed through the car's four open windows.

The car was, miraculously, still running. Elmer's foot could only coax Old Dahlin to forty-five miles per hour, and even then it ached like an old pack horse trying to reach the barn. For all they knew, the cyclone had lifted it off the ground momentarily and dropped it heavy to the pavement again. This would be its final trip, they were sure, and Elmer could only hope that it could handle the remaining miles of nothingness.

But first, eight Manifestos were burning a hole in the car.

It was now completely dark. The cyclone had smashed one headlight, and the other tried its best to pour light onto the highway. Occasionally, piles of debris appeared out of nowhere while Elmer turned the steering wheel to avoid them. Elena flipped through the eight papers, counting them over and over. She reached over and grabbed the map, peeled its two soggy pages apart, and examined the route in the weak light of the dashboard.

"We're not that far from the next town." She squinted to read its name. "Linton. 'Bout seven miles I guess."

"Is it a bigger town than Barfield?"

"Looks like." She smoothed the wet map and looked again. "The dot is twice as big."

Elmer simply nodded. The silence between them was comforting. After hiding under the overpass and hearing the entire universe explode, the quiet rattle of the car's engine felt like a lullaby. Leaning her head against the seat, Elena thought again about Elmer's mouth. The strength of that kiss had neutralized the terror of the storm, like morphine administered to a fallen soldier. Which would she remember most—the near-death trauma of the twister, or Elmer's life-giving kiss? Both sat at opposite ends of her memory. Love and fear.

Elmer was in his own dream world. He held onto the steering wheel and wrestled with his thoughts. He and Elena had no beginning and end. To kiss her was simply to love her. It was nothing more than that. He had often wondered what men thought about when they kissed a woman and assumed it was as dirty as everyone said it was. But Elena was clean. She was clean and bright, full of oxygen and sunshine, and her body was inviolate. He wanted to breathe her air and fall into her goodness. That was why he kissed her; that was why he would do it again.

And so E^2 sat in silence, side-by-side, and dreamed about each other's bodies, not from mere physical appetite, but because love compelled them.

"What is *that?*"

Elena opened her eyes and looked out at the road, startled by Elmer's tone of voice.

A dark bundle of something was piled on the right side of the shoulder, barely visible from the car. Elmer instinctively slowed the car, and as they approached, an arm reached out of the bundle and waved, followed by a thumb, the universal hitchhiker's sign.

"Elmer! Should we stop?" Elena's compassion swelled inside of her.

"No way," said Elmer. "It's always dangerous. You never know who it is. Haven't you seen movies where the hitchhikers lead people to…you know."

"To what?"

"Like bad things. Crime scenes. Or they kill them from the back seat."

"Oh, great."

"I'm serious. We can't pick him up," said Elmer. "It's just too dangerous."

"Just slow down a second. I think we should at least find out if he's okay."

Elmer pulled the car to a gradual stop and slid off the road onto the dirt shoulder. The crescent fingernail moon glowed between two clouds and they could see no other headlights in any direction.

"I don't want him in the car—" He looked at the back seat. "—but I guess we can talk to him."[1]

He put Old Dahlin in reverse and slowly rolled its wheels backward, crunching over gravel and sticks. Elena was not scared. She hung her head out of the window and twisted back to look at the man and his pile of things. He saw them coming and rose to his feet, stretching out to full height. He smiled at her, and she felt calm.

"What should we ask him?" Elena looked at Elmer who was carefully rolling the car backward.

"I won't get too close. Just ask him if he needs anything."

The bundle-man was tall and thin, but his frame was draped with objects. A backpack. Rolled fabrics. Metal things swinging from his belt. He wore a stretchy fabric beanie on his head. Beside him rested a small pile of other possessions too confusing to decipher. And as a bonus, a tiny animal was curled in the middle of it all, his tail curled around him. The brake lights illuminated him from head to toe with a crimson glow. A glowing stranger.

Elmer poked his head out of the driver's side window and looked at him. "Are you okay?" he asked.

Elmer kept his foot on the gas pedal as the stranger walked toward the car and swept the beanie off his head, crumpling it

---

1. Teenagers have a proven risk-management deficiency in their brains, and stopping for hitchhikers is one notable piece of evidence. Adults, on the other hand, avoid such dramatic events through sound judgment and the desire to stay alive.

into his hand. "How are you tonight?" he asked politely. "Are you headed to Linton?"

"Yeah." Elmer looked at Elena. He had no idea what to do. Hitchhikers only showed up in horror movies and cheesy novels needing an interesting minor character. But this one might be different; he couldn't tell yet.

He sensed their hesitation. "I'm okay if you don't want to take me there. I'm not in any hurry."

"Where do you live?" asked Elena from the other side of the car.

He turned to look at the new voice. "I live a-ways from here. But I'm just on a journey."

"Us, too," she answered. She ducked back in the car and then out again. "Just a minute…what is your name?"

"Raphael. But just call me Rafa."

"Hey, Rafa, give us a second, okay?"

They both pulled their heads inside the car and looked at each other. Elena put her hand on Elm's knee. "I know we're in a hurry. We're making bad time already—but I think we should help him out."

"What if he's got a weapon?"

"We're already driving a weapon."

"Good point." He waited a moment more. "What if he is lying?"

"I guess he's lying then."

"Honestly? I think we look like more trouble than he does." She waved her hand along the car's interior like a game show model. "Look at this. If he's willing to come along in this mess, then we should be willing to take him seven miles."

Elmer hung his head and thought with all his might. "Elena, if he hurts us—if he hurts you, then I have nothing left."

"He ain't a twister," she said. "And we already survived that."

Elmer banged the back of his head against the seat and sighed. "I'll help him with his stuff."

Saving gas, Elmer turned off the car and opened the door. The man was sitting with his knees up, leaning his back against his pile of stuff. He looked up at Elmer and smiled. "I won't be much trouble. I surely 'preciate this."

"Our car is…our car is in bad shape. We've been through plenty."

"Aw, no problem. Remember, I been walking all night." He grinned. "Damn near got swept into that storm a few hours ago."

Elmer didn't want to remember. He picked up the man's enormous backpack and it floated as if nearly empty. It was the kind of backpack that wilderness hikers carry, wide and bulky. It was fat as a house but seemed full of air. Rafa swung both a pillow and the gray canvas satchel on his back, picked up the animal, and everyone moved toward the car.

Elmer opened the door and gestured to the back seat. "It's a mess back there. The tornado blew out our windows. Wasn't even nice to start with." Rafa threw his things toward the back and then folded himself into the seat, his legs poking up like bendy straws.

"Sorry about the seat," said Elena.

Then came the next surprise. Rafa's animal was a cat. Cats are supposed to be old lady's pets, quiet, slinky creatures who live in fancy penthouses and pretend their owners are royal subjects, not tag-alongs to crazy, wandering hitchhikers. His name was Mao, named for the mispronunciation of "meow" by his six-year-old niece who preferred one-syllable words. And, he explained, he liked calling him Chairman Mao in deference to his complete authority. Even more bizarre was finding Mao on a leash. He didn't seem to mind, rubbing up next to Rafa as he pulled at the fur under her jaw. His face was the smashed-flat kind, like a cartoon feline who was hit with a shovel.

All three were deathly quiet as Old Dahlin tried its best to inhale. The engine whimpered and then breathed deeply as Elmer maneuvered it onto the highway once more, feeling the extra weight slowing their acceleration. Rafa's legs invaded the space between the front seats, and everyone was uncomfortable.

"You guys are the best. Thanks for driving me to Linton." He waited for a response and then rubbed his dirty denim knees. "What are you doing in the middle of the night so far from everything?"

Elena turned to speak to him. "We're on a field trip. For school."

The man smiled to himself and mumbled softly. "So that's what the kids are calling it these days."

Elena heard. "No really," she offered innocently. "We—we are learning new things."

"It's an accelerated program," said Elmer, recalling the phrase that Mrs. Trotter had used in his special education class. He smiled. "We are in the gifted class." He looked at Elena and she laughed out loud.

Rafa believed them. "When I was in seventh grade, I was tested, too. My teachers thought my IQ was off the chart. She was right. Except I failed six classes in two years."

"Why is that?"

"Because I was school stupid."

"School stupid?"

"You know, where your brain works everywhere else besides school." Everyone listened to the wind and then he leaned forward into the front seat and whispered low, "But now I'm almost ready to finish my grand experiment. Linton is my destination."

"Experiment?" asked Elmer.

"I fly."

Elena snorted when he said it. She didn't mean to, but it came out.

"What do you mean you *fly*?" Elmer asked.

"I am making a hot air balloon. It's almost done." The man had to speak loudly over the wind, and Elmer wondered if he had heard correctly. Of all the things that E^2 had been through—bunking in the library, driving Old Dahlin, writing a manifesto, surviving a cyclone—hearing the poky-kneed hitchhiker say he was building a hot air balloon was the grandest fiction of them all. Raphael was a nut-case, nuttier than any of them.

"Why do you want to build a hot air balloon?" asked Elena.

"Because I like to make miracles. Inventors do that. They make miracles happen." He patted his swollen backpack. "I've got it right here."

Elena could have been insulted by his absurdity, but she graciously remained in the conversation. "So how did you get started on hot air balloons?"

"You ever heard of things like flying peaches or underground rabbit holes or Emerald cities or stuff like that?"

Elena nodded out of politeness.

"Those are in stories, and in stories you can make miracles. So I figured I could pretend I was in a story and then make a hot air balloon. But as I started to sew the pieces of silk together, the balloon was real and the physics were real and I knew that some people really did fly in balloons, so why not me?"

Elmer's hands were glued to the steering wheel.

"I kept sewing and reading and sewing and researching and sewing some more. Pretty soon I had this giant balloon on my hands. It spread out across my backyard—all different colors of silky parachute fabric. I got pieces of it a little at a time. Army surplus stores, craft shops." His arms waved in the dark as he spoke. "After a couple of months, I knew that I was halfway there."

"What did your family think?"

"Oh, the whole world thought I was crazy. But I couldn't understand why. I mean, I wasn't even inventing something that hard. All these other dudes are trying to build jets and spacecraft and satellites and here I was making something *old*. People flew in hot air balloons hundreds of years ago. I wanted to fly, and since I wasn't smart enough to build a jet with my own hands, I figured I could build a balloon." He sighed and shook his head. "Everybody's trying to fly with jet fuel, but nobody is floating in balloons anymore. I figure if I want to fly, which is more beautiful?" He stopped to think. "Which is more possible?"

Elena was transfixed by his story. It was incredible. Was there really a man in her back seat telling them about balloon flight— or was this some tragic byproduct of a head injury from last night's tornado?

He continued. "So now I'm close to finishing. I will be flying over this plain before long." He swept his arm along the window. "I'm at the basket-building phase now. Won't be long. But now comes the physics research. That's a little harder, I must admit. Heated hydrogen and stuff like that. But just remember that if you want to fly, you can always do it old school. Flying is flying—don't matter how you do it. And it's crazy cool."

Elmer and Elena sat stunned. What could they say? He was certifiably insane. Maybe he did have a weapon, she thought. Maybe he was going to kill them right there or smother them with his silk balloon. Whatever it might be, she would never forget Rafa the balloon flyer.

"We're getting close," said Elmer "Where should we drop you off?"

"Wherever you want, my man. Wherever the wind blows."

Yup. He was a freak.

"Before we get there, can you answer a question?" asked Elena.

"Sure."

"Do you know much about Linton?"

"Grew up there."

"Can you tell us where a school is?" Elena turned to look at him. "We're also trying to fly, I guess." She looked down and smiled. "We're trying an old school experiment, too."

"I'll tell you what. I'll take you to not just one—but three schools in a row. That is, if you want me to stay in the car with you."

"Cool," said Elmer. "If you don't mind the pieces of glass in your butt, we're good with that."

Rafa leaned over and pulled out a shard of glass from the cushion beneath him. "Hey, any guy who's building a hot air balloon is okay with uncomfortable travel." He waited a moment and then asked, "I hope you don't mind me asking, but why are you guys going to dinky schools in the middle of nowhere? I mean, it sounds a little crazy to me." This, Elmer thought, coming from a guy who wants to launch a hot air balloon and travels with a Marxist cat?

"We are finishing our final exam," said Elmer. "Our teacher asked us to do a project." This was true. But it didn't answer Rafa's essential question: Why were two teenagers alone in the dead of night?

Rafa tried to stretch one leg through the gap in the two front seats. "What kind of project?"

"Well," he paused. "Elmer looked at Elena and she looked back at him while nodding slightly. "We wrote something called a Friendship Manifesto," he said. "Wanna see it?"

Elena turned and handed one of the copies to Rafa who could barely read in the darkness of the back seat. He took it and Mao rubbed his face against it. "A manifesto, eh? That sounds pretty fancy."

"Oh, no. It's not fancy at all," declared Elena. "We can't write very well, actually. We needed a lot of help at the library to finish it. But it's full of true things. That's one thing we know for sure. It definitely tells the truth."

"Ah, truth. Now that's what I call an awesome project. I was afraid to tell the truth when I was in school." He laughed to himself. "Most of my papers were just a lot of bullshit." He turned the paper toward the window and squinted at it. Only the wind made noise and everyone was still for a long time.

After a few minutes of reading in the dark, Rafa spoke. "Now this is genius, you guys. I mean the whole world would be different if people did these things."

Then Elena remembered number ten. "We're going to change the last one." She couldn't look at Elmer, her mind kidnapped by the memory of his kiss under the overpass.

"How come? I think this one is great." Rafa looked at them and smiled. "Oh, I get it. You guys kissed, right? So now number ten seems awkward. Listen to me. You're right about friends. They don't kiss. But when and if they finally do, they get to be friends-times-ten or something like that. I wouldn't sweat it."

Elena was relieved by his logic. "So you think friends can fall in love?"

"Heck yeah. But just like you wrote here—when they do, they have to consult another list. And the rules on that list are so complicated that you can't even put it in a Manifesto or a Declaration or a Treaty or anything like that. Face it. Love is like crazy infinity, dude. It's worse than learning physics. Believe me,

I know. But friendship? That's more like addition and subtraction. It's the right place to start."

"That's why we need your help. The schools in Linton are gonna read this."

"Oh my god, if there's ever a place that needs your gospel message, then it's Linton. I'll take you to all three—my elementary school, my middle school, and my high school—and you'll be done in no time at all."

At that moment, Mao jumped in one soft pounce to Elena's lap. "Hey, Mao," she cooed at him. He leaned his furry body along her chest and rubbed the top of his head into her hand.

"Now I know you're all right. That's the first time he's trusted anybody. And if Chairman Mao likes you? Now that's a miracle."

As he finished his sentence, a siren's wail broke through the conversation. Far ahead, emergency lights circled around the black sky, a massive interruption in the dead of night. The cat jumped back to Rafa's lap.

"Oh my god," said Elena looking ahead toward the chaos. "What happened?"

On Elmer's left side, another emergency vehicle approached at high speeds, swaying their car as it passed. "Must be something bad," said Elmer. Another five hundred feet ahead, a little orange-vested dot of a man stood out in the road up ahead lighting flares one by one. The car slowed, coming to stop right in front of him. Ahead was the outline of two twisted cars, one flipped on its back and the other smashed on one side like a stomped soda can. The flares swirled in the cool air, a romantic oddity next to so much destruction. Mr. Orange Vest walked toward them and approached their car window.

"Sorry, but you won't be able to pass for a while," he said, peering into the vehicle. He stared at Rafa for a long moment then back to Elmer. "Gotta clear this accident."

"What happened?" asked Elena.

"This crazy bastard fell asleep and crossed over the median." He pointed to the aluminum can car. "The other guy didn't have a chance."

"Are they dead?"

"Nah. But busted up pretty bad. The ambulance is taking 'em both." Elena dropped her face into her hands and started to cry. Rafa leaned over from the back seat and flopped his heavy hand on her shoulder. The highway patrolman continued. "I know. It's hard to look at. Just driving, minding your own business and *pow!* You got a guy flying over the road smack into your grill." He stopped for a moment and thought hard. "You lucky you weren't here ten minutes ago. Coulda been you right there."

They all stared at the ambulance. The patrolman shuffled his feet. Elmer looked back at Rafa and stared at him for a long time. "Ten minutes ago?"

Rafa just stroked Mao, looking out the window.

———

"Stop right here," Rafa said.

Elmer had taken the nearest exit and now Rafa was directing him to his school, *Red River Elementary*, the Home of the Hornets.

"This was your elementary school?"

Before long, Rafa was standing outside the car with his hands on his hips in the dead of night surveying the old campus which rose up against the black horizon like a haunted house. They had driven to Red River quickly, the emergency lights of the accident still whirling in their heads. "Yeah. This is it." His head,

THE MULTIPLICATION OF ELMER WHIT

like an oscillating sprinkler, moved from right to left slowly as he absorbed every panoramic foot.

"Where should we hang the paper?" asked Elmer, waving it in the air.

Rafa ignored the question, almost talking to himself. "I can't believe how small it is. I haven't been back here in years." Elena leaned against the car, holding Mao's leash, listening to him talk. "That building right there? That's the cafeteria, but gee whiz—it looks like a shoebox. When I was here, the cafeteria was the size of a stadium."

Elmer was feeling the hit-and-run urge, the desire to finish the task and move on. His father was waiting at the other side of this journey.

But Rafa kept talking, lost in his nine-year-old past. "And that right there? We used to have one of those whirly things, you know, like a carousel[2] that you could spin around and around It's gone now, but the boys used to make it go so fast that the centrifugal force would spin the prissy girls right off." He chuckled. "Gardenia was this one girl…she was so mad at us that she told the teacher on us every day. Finally, the teacher just said, 'Gardenia, how about you don't ride the carousel?' as though it never occurred to her before."

Elmer spoke up. "Yeah. Sometimes you just gotta get off the carousel yourself."

"Damn straight."

Rafa kept talking to himself. "And over here? They took most of the trees down."

---

2. Another misguided relic of 1970s playground equipment was the installation of giant animal-shaped swings hanging from metal chains. This way, you could use your massive cast iron Giraffe as a battering ram against your friend's less impressive Duck.

All three walked toward the playground in quiet respect for the ancient past. "Once, when I was in the fourth grade, a sixth-grade kid named Trenton hated me. He used to draw ugly, embarrassing pictures of me and then fold them up really tight into little squares of paper. Then he'd put them right here—" He walked over to one large tree with a V-shaped set of branches "—and tuck them under a piece of bark. Then he'd tell my friends that he found a secret treasure map. We'd run over to find it, all excited about the secret, and then when I would unfold the paper really slow in front of my friends, there was Trenton's drawings, all creepy with pictures of me."

"What kind of pictures?"

"Oh, sometimes I was wearing short shorts and a pink shirt. Once he drew one of me carrying an assault rifle. In another one he drew my face with a hatchet stuck through the middle. I never knew why he hated me."

"That's awful, Rafa," said Elena. "I'm sorry."

"No big thing, really," he lied. "It's just that he did it to a lot of the other kids, too. Even kids younger than me." Rafa picked up a stick and threw it down again. "I hope that Trenton—" he thought about what he was going to say. "I hope Trenton—well, that he's not an asshole anymore." As he walked over to Elena, he pulled a string out of his pocket and threw it down in front of the cat. "Hey, Mao? This is Trenton. Go at it." Mao swiped at the string with his claw and then mauled it for a few seconds before casually standing guard over it.

"Sounds like we picked the right school," said Elmer, still waving the paper. "Where should this go?"

"Let's put it on the building of my fourth-grade classroom. In honor of Trenton."

Rafa, Elmer, Elena, and Mao slid across the school lawn like ghosts in the moonlight toward his old classroom. The schoolyard was chilly and full of shadows, the right atmosphere for a midnight strike. Rafa twirled the circle of duct tape around his fingers as he walked, and Elmer held the manifesto in both hands. The old brick building was painted navy blue on the side with the words *Red River* blocked out on each square. The door, like a blank canvas, was ready to receive the gospel.

Elmer handed the paper to Rafa. "I think you should do this one," he announced. Elena tore off a strip of duct tape and dangled it on her finger toward him.

"Okay. I think I will."

Elmer took Mao's leash as Rafa grabbed the document with both hands. He shook his head as he looked at it with campy melodrama. "This is crazy," he said. "But I love it." Then he stared up at the sky as if to dedicate the moment's significance. "Here's to Trenton and all the boys who came after him. May they put down their put-downs and know the truth." He slapped it on the door with a flourish and swept the duct tape across the top and bottom before stepping back to look at it. Then he added, "And to me, too, who twirled Gardenia one too many times. May I grow up and realize the error of my ways."

"Perfect," said Elena.

Mao meowed and the moment was complete.

———————

At shortly past three a.m. the group had now swooped into the Kingwood Middle School parking lot. They squatted beside the car to plan their strategy. After giving Mao some water poured from the front water fountains into an inflatable bowl, Rafa had pulled a zip-bag of dried turkey-jerky out of his sack and passed it around the group in the dark like an illegal bag of weed. Elena was hungry, and Rafa's snack was heavenly.

"You know, I'm calling your document the Friend-Man," Rafa said. "Friendship Manifesto is just too long." He tore a piece of dried meat in half and shook it in front of him.

"We could just call it an FM," Elmer suggested. "Like FM radio."

"The world could use some FM radio, dude," said Rafa. "Just think about all the DJ's who could tell people how to treat others instead of playing lousy pop music."

They were quiet, listening to the soft lap of Mao's tongue in his water bowl.

"Ready for this one?" said Elmer holding up the fifth manifesto.

"Where do you want to put it this time?"

"The library, dude."

Elena sensed that Rafa had another story to tell, a reason behind choosing the library door. "You can tell us about the library while we walk there," she suggested. "C'mon—we don't have much time."

This campus was different from any of the ones they had visited before. Its low-slung architecture was fake-modern, more George Jetson than George Washington.[3] As Rafa led them to the library, his eyes grew dark and cloudy with memories.

"Can't believe it. Lived in Linton on and off all my life and this is the first time I've come back here."

---

3. Built in the Era of Dumb Ideas, its architecture bore the marks of theoreticians who believed that wall-less classrooms would foster the exchange of ideas. The kids who attended, however, knew that it actually fostered the free exchange of flying objects. On a positive note, it was also the Golden Age of ADHD diagnoses.

"What was it like here?"

"Middle school? C'mon now. Ask any person in the universe about middle school and they'll tell you the truth about it. Stick four hundred tadpoles into one small puddle of stinky algae and you'll get middle school. No toads, no eggs, just tadpoles, half of them with legs and half still just twitching in the water." Rafa slowed down and turned to his two new friends. "C'mon, you guys remember middle school, right? You must have had the same experience."

Elena was quiet, for she felt the heavy weight of being given too much in life, the guilt of being sunlight when the rest of the world was darkness. "I liked middle school," she announced. It was an audacious claim. Risky to admit.

"You did?"

"Yes. I remember my father and mother praying with me before the first day of seventh grade. I was so excited I could hardly sleep the night before."

"You didn't have a stomachache and diarrhea?"

"No. At least not that I remember." Elena reached far back into her head. "I remember the friend I met—Alexandria. She had the same backpack as me. We laughed almost every day of middle school. I didn't notice the other stuff, really. That's all I remember. Alexandria and my backpack."

Elmer and Rafa were quiet in the light of Elena's startling declaration. They had never met anyone who actually liked adolescence. It was freaky, the stuff of paranormal fiction. The trio slipped past the first building and moved quickly to the second. The air was deathly cool and still and the concrete offered no softness for their steps.

They paused in front of the library door and Elmer spoke his own truth with no exaggeration or pretense. "I was almost killed in middle school," he said.

Even Mao stopped walking when he said it.

"What do you mean killed?" asked Rafa.

"Just what I said. I was almost killed."

"Dude, are you freakin' messing with us?"

"When I was thirteen, a boy named Snyder got in trouble for calling me a retard. The teachers called his dad, and they came over to my house with a shotgun the next day—I guess to scare me. My dad answered the door while I was listening from my bedroom, and they told him that I threatened to poison Snyder's chocolate milk at lunch."

Rafa and Elena couldn't keep their eyes off Elmer as he kept going. "My dad just laughed and said 'I don't doubt it. Go ahead and be my guest. Take your best shot at him.' Then they went to the backyard and shot two times in the air—just being stupid, I guess. But that's when I knew I hated my dad. He didn't even try to defend me or anything. Just told them to shoot. I was so scared every single day of middle school after that."

"Elmer, I can't believe you went through that." Elena put both hands on his shoulders and looked into his eyes. "You should have been taken from that house. A good family should have raised you."

Then Rafa spoke the strangest words of wisdom Elena had ever heard. "No, sister—wait. I think Elmer was in exactly the right house."

"What?"

"He was in exactly the right house. I don't know why yet, but I just know."

"Rafa, you're crazy, you know that?" she said.

"People been telling me that my whole life. And everyone might be right, for all I know." He turned to face her. "Being crazy means you do stuff and think stuff that no one else has the guts to do. That's me. And now, here we are at another door, and I think that Elmer should tape this one up this time."

"You're right. This one is Elmer's."

The chilly wind caught the paper and the three of them held it down against the library door while Elmer used his other hand to stretch four more pieces of duct tape across all four sides. Then he slapped it with an open fist and said, "This one's for Snyder. May his shotgun always be empty."

"I think it is, Elmer," said Rafa. "I heard he shot his dad in the foot after he tried to poison his son's chocolate milk and the two of them were exiled to Alaska somewhere." Everybody grinned at each other while Mao clawed at the Trenton-string.

Five Friend-Mans were left. That was all.

The trio was dead-tired, not as much from the late hour but from the emotional heavy lifting. Linton's streets were barren and still as the Chevette worked its way toward Linton High School. As Rafa informed them, no one would be able to miss the hideous purple and white sign erected by the class of 1983 in honor of many decades of quality education.

Mao had fallen asleep atop Rafa's balloon backpack. Rafa had gotten so comfortable with his traveling companions that now he stretched his legs out between the front seats and rested his bare toes on the defunct car radio knobs on the dashboard.

"Ain't my feet something else?" he said, as though he admired them. "They've covered lots of miles."

"How old are you, Rafa?" asked Elena politely.

"Me? Just guess."

"I can't tell. Sometimes you seem really young and other times you seem old and very wise."

"No wisdom here. Only lucky guesses. Let's just say I'm older than nineteen and younger than forty."

"That's a pretty big gap, don't you think?" said Elmer.

"Well, that's all I'm gonna give you. As for Mao, he's about six. I don't know the mathematical formula for cat years, but I'd say he's in his prime. Just like me."

"We've got a mathematical formula, too, you know," said Elena. She picked up her canvas bag and pointed to the black E^2 that she had drawn in marker only a few days ago. "That stands for us."

"Whoa. You're' right. Elmer and Elena. E squared." He thought about this. "What are you guys multiplying?"

With his hands on the steering wheel, Elmer announced it loud and clear. "What are we multiplying? I guess we're multiplying love."

"Holy shit, that sounds so cheesy," said Rafa. "But you know what? There's things way worse you could be multiplying." He laughed at himself. "Like hate. Or anger. Or even babies."

"Or shotguns," added Elmer.

"Or germs," said Elena.

"What about insults?"

Now it was a game. Before reaching Linton High School, they thought of twenty other things they could be multiplying, including tears, punches, stick drawings of Rafa, unwanted puppies, and diseases. By the time Old Dahlin wheezed to a stop behind shop class[4], they had multiplied, at the very least, Rafa's quick wit.

"You know," said Rafa as they got out of the car, "both me and Elmer here have taken our turns posting the FM. You got this one."

"Yeah," she said, "but I posted the first two—back in Handley and Barfield."

The shut the doors to the car and made their last trek to Linton's vocational training building, the place where public relations are less important and therefore the least maintained. Tall grass and pitted concrete walkways led them to the door of the old woodshop building. Elmer suspected that the storm, which had nearly swept them out of Kansas, had messed up Linton's open fields, too, as he saw broken chunks of fence and tumbleweeds strewn about the adjoining prairie. Now the night had reached its coldest point, the air decidedly damp and chilly, and the explorers trudged to the heavy metal door.

Standing outside, Rafa made a final observation. "Well, all three of us have posted a Manifesto on a door tonight. How about in honor of animal instincts, I think that Mao should be our final poster. What do you say, cat-face?"

Mao looked up at everyone with his blunt nose and fierce whiskers and stared at them with a steady purpose. Rafa swept him up in his arms and grabbed Elena's paper with Mao's paws. "Elmer, would you do the honors of helping us with the tape?"

Elmer tore the tape, piece by piece, as Mao's paw pressed the manifesto onto the door with Rafa's help. It was a solemn

---

4. Shop class used to be a very important place where kids who were gifted with their hands could make kick-ass stuff they could actually use. Nowadays, most shop classes have been remodeled into sunless, soul-sucking test caves.

moment, made even more significant by the large moon that had risen overhead.

"To predators everywhere, we mark this night as a cease-fire," and then as Rafa looked at Mao, "—or in this case, a cease-claw in favor of love and friendship everywhere."

———————

Midnight is a strange word, for the deepest part of night is actually much later. At three o'clock in the morning, the earth spins so far away from the sun that the entire hemisphere is shadowy and cold. As the Elizabethans would say, night is a mini-death. For Elmer and the others, however, this night had brought life and a certain measure of hope. Now Old Dahlin would have to race against the sun. Daybreak meant grief and a measure of uncertainty.

But first, Rafa must be released from his duties.

Elmer had parked in front of Rafa's old Linton house where his father lived. Most hitchhikers would have been lucky to be dropped off within ten square miles of their destination, but Elmer wanted to taxi him right the door. Rafa had filled their tank at the 24-hour gasoline station and showed them the route home.

The car's engine shuddered and stopped, and Elena was nearly choked up to say goodbye. "What would we have done without you?" she said to Rafa, looking into his eyes with gratitude.

"Oh, c'mon now. Schools ain't that hard to find," he said.

"But you did more than just show us the schools," she said. "You showed us why this was so important." Her voice was soft and she put her hands in her pockets.

"What will you do now?" asked Elmer.

"I'll wait in the backyard until the night is over and then I'll surprise my dad. Don't want to give him a heart attack in the middle of the night, you know." He lifted Mao onto his lap and opened the car door. Elmer came around and took Rafa's things out of the back seat one by one, including the crazy hot air balloon in the hiker's backpack.

"Will you finish your balloon?" asked Elena.

"Of course. But you can't rush genius," he said. "I'll take as long as I need to." He suddenly thought of something and rummaged through one of his bags. "Here, hold Mao's leash for me." He put the cat on the ground and Mao stretched out like a fuzzy hammock before curling up on Elena's foot.

Pulling a wilted brown paper bag out of his pack, Rafa pushed it toward Elena and smiled. "The last guy who gave me a ride gave me this loaf of bread.

He told me that the yeast in the batter can live for hundreds of years as long as you keep it going. I guess this loaf was made from his granny's sourdough starter. It's not much but I think you should eat it for breakfast." He looked up at the swelling blue sky. "I guess that's pretty soon."

"Thanks," said Elena, taking it gently in her hands.

As his head started to whir and grind with ideas, Elmer put one finger in the air as if to halt the goodbye. "Just a sec'. I got an idea, too." He circled around to Elena's side of the car and opened up the door where just four more of the manifestos lay on the floor mat. He took one in his hands and brought it to Rafa, who was standing with his hands on his hips.

"This is our starter," he announced. "Take it and make more copies with it. Give it to whoever needs the message."

"Man, that's the coolest thing ever. I will, brother Elm, I will." They looked at each other with awkward respect. Elena leaned in and gave Rafa a hug, the kind with two full arms spread around the entire body. Then, as Elmer reached out to shake his hand, Rafa clasped it with a smooth, dope handshake, a handshake that no one ever in Elmer's entire life had thought to give to such an uncool guy as he was. Elmer loved him for it.

Reaching down to say goodbye to Mao, Elena felt his coarse little tongue slide across her chin for a split second. She wiped it clean and gave his fur a quick farewell kiss. He meowed softly and flopped his tail across her foot as if to salute her.

This would be Old Dahlin's last ride. With its single headlight barely lighting up the old road, the car carried E^2 out and away from Linton toward Elmer's final destination.

$$1 \times 6 = 6$$
$$2 \times 3 = 6$$
$$3 \times 2 = 6$$
$$6 \times 1 = 6$$

$$1 + 2 + 3 = \boxed{6}$$

CHAPTER FIFTEEN

Perfect Numbers

The one-eyed Old Dahlin with its last fading headlight was headed for Elmer's hometown with fear and trembling. The magical night in Linton was over, and it would only be an hour before the sun would rise on their journey. When the sun came up, they feared the miracles would be gone. Rafa had disappeared and with him went his life-giving optimism. Elena knew she would have to be strong for Elmer.

The barren freeway bore the marks of mid-state neglect. Unlike the roads near the cities, this one, which crisscrossed the forgotten miles, was rough and desolate. They passed one car, then another, lonely reminders that this was not a dream at all. They drove in silence. Elena pulled her legs and leaned back, trying to imagine where she was. *Was she in a bullet train racing toward some wondrous city? Was this a car—or maybe just a donkey traversing a dark canyon?* Maybe she was living in a novel, becoming some writer's second self. Her thoughts, driven by days of miscalculated sleeping and eating, were mystical, detached from reality.

Elmer, meanwhile, could think of nothing but his father, wondering if his leg had poured out its last drops of blood, wondering if his mother would be hysterical with grief, praying that their return would be met with hope instead of despair. He didn't know if his mother still loved his father; his death might bring freedom at last. But who wishes his own father would die?

"What are you thinking about?" asked Elena who had been watching Elmer's face twitch and his lips move silently.

"Nothing."

"You're a liar."

"Okay."

"Are you thinking about your dad?"

"Uh huh."

"It is happening the way it should. Things are happening just the way they should," she repeated.

He listened to her and prayed for the sun to come up. All this darkness was making him crazy. The sooner the truth was flooded with light, the faster he could accept it.

"You know what else I'm thinking about?" he said suddenly. "That police car behind us—" he turned and looked back quickly to verify the illusion"—the one that just put its lights on."

Sure enough, a police car was bearing down on them, flaunting its carnival lights.

"I'm not speeding. Geez, this car can barely go fifty," said Elm in a panic. "Where did he even come from? Did you see us pass him?"

"Oh, Elm. What are you going to tell him? You don't have a license—and we probably look like freaks."

"I don't know, but I think I have to stop."

Having never been pursued by a squad car before, Elmer panicked. *Was he supposed to pull over on the shoulder? Should he wait for an exit? If he waited, would the officer think he was hiding something?* He kept driving, seeing the front of the squad car drawing closer, the sirens cutting through the silence.

"Shouldn't you stop now, Elmer? It's really freaking me out."

"I don't know, I don't know. Give me a second to think." In his panic, Elmer gunned the gas pedal, which in this case did nothing more than cause the car to groan in pain. The policeman finally killed the sirens but the lights were torture. Elmer could see him motioning with his hand to pull over.

"You gotta stop, Elmer! Pull over right now or we'll be in bigger trouble." She grabbed his arm and started to cry. "It's okay, it's okay—just please stop!"

Elmer leaned to the shoulder of the road and slowed down. As though it were attached to Old Dahlin's hitch, the flashing squad car stayed nearly glued to its back bumper, coming to a stop while Elmer, hands shaking, wiggled the gears into park.

He leaned over and squeezed Elena's hand. "Here goes."

They watched the officer in their side mirrors, his face lighting up blue and red in the spinning drama of the emergency lights. His boots crunched on the gravel and he leaned into the front window slightly.

"Whatcha folks doing this morning?"

"We're trying to get home, sir," said Elmer, his voice twitching.

"Kinda odd time to be traveling, don't you think?"

"Yes, sir."

"Didya know you had a headlight out? Right front." Elmer said nothing and stared down in his lap. "I'll have to see your license and registration."

Panic set in. *I have no license, no registration, no paperwork except for Mr. Dahlin's pink slip. I'll be dragged to jail where they'll feed me broth and toast and make me pee in an old pot. I'll be clutching the bars of my cell every night while wailing in a minor key. I'll never see Elena again.*

"Well, it's like this..." he tried to formulate some explanation, but none came out.

Elena leaned over toward the window and poked her head around Elm's shoulder. "Sir, we are trying to get home because Elmer here's father is very sick. We've been gone for four days now and we don't have much time left." That was true. But it sounded so much like a rehearsed lie that it didn't matter.

"Do you own this car, son?"

"Sort of." He turned to face the back seat, trying to remember where he had put the pink slip Mr. Dahlin had given him.

"Why don't you please both exit the vehicle for me. Keep your hands where I can see them."

Elena came out first, showing dramatic flair by holding her hands up high like a movie criminal in a gangster film. She came around to Elmer's side and leaned against the car. The officer opened the driver's side and watched as Elmer climbed out, despondent.

"Do you have any evidence that this is your car?"

"Yes. Can I get the paper?"

"Just tell me where it is."

He pointed to the back seat and the officer opened the door. Elmer's backpack tumbled out onto the ground, and he gestured to the front pocket. "It's in there."

The officer unzipped the pocket and pulled out the pink slip. He examined it before looking back at them both. "This says it belongs to a Mrs. Beatrice Kauffman. Is that true?"

"I think she was the lady who owned it before us." He paused. "Listen, I know this sounds like we're making it all up, but somebody in Handley gave us this car. I'm sure you can call him and ask."

"His wife's real nice," offered Elena. "She let us sit on her couch." She nodded aggressively.

The officer ignored her. "Please state your full name."

"Elmer," he said forcefully. "Elmer Whit."

"Is this girl related to you?"

He wanted to say that she was actually part of him, that she ran through his blood, that they breathed the same oxygen and shared thoughts. He wished he could tell him that Elena was the reason he was alive. But instead, he just nodded.

"Okay, let me be straight with you two." His serious narrator-voice cut through the early morning hour and behind him, the faint glow of sunrise spreading over the horizon like a watercolor painting. "You both are underage, past curfew, with no identification and a car that might be stolen. We're going to take a trip to the city station and then we'll find out what's true and what isn't."

"What will happen to our car?"

"The car stays here until we find out who it belongs to." He looked at the broken windows. "You can take your things if you'd like."

And so E^2 found out in these wee morning hours that adventures take many forms, some of them requiring great courage and faith, and some requiring that you sit in the backseat of a squad car behind a metal cage listening to the buzzy radio dialogue of a small-town police officer.[1] They had ducked into the dark back seat cavern while the officer locked it down before climbing into the front seat. "Well, kids, here we go. We'll get this figured out before too long." He put his key in the ignition and then, as though feeling their fear, announced, "I'm Officer Jack, by the way."

Of all the adults they had met on this journey, most had been agents of mercy. But Officer Jack was part of the shadowy

---

1. Unlike Buddy-Cop movie mythology, most police stations can't afford to double-up in cars or make jokes.

243

unknown, an adult with the power to seize control and squeeze out every drop of their hard-fought independence. Rubio had held that power, too, but he had proven himself trustworthy. So had Mr. Dahlin. Even Rafa. Officer Jack, however, was a question mark.

Elena sat with her back rigid, her face pale with sleeplessness while Elmer held and stroked her hand. *How many criminals have sat in this car? Did a murderer ever share this seat? What would the station look like and would they be handcuffed when they got there?* Handcuffs. Who could ever handcuff Elmer Whit? Elena looked down at his pale, strong hand. She needed to feel his fingers, needed to know he would take care of her. Her own hand was small compared to his, and when he pushed his fingers in between hers, they locked into place. Her own private handcuffs.

Elmer's thoughts meanwhile were a ridiculous web of fear and adrenaline tangled up together. He repositioned Elena's hand in his palm, feeling the tension in each finger. He mouthed the words *we'll be okay* and pushed the hair away from her eyes. *I'm real scared*, she mouthed back.

"Just think of your mommy," he whispered to her. "I bet she's praying for you right now."

Elena closed her eyes and imagined that beautiful face, bent low, whispering intercession to God for the girl she loved.

———

You might imagine police stations to be gleaming white Ministries of Justice with impressive steel doors and brick walls on which hang the photographs of its handsome Chief of Police. But police stations in small towns are sad little buildings tucked into old warehouses with scuffed synthetic floors and cork tile ceilings. When Officer Jack brought Elmer and Elena into the Avery Police Station through the side door at 4:30 in the morning, the reality of the rural justice system flooded over them like so many ugly fluorescent lights. A fairly young woman with sausage-roll bangs and brown lip liner sat behind a slightly tipped desk. The place smelled of thrift store clothes, stale cigarette smoke, and pine-scented industrial floor cleaner. A number of mismatched chairs were lined up against the far wall, and two of them had been pushed together to accommodate a sleeping dude covered in a plaid wool blanket. His feet stuck out from the end like a man napping in a child's bed. Down the hall, a voice shouted something obscene.

"Hey, Officer Jack," said the woman looking up from her desk. She gave Elena the look that under-performing, insecure women give to other females when they enter the room. "You found some Ju-V's tonight?"

"Yup. We need to run some checks on these folks." He gave her Mr. Dahlin's pink slip. "We also need to verify this vehicle." He turned to Elmer. "Why don't you both have a seat right here."

Lip Liner Lady motioned her head toward the chairs and started typing on the ancient computer keyboard that *clack-clack-clacked* over the sound of Sleeping Man's breathing. Elena sat first and patted the chair next to her. Elmer was ghastly pale under the fluorescent lights. Once seated, they both leaned against each other as Elena listened to her mother's imagined prayers.

> *O, Lord, give peace and rest to my dear one*
> *Bring them home to me, bring them home*
> *Cast out the dark things that come against them*
> *And give them mercy and comfort and hope*

Elena began to hum the old Palauan lullaby in barely audible tones, and Elmer recognized it from the first night in the library. *How much time had passed from then until now?* The four days had stretched into a meandering river of experience, cascading over rocks and sand and even occasional whitewater. But this felt different, a deep and stagnant pool with no means of touching the bottom or reaching the shore.

Obscene Man was shouting down the hall again, and the receptionist rose from her desk and walked down the hallway, disappearing from sight. Elena continued to hum her tune in rhythm with Sleeping Man's rattling breaths as if to calm herself. Elmer reached over to Elena's swath of brown hair, now matted and strange, and touched it. It was not the river of chocolate that he had seen that night on her doorstep when she accepted his Oreos. But he loved it for it was part of her. He brushed his palm across it in slow movements from top to bottom, and she tucked in closer to his shoulder, closing her eyes.

"You?" He was interrupted.

The receptionist had walked into the room and stared straight at Elmer.

"Yes?"

"You need to take a picture."

"Right now?"

"C'mon. It's in here." She looked at Elena. "You need to come, too, missy."

She was overly casual, already jaded by the parade of two-bit criminals who passed through these halls every week. Life in Avery was a tough gig. She was too young to be so hardened, too old to be painting hot-pink polka dots on her fake manicured nails. She opened the door and motioned for them to step inside.

"I thought you had to be arrested first," said Elmer, looking at the mug shot placards and camera tripod set up in front of a blank wall. "I don't think we need to have our picture taken." He was right. This was a breach of justice.

"I just follow directions. Don't give me grief, now."

"Can we ask Officer Jack first?" asked Elena.

"I'll tell you what," she said. "We'll take the picture and then if you end up going home without so much as a blink, I'll delete the picture." She was frustrated, but the conflict was breaking up the monotony. She almost liked it.

"I got a better idea," said Elmer, standing up straight. "Let's not take the picture and then if we end up getting arrested, I'll give you *two* pictures."

Elena looked at him, shocked. Elmer had attitude.

"Wait right here."

They watched Lip Liner Lady twirl on the heel of her ugly brown shoes and give them a little flip of the wrist as she walked out not a little insulted.

"Whoa, Elmer," said Elena. "That was cool what you just did."

"I saw a movie once where they tried to take a mugshot and the innocent guy got them in trouble. Didn't think I'd ever have to use it."

In no time at all, Officer Jack returned with the receptionist behind him. "Laurie here tells me that you're giving her some trouble out here. Is that true?"

"No, sir. Just didn't think we had to have our pictures taken."

He looked at Laurie quizzically and then said, "Excuse us a moment."

The two of them left, leaving Elmer more confused than ever. *Was the girl in trouble? Were they in even more trouble?* Elena sat down on the old canvas director's chair and slumped over. She was hungry and terribly dirty, more worn out now than fearful. Elmer squatted down on the floor in front of her and put his hands on her knees, patting them paternally. They would have to wait and see.

When Officer Jack returned, his voice was softer, less formal. "Well, folks, I'm sorry about that. Laurie wasn't authorized to take your picture. She's kinda new at this."

Elena was secretly happy. Laurie was busted.

"When can we leave?"

Officer Jack looked at his watch. "In about ten minutes, one of our investigators is coming over to question you about the authenticity of your testimony, the breaking of our county curfew, and the details of your vehicle. We'll get you some water to drink and you can sit in his office."

The investigation room was a small, sterile space dominated by a massive desk. Officer Jack entered first and drew two chairs together. "Sit right here," he said. Lip Liner Laurie brought in two glasses of water and set them, grudgingly, on the desk without looking at either of them. *She needs a Manifesto,* thought Elena.

Ah, another bureaucratic space designed for more soul-numbing waiting.

Elena thought about Old Dahlin on the side of the road, abandoned and lonely for company. Chances were good that it would be towed away to Avery's Auto Salvage where it would be picked over like a carcass in the company of vultures. Of course, with no car to carry them home, her father would then have to be called. He would answer the phone and his heart would stop beating at the sound of a policeman's voice. *I have your daughter here,* Officer Jack would say. Elmer would be implicated in the plot, shamed by the failure of it all. It was too much to imagine what would happen next.

Elmer imagined far worse. His father was dying, and he had no way of reaching him. What if Mr. Dahlin was a fraud, having given them a stolen car? They would then be taken to jail, given lashes with leather cords, made to sit in front of white walls for hours at a time, and instructed to hammer license plates for the entire state of South Dakota. Elena would have to share a cell with five other women—all with endless criminal records—and she would cry each night for her mother. His only chance would be to scrape away the plaster under his bed (one labored spoonful per night) until he made a hole big enough to escape. By then he would be thirty—far too old to sprint—and the guards would lasso him like a calf in the prison courtyard.

So went the imaginations of two weary travelers in the Land of Nowhere.

Then the door opened. As Elmer turned to look at the investigator, his eyes saw something that his mind could not comprehend. The man who opened the door was not real—couldn't be real. His unshaven face was familiar; his body a ghost from the past. The young man carrying a clipboard was nothing less than his brother Ed.

It was the rarest of surprises.
It was a wonder of wonders.
It was a miraculous occurrence.
It was the world's greatest impossibility.

When they saw each other, the recognition exploded in a great light. The rest of the world disappeared into nothingness, and Elmer's brain waves stopped their flickering. The door floated slowly on its hinges, the only movement in the room. Ed stared into the face of his brother—a rumpled, dirty, weary young man who bore no resemblance to the kid he had said goodbye to two years ago.

"Elmer Whit," he said. "My god."

"Ed? Is it really you?"

Elena could only sit and stare at the transformation between them. Ed shook his head and went straight away to Elmer's chair where he practically lifted him up and enclosed him in his arms. The two young men lingered there for a miraculous second or two until Ed released him and stood back to take another look.

"You found me."

Elmer couldn't imagine what to say. He had been on a journey to find his brother that morphed into a journey to find himself. But it really happened as they planned, a miracle more astonishing than finding money or food or hitchhikers or a car. He had always loved his brother and now he was staring into the face of his family.

The first thing he thought to say was, "Do you know about Dad?"

"Yes."

"I am going home to see him. If I can."

Up to this point, Ed had hardly seen Elena, an accessory in this moment that hadn't seemed critical. But now he looked at her, frail and frightened on the edge of her chair, a beautiful girl glowing through the matted hair and unwashed clothes. "Who are you?" he asked, not accusingly, but with a genuine curiosity.

"This is Elena," said Elmer. "She has come with me."

Ed's mind was so full of disconnected dots that he could hardly choose which one to pursue first. He sat down on the other side of the desk and leaned back in his chair. "Honestly, Elm, how did you get here?"

"I can't answer that."

"Can I try?" asked Elena. She was almost unreal, a lovely illusion in Elmer's best dreams.

"Yes."

And with the simple beauty of her voice and the space of nearly an hour, she told Ed about the school experiment and fake friends, how they took the lonely bus ride to Handley, the power of unexpected grace, writing Friendship Manifestos, and cats on leashes. From her tongue came the path toward friendship, the blessed Twister, a broken-down vehicle, and Oreo cookies with wildflowers. She explained peacemakers and Rwanda, a chilly baptism, the nights in the library with mind-blowing books, and the news of a nearly-severed limb. All of this she did with a pureness of heart that hypnotized Ed as he sat and listened to the unbelievable journey of his never forgotten brother. It took a very long time.

When she finally finished, she looked at Elmer and asked, "Did I do all right?"

All he could do was nod.

Ed was stunned. He kept looking at his brother and back at Elena as though they would disappear if he blinked too long. It was still Elmer sitting there, the little punk brother who wore his clothes strangely and his feelings awkwardly, but it was not Elmer at the same time. He was older, certainly, but it wasn't just his taller stature or the stubbly beard that made him take a second look. It was an essence of something reborn in him, the beauty of a life being lived well at last, the joy of simply being a young man whom someone loved. This was the born again Elmer, and his brother felt joy.

The shock of seeing him had taken his voice, but at last he spoke. "I can't believe you're here. Something must have told you."

"Maybe," said Elena. "Maybe it was God."

This hadn't occurred to Ed, but she said it with such conviction that it seemed like a viable option. In Elena's world, God had complete sovereignty.

"What about you?" asked Elmer. "Why are you in here Avery—and how did you become a police investigator?"

"When I left home, I was a stinking mess. All I had was my diploma and that crappy Chrysler LeBaron. The first three months I spent in Handley doing next to nothing, drinking with losers, doing a few stupid jobs here and there. But I knew I wanted to join the police academy." Ed stopped and drummed his fingers on the desk. "It was a long shot. Then I met this girl…" he trailed off. "Her name was Allison and she told me I would make a great policeman." He stopped and looked at Elena. "She was the greatest person I'd ever met. We didn't end up together but if it wasn't for her, I wouldn't have made it through the academy."

"Wasn't it hard?" Elmer's respect for his brother swelled.

"Shit, yeah. It was harder than living with dad, harder than anything. Heck, it was harder than leaving you behind in mom's house. But I did it. Quit drinking, quit feeling sorry for myself. Mostly I just quit pissing on my dreams. I wasn't the best cadet, I'll tell you that. I barely made it. But when I graduated, they told me about an opening here in Avery. Nobody else wanted it. It ain't glamorous here, but it's a decent job. I get a pretty good paycheck and decent hours." Elena looked at the clock: 6:17 a.m. "Oh, except for today. I'm never here this early. . . " He stopped cold." Officer Jack is a sub they called in from down south. He was supposed to stay until noon today, but he called me at home early this morning—told me I hadda come in early and take care of two juveniles he found near the highway. Otherwise, I tell ya, I'd been snoozing."

All three said nothing, sitting in the wonder of it all. Maybe God did know about them after all.

"So how can we get home?" asked Elmer.

"Well, first I gotta get your story confirmed. I know you're my brother and all, but I can't lie for you. It's the code we keep."

"That's cool. But it's all true, I swear it's all true."

"Who can I call about this piece of junk car you got out on the highway?" Ed looked at his clipboard and flipped through Officer Jack's notes.

"His name is Mr. Dahlin. I swear he gave us this car."

"Gave you a car? Listen, I love you and all, but I would never give you a car if I only just met you."

Elena spoke up. "Well, he did. Elmer's not lying to you. I was there when it happened."

"Okay. Do you have the guy's number?"

"No, but we can find it."

Ed put Laurie to work finding the Dahlins' number. Once the phone rang back in Handley, the old couple was happy to share the good news that Elmer's car was perfectly legitimate (while adding some details about their neighbor's new bicycle and the cost of asparagus).

In the space of an hour, Elmer had been released twice. Once from possible jail time and a second time from his brother's silence. Now if only he could manage one more ticket to freedom.

$$\frac{C}{D} = \pi \qquad 3.14159265358$$
$$9793238462\ldots$$

CHAPTER SIXTEEN

Infinite Numbers

Old Dahlin had finally been put down. Like a longsuffering horse with a broken leg, he was taken to the back of the farm and shot with a compassionate neighbor's shotgun while the owners sat in the house and cried--or in the case of Old Dahlin, hauled off to the *Avery Reclamation and Salvage* on the back of Manny's tow truck.

They really did cry. That car had been the reason for being here, the first taste of freedom Elmer had ever known. It's where they had studied about Desmond Tutu and the peacekeepers, and it's where Elena had dreamt about pink angels and apple trees on the napping day. In its backseat Elmer had changed clothes the night of the infamous secret bath in the high school swimming pool. The back seat had borne the wrath of the Great Noise and collected Chairman Mao's cat hair.

"It's okay," said Ed as all three watched Manny latch his towing chain to the axle. "It was time for it to go."

"I know," said Elena. "But he was almost like...he was almost like a friend." Manny had helped them detach the rear-view mirror; it would be Old Dahlin's gravestone, and when they returned home, Elena planned to place it in her backyard under their oak tree out of respect.

Ed was taking them home. With only two hours left on their journey, all three would arrive at Carl Whit's hospital by noon. Elena had called her mother, hysterical with joy, and told her she would be home that night for dinner. Mrs. Moon shrieked and fussed and kissed her over and over through the phone. "I have so much to tell you, mommy," Elena had said to which her mother replied, "Of course you do."

There was no such phone call to Mrs. Whit. She answered Ed's call with sullen self-pity and told them that their father would be dead by tomorrow. Ed told her that they were going to make peace with him, and she could choose whether she wanted to do the same. Her answer, of course, was the same one she always gave: *nobody else cares, so why should I.*

Before they left the police station, Elena had felt the conviction to leave one of the last two Manifestos on Laurie's desk. When she ran back to the desk, Laurie was not there. Elena slid it under her hot pink nail polish bottle with a note paper clipped to the top: *This is for you. Give it away if you do not need it.*

———————

After spending days in a car full of punched holes, sitting in Ed's truck was like riding in a watertight tank. It was nothing fancy—just a used Ford with chunky tires and a bed cover— but it felt like world class transportation. All three sat across the front cab listening to country music crackling softly through the old speakers. Elmer and Elena held paper cups with straws, sucking them from time to time. The light of day had burst through the clouds in a spectacular display, a curious setting in which to re-live a haunted childhood.

"It's hard to imagine I found you," said Elmer. "I can't remember being a boy without you around."

"Me neither."

Then Elmer asked the impossible question, the question that everyone with a half-brother wonders at some time. "Do you think mom loves you more than me?"

"Mom doesn't know how to love, Elmer. But because you were part of her DNA she tried to."

"She was fifteen. Younger than me. Probably scared out of her freakin' mind."

"I don't like this," interrupted Elena.

"You don't get what it's like for guys like us," replied Ed, turning to Elena. "You had a good mother." Ed wasn't jealous, just truthful. "And you probably had *double*, for God's sake. A dad, too."

Was love really a system of addition and subtraction where man is whole or partial, plus or minus, depending on who loves him? If so, then Elena was bursting with infinite possibilities while Elmer was lucky to be alive.

"All's I know is that I didn't die from my tough life," said Ed. "Look at me. I'm alive."

"Yes, you are," said Elena. "You are very much alive."

Elmer asked another difficult question. "What will you say to him when you see him?

"I dunno. Won't know till I'm there."

"I think I know."

"You do?"

"Uh huh."

"Go for it, little brother. Don't hold back neither. He's a big boy. He can handle it even if he is dying."

A red light, far in the distance, proved that the long stretches of open highway were beginning to shorten, the sign that they were approaching home. Ed fiddled with the radio, looking down at the stations for a split second, and looking up, noticed they were bearing down on the car in front of them. Ed popped the brake, and Elmer's cup flew onto the dash, pouring soda in one ugly puddle on the floor of Ed's truck. Elmer froze, the specter of his father rising up in his heart. He remembered that horrible day from his childhood.

But at the stoplight Ed simply reached under his seat for an old towel. "Just chill. We got it, bro," he said.

———

When they had arrived back home, Elena's parents met them at the front porch, skipping the introductions with Ed and going directly toward their daughter and raining love down in torrents. Elmer had choked on his smile, amazed at the wonder of a set of parents with such focused affection. He and Ed stood by the car, awkward and gawking, like two flightless birds watching a condor fly.

Ed and Elmer must get to the hospital at once, she had told her parents. They all shared a quick, clumsy greeting and good-bye before Elena walked to the truck and put both hands on Elmer's shoulder, standing just below eye level. She looked up into his streaked and weary face, noticing only the curve of his mouth, the strength of his jaw. "You go do this thing," she said. "You must see him."

"I can," he whispered, "because you love me."

She smiled and then turned to her parents who, arm in arm, escorted her to the door of their snug little house. Before the front door closed, she turned to look at Elmer who had not stopped looking at her. She reached out her hand with one of those lovely little waves that girls give.

Carl Whit had been tearing stuff down since the seventh grade. Demolition, when it's reserved for old buildings and broken equipment, is a necessary task, but when it extends to the soul, it ruins everything. Now it was destroying his body. Elmer's father lay in the bed like a razed house, ugly bits and parts piled in the center of an abandoned lot, quietly waiting to be cleared.

Alone, Elmer entered the room. He noticed the patient's eyes were closed, noticed the asymmetrical shape of his body. Mr. Whit's leg had been heavily bandaged, and a wad of medical who-knows-what mercifully concealed the mangled stump at the knee. Digital hums and beeps of strange machines floated around the room. The nurse had opened the door for Elmer and told him he could speak privately. *Would he have the strength?*

Elm moved closer and examined his face. In all the years of knowing his father, never did he remember staring directly into his face. It had been a moving target of pain and anger, a fleeting image moving across Elmer's cinematic life, but never a personal set of eyes, an actual nose, a soft mouth. Now his face seemed real. Elmer leaned curiously into it, closer and closer until he was four inches from his eyelids. The skin around his eyes, pale and fatty, looked vaguely like that of a plucked chicken. His nose was slightly blotched with redness, and from the corner of his mouth dripped a slow-moving bead of saliva, perhaps the only evidence of his being alive. Had his mother ever found him handsome so many years ago?

Then, in an instant, his father opened his eyes. The effect was startling, to say the least. With Elmer's face hovering so closely to his, Elm moved away suddenly, afraid of being discovered in such intimate territory.

"Dad?"

Carl said nothing but tracked Elmer with his eyes.

"Can you hear me?"

Nothing.

"Your leg—does it hurt?"

Only his eyes blinked, but who could tell the difference between reflex and realization?

"It's Elmer. I came to tell you something."

And God answered his dream. Standing at the front of the high school auditorium, Elmer summoned his courage and began. "I've come back to tell you the truth. You must listen to me." The young audience rippled with curiosity, each conversation dying out across the crowd one by one until the final shriek of a ditzy girl fell into the chasm of silence. Their faces tilted upward toward the stage and stared at this strange boy about to spill his words. "The world is full of people. Some are good and some are evil, but most are both. You will hurt your friends and you will try to kill your enemies. Some of you do it with your hands and feet, but most of you do it with your mouth."

The audience was stunned by his presence of mind, his clarity of speech. Where was the boy they once knew, the one with the strange birthmark? Could this really be him? He continued, more like an orator addressing a vast country and its citizens. "All over the world, for thousands of years, people have been evil. And you are part of it. You didn't know this because your wars are tiny. Your strikes are small. But your evil is no different from all the rest." Elmer looked at Kelton and pointed his index finger directly at him. "You—you have been a part of this." A collective gasp shuddered through the crowd as their shoulders shifted and their heads looked to see who was at the end of his pointed finger. "And you…and you over there—and that one, too." Elmer scanned the crowd for the dozens of bandits, saboteurs, assassins, and adversaries that had plagued his village, overtaken his country. "You have been part of this evil." The people began to wilt beneath his speech, breaking eye contact, praying that they would not be indicted for these war crimes.

"Dad, you tried to ruin me," Elmer said. "You hated me for so long. I felt small in your house." Carl didn't move in the bed. "I embarrassed you, made you feel worse than you did before. But your dad hated you, too. I know that now."

Elmer's courage rose and he moved closer to his father's side.

"When I was very small, you yelled and shouted and smelled bad. You didn't protect mom. You and Ed would fight with each other. My brother would run away from you, come to me so scared that he grabbed me and we hid in our closet." His hand floated to rest on his father's good leg. "Do you remember that, dad?"

His father's body did nothing.

"The nightmares came all the time. I had nightmares. Did you ever know that? You were not a good man. You were a monster, and in my dreams, I tried to kill you sometimes. You had wings and teeth and you hissed at me. I wanted you to love me. I didn't want a monster in my house. I wanted a father. But you couldn't hear me because I was asleep and so were you. We never talked together. Not at home, not in your truck. You just talked to me and I had to listen. You came in and out of my house, ruining my mother and hating my brother." Elmer leaned in closer, braver. "You were not a good man."

"When you did these things to each other, you were not hurting the enemy. You became the hater, the criminal. Did you know you were becoming what you hated?" The crowd, in its stunned realization of the truth, sank down into the floor, moving inward. He spoke a grave truth. He had opened a box, its contents once secret but now exposed for all to see.

"I was strange and different while you were lonely and afraid. So when you saw me, you saw a chance to strike. And it happened again and again. Your hearts are not pure. You looked for an enemy and found him. You found him in me. It seems so easy to hurt somebody who cannot strike back. But this is only for the weak. It is for people who are afraid, not strong."

Elmer walked backward, slowly, moving away from the crowd. He had silenced them.

"I cannot change what you did to me. I cannot change my mother either." said Elmer. He crossed the barrier of life and death and sat, tentatively, on the edge of his father's bed. A barely perceptible shudder passed through the man's body as his son leaned his face closer. "I cannot change this birthmark, and I can't change what's in my head—" and then added "—or not in my head. These are things that were given to me."

Elmer swallowed and blinked away the tears puddling in the corners of his eyes. "But I can change other things. I can forgive you. And if I forgive you, I can love you."

At this word, Mr. Whit lifted his hand and clutched at his son's forearm. Only the brokenness of his body allowed him to glimpse the power that every peacemaker in the world had come to know, the sheer divinity of undeserved grace, and in this new blinding light he pulled his son to his face and asked him in a wheezy whisper *How?*

Elmer whispered back. "Because someone else loved me."

Then Elmer burst to the front of the stage with deliberate energy and courage. His eyes reached into everyone's soul and the crowd latched onto his words, listening to every good thing, listening to every word he spoke. It was not his voice, his speech, but someone greater's. He was not Elmer, but something more.

"But you must know that this is not the way to live. Your Creator gave you love, goodness, hope. He did not make you evil. You are light." He pointed to one whose eyes were fixed on Elmer's face. "He made you that way, do you know that?"

Then to another he said, "He gave that love to you. You have this gift—do you understand me? And you... The words you say and the things you do here on earth either praise that gift or trample it. You can raise another up or you can bring him to his knees. Of all the things God gave you, he gave you the right to choose the light or the darkness." He gestured to one sitting on the side. "That one beside you? He is desperate and lonely and scared just like you. He wants to find peace just like you. Which way will you choose?"

As he stretched out his hand to each face that looked up, he made the promise that was made to him and everyone before him. "Choose this peace, I tell you, and live. Even if you die."

Carl Whit laid his head back on the pillow and his breath wheezed out of him like the bellows on an ancient furnace. Elmer dropped to his knees and leaned his forehead into the sheets as his father's hand finally fell softly on his head.

———————

The manifestos eventually multiplied, like all organisms do when they are properly fed and watered.

Out in Barfield, Cashier Guy and Corndog Boy never forgot the strange couple who arrived the day of the notorious Twister looking for plastic bags. They read Elena's document carefully, leaving it behind the counter for a week before the cashier took it home to his stepsister. That little girl then colored the margins with pastel markers, making curlicues and flowers around the sides, and showed it to her friends. Those girls memorized most of the instructions and made a club in its honor, which lasted, unbelievably, until they graduated from high school. It's hard to know the mathematical formula, but it's quite possible that 247 acts of meanness had been averted as a result. At least seventeen yearbooks that year contained the cryptic message *Long live the Manifesto!* scribbled along the top margin of each member's book.

Linton's fourth grade class at Red River Elementary found its document when Jerry Fodoro arrived at his classroom door. The son of a single mother who managed the Dairy Queen, Jerry was often the first one on campus. He tiptoed up to read the paper and wondered who had put it there. His teacher? The principal? One by one, each classmate who arrived gathered to see what was hanging on the door, and when his teacher finally showed up, she thought some mischief had broken out among the cluster of students crowded around. Jerry announced that he was the first to find "the note," and Mrs. Perry peeled it off and brought it inside. In a stroke of creative genius and not a little act of State rebellion, Mrs. Perry threw off the morning's lessons in favor of discussing the manifesto's ten points. The class debated the merits of such a list, and Jerry, miraculously, wondered if he had been a crappy friend all this time. At the same time Sherry and Elise looked at each other and smiled, but Pablo and Kevin only dreamed of kickball. In the end, Mrs. Perry shared the mysterious paper with her colleagues at lunchtime and the strange little "Friendship List" went on to become part of the school district's core curriculum under the label *Character Development and the Art of Friendship.*

Laurie's manifesto sat on her desk at the Avery police station for a long time after Elena left it there so early in the morning. She read it over and over again. One day a bottle of nail polish toppled over it, spreading out in a pearlescent river of *Purple Passion!* over the delicate words. She rewrote it the next day from memory and tacked the new copy above the picture of her boyfriend Manny the tow truck driver. Ed's new wife Gloria liked it so much that she made copies for her second-grade class at Avery Elementary School.

Meanwhile Mr. Carlyle at the high school, the kind of shop teacher whose long, gray beard was the subject of many conversations, found his manifesto while unlocking his classroom door early in the morning. He was so taken with its simplicity and power—and its mysterious origins—that he assigned his second period class the task of building a special wooden case for it. They spent a month measuring and mitering their wooden planks before finally installing a lock on the glass cover. As the grand finale, they shellacked and mounted the paper into the case and installed it in the high school's front lobby.

The one taped to the door of the Handley Library hung for seven days at first, developing a strange following among the curious. No one knew who wrote it or why it was left there, but some began to say that a child's ghost left it there at midnight. Others said that they saw a strange man tape it there shortly before sunrise, and still more speculated that the librarians were behind the mischief.

After the tape started to peel off and the edges of the paper began to curl, Mrs. Ottowald took it inside and placed it inside the pages of a heavy book for three days for flattening. On the morning of the fourth day, she took it out and placed it in a shiny oak frame. The library staff, after several meetings, said it would be good to take the mysterious document and hang it upstairs in the children's room where people could continue to read it for years to come. It is still there today.

Elmer and Elena returned to Sun City High School to the whispers and confusion of their peers. Only Miss Chris knew the secrets behind their mysterious disappearance. She and Team Elm had no disappointments about the failed day at Coaster City. Elmer had, in fact, found his best friend. Miss Chris posted their Friendship Manifesto outside her classroom where no one dared touch it. Every day, several people gathered around it to point and whisper. E^2 still kept meaning to change #10, but every time they thought about it, they ended up kissing.

(If we're being truthful, one of the Manifestos sadly came to nothing. At Kingwood Middle school, aspiring arsonist Jonathan Jones found it and promptly used it to light his monthly trash fire.)

Rafa long remembered his good friends and the magic night in which they shared the gospel of love. He made fifty copies of it the "starter," giving one to every stranger he met. He worked on his hot air balloon for months, even traveling to Handley to visit with an odd professor who taught him the physics of ballooning. He spent six months there, eating pancakes at the senior society and spending afternoons in the park with Chairman Mao.

When he finally made his maiden voyage on a real balloon many years later, he tossed ten FM's out of the basket at three hundred feet, watching them drift like white feathers to the landscape below. No one knows if they were ever found, but he dreamed they multiplied into a hundred more.

Many voices. One message.

For more information, please visit
www.quoir.com

CPSIA information can be obtained
at www.ICGtesting.com
Printed in the USA
FSHW021911260419
57620FS